I0452828

Breaking the Rules

Written by

Tinthia Clemant

Breaking the Rules
by Tinthia Clemant

Copyright © 2019 by Tinthia Clemant
Published by River Lady Press
www.riverladypress.com
All Rights Reserved.

This book is a work of fiction. Names, characters, places, and events
are products of the author's imagination.
Any resemblance to actual persons, living or dead, locations or
events, is strictly coincidental.
No part of this publication may be reproduced, stored, or transmit-
ted, in any form or by any means, without the prior permission in
writing of the author, nor be otherwise circulated in any form of
binding or cover other than that in which it is published and
without this condition being imposed on any subsequent purchaser.
All rights reserved by the author and publisher.

First edition 2019
Library of Congress Catalog Card No. 2019940972

Editing by alyssakressbookediting.com
Cover design and formatting by coversbykaren.com

ISBN-13: 978-0-9974371-7-1

This book is dedicated to every woman who believes she lacks the courage to take back her life.
Never forget: you are a warrior.

Breaking the Rules

Prologue

"Life is short, break the rules, forgive quickly, kiss slowly, love truly, laugh uncontrollably, and never regret anything that made you smile."
Mark Twain

September 2005

Shannon fiddled with the buttons of her dress as she and Justin waited for their coffees. Outside, rain fell on people rushing by the window of the coffee shop. She moved her attention from the scene outside to her two-month-old son in the carrier next to her. He was the most beautiful baby she'd ever seen, and it still amazed her that he'd formed inside her body.

"Are you listening to me?"

She looked up at her husband of one year sitting on the opposite side of the booth and nodded. A sense of hopelessness washed over her. She'd tried to do everything right—paid for the train tickets with cash and not her credit card, hadn't used her real name, all the little tricks she'd picked up from watching movies over the years. She'd even cut her hair. Yet Justin had found her after only two days. She wouldn't make a very good spy.

"Say something," Justin demanded, loud enough that the people across from the booth glanced over.

Shannon rubbed at her forehead. "I'm sorry, my head is pounding." Hopefully, the lie would keep his anger at bay.

"Do you have anything you can take?"

"Yes."

He reached across the table and grabbed the diaper bag.

After rifling the contents, he removed a pocket-sized tube of Advil, along with her cell phone.

She watched her phone slide into his coat pocket. "What are you doing?"

"I'll hold on to your phone. Now that I've found the two of you, you won't be needing it." He poured four pills into his palm and held them out. "So, what do you think?"

"I need my phone."

"Why?"

"I...I'm expecting a call."

"From who?"

She struggled to come up with a name that wouldn't set him off. "Maureen," she lied a second time, hoping he didn't know she hadn't spoken to her coworker since quitting the ad agency.

"If she calls, I'll give it to you. Now, back to what I said. What do you think?"

"What do I think about what?"

She received a severe frown as a response before he said, "You're doing it again."

"Doing what?"

"Not listening to me. How about thinking about me for once and not always yourself?"

"I...I'm sorry?"

"Yeah, you're always sorry *after* you do something."

She glanced at the baby. Satisfied he was still sleeping, she adjusted his blanket and returned her attention to the table, where she stared at her coffee.

Justin's tone softened. "You make me do and say things. If you acted better, I wouldn't be so hard on you." He reached across the table again, this time offering his hand.

Shannon bit into her lower lip in the exact spot she'd recently opened with her right canine. Blood meandered through her teeth, and she slowly placed her hand in his.

"That's my girl. What I said was, if you and Chad come back home where you belong, I'll go to couples counseling like you asked. I can change."

"I don't know."

"You don't know what?"

"I don't know what to do."

He lifted her hand and kissed her knuckles but then squeezed her fingers, driving her wedding band into the side of her pinkie. "I'm not the bad guy, Shannon. Most of the time I'm only joking around, but you take things much too serious. You know what your problem is? You're too sensitive. You need to lighten up."

The baby squirmed and drew her attention. Chad scrunched his face, coloring the round cheeks so that he resembled an angry plum. "I have to clean him." She moved from the booth and looped the strap of the diaper bag over her shoulder. "I'll be right back."

Justin pushed his chair back from the table and walked with her to the bathroom. "I'll wait right here," he said, positioning himself against the wall. She pulled on the door, but he blocked it. "I'm taking you back, Shannon. You need me— you're too weak to raise a kid on your own."

He released the door, and she entered the bathroom.

While changing Chad's diaper, distant voices filled her ears, voices that belonged to ghosts who wouldn't stay vanquished. In her mind she was a child of six and hiding under her grandmother's heavy, wooden desk.

'Don't you walk away from me, young lady.'

The memory of the voice was like a cold wind, the kind that could get under her coat and raise goosebumps up her back.

She knew her mother would speak next; the memory was always the same—never changing because the dead wouldn't allow it.

'For Christ's sake, Mother, I just buried my husband.'

'*Keep your voice down, Katherine. Do you want everyone to think you're hysterical?*'

'*I don't care what people think. This is not the time to have this conversation.*'

'*This is the perfect time. What are you planning on doing? Raising the child on your own? You know you're not equipped for that.*'

'*I'm perfectly capable of taking care of my daughter.*'

'*No, you're not; you're too weak. You need me.*'

In the restaurant bathroom, Shannon squeezed her eyes closed, recalling the spider that had crawled up her young shin and how she'd placed her hand in its path and lowered it back to the floor. It had scurried out from under the desk, and her grandmother's thick-soled shoe had turned it into a black splotch. That was how she felt now, like a spider with a dark shadow hanging over her head, ready to drop and crush both her and Chad.

"Shannon." The doorknob rattled. "Hurry up."

"I'll be right out." She unbuckled Chad from the changing table, returned him to his carrier, and paused to stroke his dark brown hair. In exchange for her tender touch, he cooed. She kissed his cheek and whispered, "I'm sorry munchkin. I tried."

Chapter 1

*"Being deeply loved by someone gives you strength, while
loving someone deeply gives you courage."*
Lao Tzu

June 2011

Blog Post Topic: Endings and Beginnings

*I like to think of endings as beginnings. This may seem
confusing but stay with me and I'll explain.*

*With each new beginning, there had to have been an end-
ing beforehand. A time may have come when we said, 'Enough!'
and tossed something, someone, someplace, or some emotion,
to the curb; for without bringing to a close that which we no
longer accept as our reality, we lack the freedom to enjoy that
which we want to begin. One cannot start unless one has
stopped, first.*

*Endings are the fertile soil in which we plant the seeds of
possibilities. (Tweet this)*

*Before you enjoy your stew, take the bay leaf outside and
bury it in your garden. If you don't have a garden, any soil
will do. As you cover the leaf, repeat your goal and say 'always
a blessing'. Now it's time to enjoy your stew. Your wish has
been infused into the wonderful goodness of the ingredients
and is ready to fill you with nourishment and clarity. Ladle
a heaping serving of stew into your bowl, accompany with a
generous chunk of rustic cornbread, and pour a glass of apple
cider wine. Head outside, face the setting sun, and bless the*

road ahead. Celebrate your endings, my dear friend. Raise your glass to the courage you found to say goodbye to whatever you're ending and to the magic that lies ahead.

Your journey awaits. Until next time, S

To: sm@gmail.com
From: vk@gmail.com
Subject: Nomination and Newest post
Hi, Shannon. Great news, your blog has been nominated for a SAVEUR award in the Food and Culture division. The winners won't be announced until fall, but I'll be able to get plenty of marketing momentum with just the nomination. I've attached all the information. Have some champagne and do a happy dance. **The Grateful Earth** has made it to the big time. You also have a new company that wants to advertise on the blog (information attached). When you have the next post ready, send it over. Cheers, Val

To: vk@gmail.com
From: sm@gmail.com
Subject: Nomination and Newest Post
Hey, Valarie, squeee... I've been secretly coveting a SAVEUR award for a while. Even if I don't win, I'm blessed to be nominated. Let's get the company on board; I like their mission statement. The blog post is attached to this email along with recipe for Journey Stew and necessary photographs. Please link to the rustic corn bread and apple cider wine recipes I mention in the body of the post. As always, thank you for your hard work; I couldn't do this without you. Blessed be, S

Shannon hit the send button and silently congratulated herself. Nominated for a SAVEUR—hot damn. Winning the award would attract more viewers to the blog which would attract more advertisers, resulting in more money flowing into her bank account and ultimately freeing her and Chad from Justin's grasp. It was scary, thinking about supporting Chad on her own, but the option of staying with Justin was even more frightening.

When she'd started the blog, Chad had been an infant.

The all-too-familiar pang of unease clenched her belly as it did every time she gave those early years a thought, no matter how fleeting. She'd been Justin's prisoner, both physically and emotionally. The blog had been a way to maintain a connection to the outside world. That time in her life when she'd been locked in the townhouse with no car, no phone, no one to talk to except for a newborn—those were the darkest times she could remember, darker than the years spent living with her grandmother Arlene, which were as black as obsidian.

After she'd left her grandmother's house, more like ran away from it, she'd promised herself she'd never let anyone have power over her again. She'd been eighteen and confident she'd do a better job of taking care of herself than her mother and grandmother had done. And she had, until she'd turned thirty-two and Justin had walked into her life. He'd promised safety; that he was someone she could trust. But he'd lied, and his true personality, like some ugly creature rising from a swamp, had emerged. By the time she figured out he was no different than her domineering grandmother, she was trapped.

There were only two people in her life whom she could trust: herself, although at times she doubted her own motives, and the child standing behind her chair. He was someone who wouldn't let her down.

He'd been there for the past ten minutes, waiting for the right moment to strike. His fortitude amazed her. Well, he wasn't going to win, not this morning. Today, she was going to be the victor.

She yawned and reached out into a slow stretch, then spun her chair and flung herself at her son, taking them both down to the carpet.

Chad released a high-pitched squeal of delight and tried to wiggle away, begging for mercy as he squirmed.

"Help me, Jasper," he called out between bouts of laughter.

His plea fell on deaf ears. Their chocolate Lab remained immobile, eyes closed, snout positioned between his large paws.

"You're an old poop," she said to the dog and then to her victim, "Had enough?"

"No way."

Of course he hadn't; he never tired. Her? She needed to step up her cardio if she was going to keep pace with him. Hopefully, he'd remember what she'd taught him about calling 911.

She admitted defeat and said, "Uncle." Then she sat back on her heels to stare into round eyes the color of Madagascar cocoa. They offered her unconditional love...and trust. He relied on her; she was his bastion against the harshness of the world. He still had no clue that his mother was a phony; that every day she let him down a little more by keeping him in the toxic environment where they lived.

She switched to sitting, and Chad crawled onto her lap, his young body fitting perfectly in her arms. Once he was there, she inhaled—bubble gum bath soap and little boy. One day she'd figure out how to bottle his aroma; that way she could keep him with her no matter where his journey took him. He was her reason for living.

Why, then, wouldn't she do what had to be done?

"Are you giving up, Mama?"

"Absolutely not. I just need a rest, that's all." She blinked back a tear. Having him see her cry was not an option. Her mother had cried, endless streams of tears while her young daughter had watched, powerless to stem the flow.

Chad left her embrace and joined Jasper, whose tail thumped a greeting on the carpet.

"Mama, why are you looking at me?" Chad's head rested against Jasper's glossy fur.

His question was simple enough, unlike the answer. If she said she was staring because she wanted to seal in her mind his beauty—the long, black lashes that fanned his cheeks while he slept or the shape of his nose—would he think she'd lost her mind?

Or that she was checking for a fractured spirit?

"I'm watching you because I want to count your warm cheekies," she replied, doing her best imitation of *The Count* from Sesame Street. She gathered her skirt. "One cheeky..." she said, crawling his way.

"Mama," he managed between giggles. "Don't eat me."

"Two cheekies," she said.

"Help, Jasper, save me." Chad hugged Jasper.

"He cannot save you. You're mine, all mine."

She kissed his neck and chin. When her nibbling ended, she carried him to the far wall and collapsed on the loveseat, his body resting against hers.

"Mama, how did you know I was behind you?"

"I heard your big feet, that's how." She raised his foot. "See this foot? It's *huge*."

Chad laughed and kicked his legs playfully. "Tell me, how did you know?"

"I'm a mama. Mama's have special senses."

"Like Spider-Man?"

"Just like Spider-Man."

He lifted her hand that had been resting on his chest and traced the lines of her palm with his index finger. "Will I have spidey senses when I'm a daddy?"

"Yup, just like Daddy."

With his focus still on her palm, he said, "Daddy doesn't have spidey-senses. He's too mean."

She leaned over and tried to see his eyes. "Why would you say that?"

Her question received a shrug.

"Chad, look at me, please."

The expression she received was powerful enough to silence all other sounds except for her beating heart.

"Sweetie, Daddy's not mean."

A flicker of sadness passed through the young eyes staring back at her, gone as suddenly as it had appeared. It had been the same look she'd seen in her mother's eyes... And lately saw in her own.

She cupped his face. "Daddy works very hard, and he gets tired."

His shrug told her he didn't care about her explanation.

"I have to pee," he said and crawled off her lap.

With Jasper in tow, he ran from the room, leaving her to reason through what she'd just heard. Children didn't miss a thing; she should have learned that from her own experiences as a child. They were like sponges, absorbing everything they heard and saw—the good *and* the bad. She stood and moved to her desk. She'd been a frigging fool to think she'd protected Chad from Justin's ugliness. Her cowardice would end up doing more damage to them both than Justin's toxic tongue ever would.

Taking in a deep inhalation, she closed her eyes and whispered, "No more darkness, no more black; open the door and we'll never look back. Reveal our path, light the way, and Chad and I will travel to better days. So mote it be."

She gave the silver bell she kept on her desk a quick shake, sealing the spell. Perhaps it was time to share what her married life had been like with Dee and Peg. Her two friends might be able to offer some advice she could use. Well, Peg might. Dee would most likely say suck it up and deal; after all, Justin *was* the husband.

Her choice in Dee as a friend was baffling. Oh, sure, Dee was generous to a fault, but her personality could be overbearing at times. In many ways she was like Justin—domineering, opinionated. Peg wasn't like that; she was easier to talk to.

Life would be a whole lot easier if Justin would just leave. It was clear he no longer loved her, although she doubted he ever had, and her feelings for him were long dead. Plus, he didn't even try to hide his affair. The whole town knew about him and Shelby. Nothing suggested that would be ending anytime soon, so why was he still around?

She'd stopped caring about his running around long before now. Back when he'd explained the other women provided what she couldn't, she'd tried harder to please him in the bedroom. But his philandering hadn't stopped, and much to her self-disgust, she'd simply accepted his cheating as a way of life. He'd even stopped sleeping with her, which was a relief. She liked sex, a lot, just not sex with Justin. Someday a man would come along who'd rock her world. First things first, though. Leaving Justin had to be her priority.

The rumble of the garage door riding on its tracks crawled up her spine. What the frig was he doing here? On any other morning, she and Chad would be long gone by the time he got home.

Chad shouted from the kitchen, "Mama, Daddy's home."

Her response was less than enthusiastic. "Yes, sweetie, I know."

Chapter 2

"The secret to happiness is freedom... And the secret to freedom is courage."
Thucydides

Chad asked his father if he'd brought donuts and Shannon listened from her office to Justin's incoherent grumble, indicating he was in a foul mood. No surprise there. Lately, if Chad blinked, Justin growled. As Chad got older, it became harder and harder for her to maintain a distance between them. Boys wanted to be with their fathers, and Chad was no different. Unfortunately for Chad, Justin didn't return the sentiment.

Chad continued with a line of questioning that would have thrilled an FBI interrogator. "Daddy, did you get donuts? Is there chocolate? Where are they? Are they in the car? May I have one, please? Can I? Daddy, where are the donuts?"

"For Christ's sake Chad," came Justin's angry response. "Let me get in the goddamn house."

Shannon entered the kitchen and guided Chad away from Justin and positioned him facing the front hallway. "Sweetie, go upstairs and get yourself dressed. Brush your teeth, too."

Chad frowned, a tiny crease forming between his brows. "But Mama, where are the donuts?"

A set of keys slammed against the counter, and Justin's face twisted. "Enough about the donuts. Do what your mother says."

Undaunted by his father's outburst, Chad escaped Shannon's arms and stood at Justin's feet. "Daddy, where were you? Did you go out? Where did you go?"

Justin walked away from Chad and reached in the cabinet for a mug. "It's none of your business where I was. You're a kid. You don't get to ask me questions. Go upstairs before I really lose my temper."

"Sweetie." Shannon whisked Chad into the hallway. "If you hurry and get dressed, we'll stop for donuts on the way to school."

"Yay, donuts!" Chad charged up the staircase.

Shannon waited as Jasper followed, dog tags jangling in his hurry to catch Chad. Once she felt sure Chad was out of earshot, she faced her maybe-someday-hopefully-please-god-dess-make-it-happen-ex-husband. "What are you doing here?" Had her question come across as accusatory as it sounded to her ears? She hadn't meant it to. Or maybe she had. At this point, it was hard to separate her true feelings from her cowardly ones.

"Jesus Christ, can't I come home without being attacked? What are *you* doing here? Why isn't Chad in school?"

She watched his nostrils flare, a sure sign his anger was ready to spill her way.

"It's too early. We leave at seven."

"Yeah, well, get him dressed and get the fuck out of here."

"But—"

"But, but." He spat the words, using a mocking, falsetto tone. "I'm Shannon, and all I can say is 'but.' I think I'm special, but I'm really stupid."

He tossed more insults her way. The words she wanted to volley back at him cowered in her throat. Actually, there weren't that many words, three to be exact: I am leaving you. Okay, four, if she counted the 'am.' Three, four, tomatoes, tomahtoes, what did it matter? She was no closer to saying them than she'd been yesterday...last week...last month...last year. Each time, when she felt the phrase slipping out, she swallowed it. Like a deer accepting its fate as a sixteen-wheeler careened its way, she remained mute and allowed Justin to mow her down. All she could do was stare at him.

When she'd first met him, she'd thought he was handsome. With a strong, lantern jaw, and blue-black, wavy hair, he'd possessed a movie-star quality to his looks. But lately, his mouth was set in a permanent scowl and his eyes—if only she'd paid attention to his eyes. Almost crystal clear in color, the faint hint of blue had once been intriguing, but now... Well, now they reminded her of a doll's eyes: lifeless, vacant...dead.

Justin ended his list of demeaning insults with, "Just once I wish you could make a decision without my help, but no, I have to do everything because you screw things up."

"Excuse me? What are you talking about? What didn't I do?"

He shoved the mug at her. "Forget it. Get me some coffee."

She nodded. She used to run from guys who wanted relationships, preferring men who were only interested in screwing. No commitment meant no chance of her being controlled. All those years of avoiding emotional intimacy—they'd been a big, fat waste of time. She'd run away from attachments because she'd feared she'd end up under someone's thumb, and here she was getting squashed like a bug.

"Are you listening to me?"

"I'm sorry," she said, giving her head a shake. "Why are you so angry? What's wrong?"

He marched over to her. "What's wrong? Why do you think there's always something wrong with me? What's wrong with *you*?"

"I didn't say there was something wrong with *you*. I asked—"

"Shut the fuck up and let me talk. I can never get a word in with you always yammering." He kicked a stool away from the center island and sat. "I was having breakfast at the lodge, and that asshole St. John came in."

"St. John, the developer?"

"Yeah, St. John, the developer; do you know of any other

St. John? The guy's a blowhard, always bragging about his money and how he owns Wexford. I wanted to smash his face in."

She poured coffee into the mug and held it out. "I agree he's a jerk, bulldozing Wexford's open land the way he does. By the time he's finished, there'll be no trees left standing."

"Are you stupid?" He whipped the mug from her hand. "I'm telling you what happened to me, and all you can babble about is trees?" He slammed the mug on the island's tiled surface. "And I don't want stale coffee."

"I was just—"

"Save it. I can't even have an educated conversation with you. At least Shelby went to college. I should leave you and marry her."

If she was smart, she'd let the comment pass, but as he'd pointed out many times, she was a dummy. So instead of holding her tongue, she poured gasoline on an already-raging, five-alarm fire. Maybe getting incinerated was what she needed. *"Do it,"* she seethed. "I'm begging you, grow a set of balls and do it. Divorce me and get the fuck out of my life." She'd kept her voice low so Chad wouldn't hear her, but in her head she'd screamed loud enough to wake the entire State of New Hampshire.

His hand came narrowly close to her face, but she refused to back down.

"I would never leave you," he said.

A smile replaced his scowl, sending cold shivers up her spine.

"Even back when I asked you to marry me," he continued, "I knew you were wrong for me, but you got yourself pregnant, and I would have been a heel to run out on you. I suppose you could leave me, but there's no chance of that happening." He released a snicker. "You're too weak, so I guess I'm stuck with you."

She chewed her bottom lip, her teeth cutting into the skin, releasing the metallic taste of blood.

He exhaled a heavy sigh and moved close. "I said, you'll never leave me, *will you*?"

She nodded. There wasn't anything to say. He was right: she *was* weak. Oh, goddess, how she wished she had the courage to stand up to him.

"I'm going to take my shower," he said. "I'll send Chad down, and when you're done making my coffee, I want you both out of here."

A heavy weariness settled over her, and she nodded again and faced the sink, sickened by her gutlessness.

Shouting and frantic barking startled Shannon, and the coffee canister dropped from her hand. By the time it hit the floor, her foot was already on the first step, and she ran up the rest of the staircase to the second floor. Justin stood in the doorway leading to Chad's room, Jasper's collar twisted in his hands.

"Justin, stop, you're choking him."

"Go downstairs, Shannon. This doesn't concern you."

She tried to push past Justin, but he used his free arm to block her.

"Let me through." She caught a glimpse of Chad standing by the window. He was wearing only underwear and socks, and toys were lined up along the ledge.

Justin dragged her and Jasper to the top of the staircase and sent them stumbling halfway down. Then he scrambled to Chad's room and slammed the door.

Shannon and Jasper rushed back up the steps, and she pushed against Chad's door. "Justin, let me in."

Justin shouted at Chad from inside the bedroom. "Why can't you do simple things? Are you stupid?"

"Justin, open the door," she cried, pounding with her fists.

She remained barred from the room as threats of burning

toys and boarding school followed She sank to the floor. "Dear goddess, hear my plea, protect my son; he is innocent in this ugliness I have brought upon him. Please, he is just a child."

Justin's raving stopped, and he calmly instructed Chad to get dressed. The door opened, and Justin glared at her. "Don't you ever interfere when I'm disciplining my son, do you hear me?"

Jasper growled, and Justin kicked at him. "Go downstairs and take that fucking dog with you before I call the pound and have him put down.

Shannon staggered down the steps, unable to stop her thoughts from traveling to a time when she'd prayed outside another closed door, after thirty years, her grandmother's screeches still fresh in her mind. 'You're selfish; you never think of anyone else but yourself.'

Back then, her young age had been her excuse for not being able to help her mother, but she wasn't a little girl anymore. She was thirty-nine—an adult. What was her excuse now?

"I'm sorry I couldn't save you," she murmured as she swept up the coffee grounds.

"Mama, who's here?"

She set the dustpan on the counter and pulled Chad into a fierce embrace. "Are you okay?" She checked his face and arms though she knew there were many ways to harm a person that didn't involve physical injury.

Chad wiggled from her grasp. "Mama, who's here?"

"No one, sweetie."

"But I heard you."

"Oh, I was talking to my mama."

"And what did your mama say?"

"She said we should get going if we want donuts."

With a clap of his hands, Chad jumped in place. "She did? Can we?"

"You bet. Let me look at you first."

He stood for inspection, arms by his side, a big grin on his face. Striped T-shirt, plaid shorts, mismatched socks. At least his sneakers matched.

"Daddy said I look like a clown."

"Well, I think you look marvelous, exactly how an almost-six-year-old boy should look right before summer vacation. Where's your backpack?"

"Silly Mama, right there."

She glanced at SpongeBob's goofy face loitering on the floor. "Okay, take Jasper and get in the car. You may open the garage door too. It's donut time."

He bounced to the foyer door, a song about donuts leaping off his lips. Singing meant he was happy. Hopefully, he'd never have a reason to stop.

After placing a new filter in the coffee maker, she added the grounds she'd scooped up off the floor and water to the chamber. She pressed BREW, slipped her bag off the counter, and fished out her phone. *Meet at the Beans after we drop the kids off at school? I need help*, she texted and entered the garage. Chad's singing sounded loud and clear through the SUV's open door.

Chapter 3

"Nobody can make you feel inferior without your consent."
Eleanor Roosevelt

The voices of the patrons inside *Brewin' Beans* hummed steadily against the whirring and sputtering of the espresso machine. Like bees around a hive, customers waiting for their morning fix of caffeine hovered by the counter. From where she sat, Shannon had a full view of the entire inside of the café. Jimbo hated when she called the *Beans* a café. 'For the love of Pete,' he'd complain. 'Call it what it is, a goddamn coffee shop.'

Of the handful of establishments in Wexford, the *Beans* was her favorite place to be. A friendly staff was always ready to serve her, and the coffee was as good as any European bistro. Of course, she'd never been to Europe, but she imagined it to be true. Plus, her scones were featured daily in the bakery case.

And, of course, there was Jimbo. She sipped her lukewarm espresso and followed his movements. At six feet seven inches tall, three feet wide, with a shock of white hair, matching bushy eyebrows, and a chest-length beard, he was hard to miss. When she'd first met him, she'd immediately thought Old Saint Nick had decided owning a coffee shop in a small town in New Hampshire was the way to spend his off-time from the North Pole. Jimbo even sported the portly belly that shook whenever he laughed, which was often.

A local kid who would 'never amount to anything,' Jimbo Albie had spent his middle- and high-school years playing football, stealing cars, and getting high. After he graduated, he bought a motorcycle and moved to Manchester, where he partied, sold drugs, and spent a good deal of time behind bars.

If it hadn't been for Adam St. John dragging Jimbo into

rehab and then back to Wexford, he would have wasted away in some obscure alley. The developer had helped Jimbo buy the building she was sitting in and had handled all the renovations.

Shannon wrinkled her nose, distaste tinging her saliva. Being a good friend to Jimbo didn't excuse St. John for what he really was: a money-hungry, land-grabbing jerk.

She felt no love for the residents of Wexford, but the wooded areas were magnificent, and St. John was mowing them down for his grotesque housing developments. If she'd been allowed to join the Conservation Committee, she'd be working hard to stop him, but nope, witches need not apply. She'd curtly been informed this by the committee's chairperson and self-appointed witch hunter, Leeann, two e's-two n's. The woman needed to get a better way of introducing herself: 'Hi, I'm Leeann—two e's-two n's—Chambers.' Seriously, who introduces themselves like that? Every town had someone like her, the busybody who made sure her perky little nose was in everything.

Shannon signaled toward the two women who entered the café. The larger of the women walked up to the booth with a determined stride, unkempt frosted hair pushed behind her ears, cheeks, normally flushed, blazing cherry red. "I have a showing, so we need to make this snappy." Cantankerous at times, opinionated often, and Irish to the core, Denise 'Dee' Boyle had a take-charge manner, and that morning was no different. Peering out from under hooded eyelids, she studied Shannon's petite coffee cup. "You're drinking espresso?" Her husky voice was thicker than usual, indicating a hangover. "Why don't you drink real coffee like normal people?" Dee waved her hand at Shannon. "Switch sides, I need to see the door."

"It's great to see you too, Dee," Shannon said, exiting her seat. "Morning, Peg." She paused to hug the tall redhead standing behind Dee.

"Everything okay, Shan?" Peg stooped to place a light kiss on Shannon's cheek.

"Yeah, fine. I—"

"Stop talking," Dee said. "Peg, sit. What do you both want? My treat. The Holstein house sold, and my commission check was through the roof. Jeff and I stayed up late celebrating, and now I can't get rid of this stinking headache. Shan, do you have any of your magic shit with you?"

"Hmm, let me see, what do I want?" Peg said, tapping her chin with her index finger.

"This isn't rocket science, Peg," Dee snapped. "Make a decision."

"I'll have a double latte and one of Shannon's scones," Peg decided.

"Same for me," Shannon added. "But no scone." She handed Dee a small packet of white powder. "For your headache."

"Why the two of you can't drink normal coffee is beyond me." Dee took the powder and looked at the line near the counter. "That's bullshit. I'm not waiting in that. I'll go round and corral Jimbo from behind."

Dee marched away, leaving Peg to roll her eyes and Shannon chuckling.

"I wouldn't want to be Jimbo."

"He's a big boy; he can handle Dee." Peg removed a mirror from her purse and handed it to Shannon. "Hold this, will you?"

Peg—christened Margaret—O'Neil was the princess of the group. Tall and slender, with the grace of a swan, she was also the referee, often separating Shannon and Dee when they locked horns. She positioned Shannon's hand in the exact right spot and smiled, revealing straight, polished-to-a-brilliant-shine teeth. "Perfect, don't move." She removed a hair clip, and a mass of curls the color of an October sunset tumbled over slender shoulders covered by a pink cotton hoodie. Repositioning the lion's mane back on top of her head, she loosened a few strands and allowed them to coil around her neck. Frowning, she said, "I hate my nose." She took the mirror and closed it with a decisive snap. "When I'm rich, I'm going to get it fixed."

"I wouldn't," Shannon advised. "Your nose gives you a Greek-goddess look."

"Thanks, Shan, but I've never liked it. I guess it goes back to being given nicknames like Honker when I was in grade school."

"Yeah, well, grade school can be a tough time for kids," Shannon said. "How's the studio? I keep meaning to get over there, but I never seem to find the time." She diverted her eyes, not wanting Peg to see that she was lying. She had plenty of time to visit her friend's yoga studio, but when Justin had found her mat in the closet, he'd torn it in half, telling her to clean the house if she needed exercise.

"Don't worry about it. Yoga isn't for everyone."

"I like yoga. I used to do it when Chad was first born. It's just that..."

Peg reached out and patted Shannon's hand. "Really, I mean it. It's okay."

Shannon bit at her lip and nodded. Hoping a change of topic might appease her guilt at being a shit friend, she asked, "How's Haley?"

"She's a fucking witch." Peg covered her mouth with her fingers. "Oh, sorry, I don't mean your kind of witch. I'm thinking of the ones with pointy noses and green skin."

"I get it, but try and find another word. What's she done this time?"

"She picks fights with me constantly. I can't even breathe without her having something nasty to say."

"Has she started her...?"

"Her period? Yes, and that's part of the problem. She and I have the same cycle, so we're both wit—bitches at the same time of the month. The other day she called me..." Peg leaned forward, her voice lower than a whisper. "...a cunt." Sitting back, she added, "What do you think about that?"

"I think my grandmother would have washed my mouth out with a gallon of bleach if I had called her that, though I wanted to. What'd you do?"

"I locked her in her bedroom, which was a waste of time because she went out her window. I swear, I'm at the end of my rope."

It was Shannon's turn to pat Peg's hand. "I'm sure it'll get better, but I'm glad it's you and not me. Girls can be mean." And adults, she'd almost added, her thoughts cycling back to Justin. The names he'd called her over the years would shock Peg.

"Tell me about it. I'd love to send her to a camp this summer. Someplace far away, like China."

Dee flopped onto the seat next to Peg and reached for a napkin. She wiped her face and complained, "It's a madhouse up there. You should have seen the looks I got when I walked behind the counter." The damp napkin dropped on the table. "Shannon, your scones are sold out. I guess the new flavor was a hit. And I ordered a pot of real coffee. You two can take it or leave it."

"I'll make more tonight," Shannon said. "Where's the coffee?"

"Jimbo's daughter is bringing them over with some bagels. He needs to do something about the AC in this place." A second crumpled napkin joined the first. "What were you two talking about?"

"Nothing, really," Peg answered. "My evil daughter and that you two haven't come by for a free class."

"You know I don't like yoga." Dee centered her hazel eyes on Shannon. "Right now I want to know why the urgent meeting? Is Justin divorcing you so he can marry Shelby?" Based on her laughter, Dee seemed to enjoy her little joke.

Peg bumped Dee's shoulder, clearly not amused. "Not funny."

"Whatever. So what's up, Shan? Wait a minute. Here comes our food."

A petite young girl arrived at the table and set down a coffee pot, mugs, and food. "Here you go, ladies. Dad said to yell if you want anything else." She did a *pirouette* on her white Keds and almost skipped back to the front counter.

"I can't even imagine how that cute little wisp has Jimbo's genes." Dee snorted and grabbed the cinnamon raisin bagel. "Maybe she's the mailman's."

Peg daintily selected the plain bagel. "You might recall Jimbo was a good-looking guy in his younger days."

"Yeah, was," Dee answered. "Not any more. That's what drugs and alcohol does to a person. Maybe it's true that St. John got it on with Jimbo's wife."

"Dee, don't even kid about things like that," Peg said.

Dumbfounded, Shannon stared at Dee. "I can't believe you said that."

"What? It's always been a rumor. Ask Jimbo. He'll tell you."

"That's not the point," Peg continued. "Adam wouldn't do something like that to his friend."

Dee snorted and smeared a piece of her bagel with cream cheese. "He's St. John. He'd fuck Malcolm's wife if given the chance."

"Who's Malcolm?" Shannon asked.

Peg gave Dee an incensed glare. "Adam's half-brother, and he wouldn't sleep with another man's wife."

The two entered into an argument about St. John's integrity while Shannon sipped her coffee. If the rumors were true, Adam St. John was a manwhore. Not that there was anything wrong with sleeping around. Back in the day, she'd played a robust game of musical beds...and hallways...and cars, along with an elevator or two, sleeping bags, and even a rowboat. At any rate, his promiscuity had nothing to do with her reasons for not liking him. Since she'd never even met the man, she had no idea if he was a blowhard, as Justin called him; her opinion was based purely on what the developer was doing to the town.

Dee waved her spoon. "Snap to it, Shan. I'll be leaving soon."

Shannon lowered her cup.

"Give her time," Peg said. "She's thinking."

"She's not thinking; she's daydreaming. Come on, Shan, spit it out, whatever you called us here for."

Shannon inhaled and released air through her teeth. She shouldn't share information like wanting a divorce; it was a private matter. If she'd learned one thing from her grandmother, it was not to air dirty laundry for the world to see.

Dee stirred her coffee with an impatient tapping. "Any day now."

Shannon lowered her hands to her lap. "It's nothing. I shouldn't have bothered you two. I'm sorry."

"Bull. Come on, tell us. I promise I'll keep my big mouth shut," Dee said.

With a quick intake of air, Shannon blurted, "I'm thinking of leaving Justin."

The gaping mouths facing her told her she should have started with a more subtle lead-in.

Chapter 4

"Always be a first-rate version of yourself, instead of a second-rate version of somebody else."
Judy Garland

Dee's spoon clattered against her plate. "I must still be drunk because I could swear I just heard you say you're leaving Justin."

Shannon was quick to offer a correction. "I didn't say I *was* leaving him; I said I was thinking about it."

"Is this because of Shelby?" Peg cast a look of concern across the table.

Cutting over Peg's question, Dee asked, "Why all of a sudden do you want a divorce?"

"This isn't all of a sudden," Shannon said. "It's been coming for a while, before Justin and I even moved up here. I should have done this a long time ago, but I didn't."

"And you figured now's a good time to throw your marriage away," Dee concluded. "Are you sleeping with someone? Is that it? You have someone on the side, don't you?"

Shannon's eyes widened. "No, that's not it at all. I'm trying to save Chad and me. If I don't do something, we'll..." She slowly shook her head. It was useless trying to explain what she herself couldn't figure out. She should have sewed her mouth shut. "Just forget about it."

"No, Shannon." Dee pushed her mug aside. "We can't forget about this. I've known you for two years, and you've never said boo about your marriage, and all of a sudden you're leaving Justin. What about Chad? Have you even thought about him?"

"Yes, I have and, as to your question, Peg, this has nothing to do with Justin's infidelity; I don't care who he screws."

Dee folded her arms and smirked. "So, this *is* because of Shelby."

"This isn't about Shelby," Shannon replied, her voice insistent. "This is about me..." She paused and then said, "I'm disappearing."

"Disappearing?" Dee snapped back.

Peg held her hand on Dee's arm. "Dee, shush. The whole place can hear you."

"I don't care." Dee's tone was firm. "You're being selfish, Shannon, completely selfish. If this isn't about Shelby and you're not screwing around, then what exactly is wrong? Is it sex? Yeah, sex sucks when you've been married for a while. So what? Why don't you try the Aphrodite's brownies you gave me for my last anniversary? They certainly did the trick; Jeff was as randy as a horse. By the way, I need another batch."

"This goes deeper than brownies," Shannon insisted. "You have no idea what kind of man Justin really is."

Dee refused to give up. "I admit Justin can be an asshole at times, but he's your husband, and you took a vow to stand by him. Why don't you speak to Pastor Hannity? I bet he'll see you, despite you being a witch."

"I don't need a priest." Shannon stabbed the mound of cream cheese on the side of her plate. "I need a frigging spine, so I can save myself and Chad."

"Okay, no more talk about priests," Peg said, assuming her role as referee. "Shannon, you said you'd wanted to leave him before you guys moved to Wexford but you didn't, so why now?"

Shannon puffed her cheeks and blew out a stream of air. Peg's question was the million-dollar one, wasn't it? Why now? "I did leave," she answered. "And, before you ask, yes, I went back."

"Why?" Dee shot out.

"It's complicated."

Peg said, her voice gentle and coaxing, "We'll listen, Shan; no judgment."

Shannon slapped the cream cheese with the side of the knife, flattening the mound into a pancake. She should know the answers by now; she'd asked herself the same questions a million times over the past six years. "I thought it was better to keep Chad in a family unit—a mother and a father. It was something I'd lost when I was young."

"This doesn't make sense," Dee said. "Chad *still* needs his father. Shan, every guy cheats; that's just what they do. It's how they're wired."

"I already told the both of you this isn't about Shelby. I don't care if Justin screws the entire female population of New Hampshire. This is about his treatment of Chad and me, and now that Chad's getting older, he's annoying Justin...a lot." Shannon frowned and shook her head. If only she could make them understand.

"I get it. Kids suck," Dee snorted. "They put stress on a marriage like nothing else. You should get rid of Chad; send him to camp for the summer. That way you and Justin can spend time together like a normal couple."

Shannon dropped the knife and let it clatter on the plate. "I'd rather get rid of Justin." She smoothed the folds of her skirt, giving herself a moment to gather her thoughts. She'd try one more time, and if they didn't understand when she finished, she'd give up. She cleared her throat and said, "I loved Justin, or at least I loved the version of Justin he presented to me. In the beginning, he was wonderful—and I felt safe. We were happy. Sure, he cheated on me, and he had a bit of a temper..." She tugged at her wedding ring. "Who doesn't? When I got pregnant, he asked me to marry him, and I accepted, choosing to ignore the cheating. I moved into his townhouse in Charlestown, and until Chad was born, he treated me like a queen, but after...he changed." She hugged her arms, recalling how frightened she'd been of Justin's rantings.

"How, Shan?" Peg asked. "What would he do?"

"Oh, each day it was something new that would set him off: he didn't like the skirts I wore or what I cooked for dinner or the house was too cold, too hot, too bright, too dark—name something, and he hated it. He insulted me, told me I was brainless and an imbecile. And he played mind games, insisting he'd told me something when I knew he hadn't." Shannon bit at her lip. She had to lower her voice, or soon the entire café would know her business. "By the time Chad was three months, I'd had enough, and I left. Justin found us and took us back home."

"I still don't get why you went back," Dee said. "And if things are as bad as you say, why are you still with him now?"

Shannon looped the straps of her bag around her arm and stood. "I'll be right back. I need the ladies' room." Before she left the table, she faced Dee. "Walking away from a marriage, even if it's toxic, isn't easy."

After locking herself in one of the two unisex bathrooms, Shannon leaned her back against the door. Sharing her news went about as well as trying to grate a lemon with a feather.

She used the toilet and washed her hands, scowling at the mirror. It was difficult to face herself lately because when she did, she saw emerald eyes clouded by a defeat that was alarmingly pronounced. Maybe she should accept that she's trapped, buy a box of condoms, and visit some seedy lounge in Manchester; line up six of the foil packets on the bar, and ask if there are any takers.

As for love, screw it. She didn't need it. Justin had professed love, and look where it had gotten her. Even her grandmother had droned on about love. All words, nothing more. Bottom line, people say they love someone so they can get close enough to inflict emotional pain.

A quick romp was what she needed, someone to help distract her. Clear her head... Blow out the pipes... Center her *chi*... And give her vibrator a much-needed vacation. Sitting on some stud's tongue would sure make the situation with Justin a lot more bearable.

The light tapping against the bathroom door ended the fantasy. "I'll be right out," she said and faced her reflection one last time. "What you need is to grow the fuck up. You got yourself into this situation, so get yourself out of it."

She exited the bathroom and walked over to the counter.

Jimbo's grin faded, his gray eyes quickly taking on concern. "You okay?"

"Yeah." She offered a ten-dollar bill. "May I have three bottles of water, please?"

"Anything for you, sunshine." He slid the cash her way. "Keep your money; I need double the amount of those Tropical Breeze scones you brought me yesterday. Can I have them ready tomorrow morning?"

"Sure thing. I was planning on it."

"Have you reconsidered my offer to come on as a partner?"

"I appreciate what you're trying to do, I really do, but Justin already said no."

Jimbo waved for her to meet him at the rear of the counter. When they were in a more private area, he said, "Justin's a schmuck. Divorce him, and get on with your life."

"It's not that simple."

"Sure it is. You say, 'Justin, sweetie-pie, I'm divorcing your ass,' then you grab the little bucko, live in a snazzy townhouse in the Commons, and you do your cooking and baking here."

"I've thought about it, I really have. Not the cooking and baking part, and thank you, but the divorce. I know it's the best thing for Chad and me." She chose to add what Dee had said in the hopes he'd agree, which would make one more person on the side of staying with Justin. If everyone she talked to thought leaving was a bad idea, then it must be. "But Chad will get hurt."

Jimbo wiped a towel over the counter and grumbled. "Aw, you sound like Denise. She's the one with the glass-half-empty attitude, not you. You're one of the strongest women I know, next to my own sweet Mary Jane. I tell you what, I have a friend who knows a bangin' divorce lawyer. Want I should give him your number?"

"Not yet. I still have to think everything through; a divorce would get messy."

He pulled on her hands and stared her straight in the eyes. "Life's messy, so why should this be any different? And Chad won't get hurt, not with you watching out for him."

She stood on her toes, wrapped her arms around his neck, and kissed the area of exposed skin above the white whiskers. "Thank you. What would I do without you?"

"You'd be lost."

Jimbo went to fetch the waters. She moved to the front counter and chewed her lip. Two hours gone, and she was still in limbo.

Jimbo set three bottles on the counter. "Promise you'll come to me for help if you need it?"

"I will, and thank you again."

Jimbo's massive hands folded around hers. "Chin up, sunshine. What's gonna happen will happen. What is it you Wiccans say?"

"You mean 'so mote it be'?"

"Yeah, that's it. So mote it be and amen to that."

Shannon thanked Jimbo and headed back to the booth.

Before her butt hit the cushion, Peg announced, "Dee and I think you should have an affair."

Chapter 5

*"The real lover is the man who can thrill you by kissing your
forehead or smiling into your eyes or just staring into space."*
Marilyn Monroe

Dee collected the dishes and stacked them at the edge of the
table. "No, Peg thinks you should have an affair. I think you
should be happy you have someone to take care of you and Chad
and call it a day. Life on the outside sucks. I've placed enough
divorcees in condos in this town to know. They're all lonely—out
drinking and partying; they're miserable."

Peg chuckled. "Drinking and partying sounds like fun to
me."

"This isn't funny, Peg. Shannon will never find someone
like Justin again."

"I hope not," Shannon replied.

Dee tapped the table with her finger. "Listen, Shannon, I
know you don't believe in God, so I suggest you pray to whoever
or whatever you worship. Pray to the trees or a rock for all I
care but do not tell Justin you want a divorce. You will be making the biggest mistake of your life."

"Back to my suggestion," Peg said. "What you need is a hot
guy to help smooth the ragged edges. Believe me when I tell
you it works."

Shannon and Dee turned their eyes on Peg. "Do tell?" Shannon asked.

Waving away the question with a flip of her hand, Peg said,
"Some other time. Right now we're discussing you." Peg nudged
Dee. "Do you think he'll do it?"

"Leave him, and me, out of this. An affair is against the
church's rules."

"Screw the rules. Guys do it, so why can't we?" Peg was a

woman on a mission. "Pretend for a moment we ask him. Do you think he'll do it?"

"If a woman is breathing, he'll sleep with her. However, he has his own rules, and hooking up with Shannon would be breaking the top two. Besides, Shannon is no match for him. She'll get trampled." Dee picked up the dishes and slid from the booth.

A quick glance at the front door put a scowl on Dee's face, and she demanded they drop the entire conversation. She then carried the dishes over to the server's station where they landed with a crash.

Peg looked at the entrance and clapped her hands like a child at Disneyland. "This is great. You'll get to finally meet him."

Dee returned to the booth and pointed at Peg. "This has gone too far, so stop it."

"You're a poop."

"Who are you talking about?"

Shannon tried to stand, but Dee forced her to stay seated.

"We're not talking about anybody." Dee grabbed her bag. "Shan, promise me you won't do anything until we've talked about this some more."

"I promise. Now tell me who you're talking about." Shannon half-stood and rested a knee on the seat. "Dee, move. You're blocking my...oh, my." The guy shaking hands with Jimbo was vaguely familiar, but his head was angled, so she couldn't get a good look at his face. However, she liked what she *could* see. He wasn't as tall as Jimbo, maybe Justin's six-foot height, and he had broad shoulders, and an ass worthy of grabbing. "Who is he?"

While he talked, Mr. Hotty ran his hand through his straight, dirty-blond hair. A stray piece fell over his forehead, and a thrill raced through her body as she imagined that very strand hanging over her as he drilled her.

Jimbo leaned across the counter and said something, to which Mr. Hotty laughed, releasing rolling waves that made their way across the room and into her blood. She couldn't see the color of his eyes but enjoyed the way he rubbed at the scruff on his chin before he spoke, a gesture that elicited a bellow of laughter from the owner of the *Beans*. She'd be able to endure anything Justin dished out if she had this guy to run to. Maybe an affair wasn't such a bad idea... Or, a one-night fling? The tanned, defined arms extending out from the rolled-up sleeves looked quite capable of holding her against a door, wall, tree... anything sturdy—even a dumpster would work.

Jimbo pointed toward their booth, and Mr. Hotty settled on her a pair of the bluest eyes she'd ever seen and suddenly a vision of a snowy afternoon opened up in her brain. She was in the car with Chad while Justin walked around the property with the developer who'd built the massive house where they now lived. "No, no, no. Absolutely not." She sat and folded her arms. "I can't believe you two thought I would sleep with Adam St. John."

"I didn't—it was Peg's idea," Dee said. "Anyway, I'm leaving before Miss Blabbermouth makes things worse. I'll call you tonight."

Dee walked away. Shannon rose, and Peg joined her. St. John met Dee and gave her a peck on the cheek. It was obvious from the way Dee was waving her hands at the door she was trying to get him back outside. And from the way he was shaking his head, he wasn't having any part of it. He nodded toward the table and hooked his hand under her elbow.

As they walked in her direction, Shannon held her lip between her teeth and gripped Peg's forearm. St. John had a deliberate way of walking, not quite a swagger but a movement that said he was confident in himself. His eyes held her in place. If she'd wanted to look away, she wouldn't have been able to, his pull that strong. But who said she wanted to look away?

Sure, the guy was a land-grabber, but he certainly had a way of getting the old heart pumping and the juices flowing, especially to her groin.

"You're drooling," Peg chided.

"I am not." Shannon released Peg. "I admit he's smoking hot, but he's still Adam St. John." She met Peg's satisfied-looking grin. "He's a jerk, and I already have one of those, thank you very much."

Peg gave Shannon a hip bump. "Never believe gossip, especially Dee's gossip. Adam's a sweetheart. Besides, I'm not suggesting you fall in love. Just use him when things at home get out of whack. Think about it. I'll be right back." She added a pat to Shannon's shoulder and joined Dee and St. John.

Shannon sat with her back to the trio. In a matter of seconds, she'd officially meet Wexford's developer extraordinaire. Even if she did sleep with him, which she shouldn't...wouldn't... what did they have in common? She was a hedge witch, and him... well, to him, the only good tree was one in the shape of a two-by-four. But then again, if he was as good in bed as he looked like he might be, there wouldn't be a need for conversation. No, she sighed, she couldn't sleep with him, and besides, he probably had a tiny penis. That was why he built such huge houses; he used them to compensate for his pitiful manhood.

By the time she'd chased her thoughts like a dog chasing its tail, the trio had moved to the table's edge, continuing their exchange above her head: Peg asked St. John if he was dating anyone, and Dee told Peg to stop and insisted they didn't have time for chitchat. St. John stated he hadn't met their friend, and Dee doubly insisted he and she needed to leave.

While they talked, Shannon kept her eyes on the inky liquid in her mug. She tried to calm her frantic heart rhythm by counting her breaths, but St. John's scent distracted her. A tanned, strong-looking hand extended under her eyes, and she sucked in her breath. He had a great hand. Rugged looking. Not too big. Fingers perfectly shaped for delivering mind-blowing pleasure.

"We haven't met. I'm Adam St. John, but most people call me St. John."

His voice, smooth and fluid like melted chocolate, flowed under her skin and into her core.

She opened her water and let her eyes follow the length of his arm up to his face where she met a lopsided grin that reached the corners of his eyes, the weathered skin crinkling along the edges. In another life, he'd have owned a pirate ship. And she would have gladly been his wench.

She placed her hand in his and jolted at the charge that shot through her, understanding perfectly why so many women fell to their knees when they met him.

Dee shoved St. John. "Okay, you've met Shannon. Let's go."

St. John kept hold of Shannon's hand. "What's the hurry? If nobody has to leave, I'd like some coffee."

"Fine with me," Peg said and reclaimed her seat. "Adam, Dee's sitting next to me, so you sit next to Shannon."

Dee flashed Peg a look that said she'd deal with Peg later, to which Peg shrugged and smiled.

"Fine," Dee said. "One cup, but St. John, you sit *here*." Dee tugged on St. John's arm, trying to direct him into her spot.

St. John claimed the end of Shannon's side of the booth. "Too slow, Denise, and relax. I'm not going to eat the poor woman." He turned his attention to Shannon and grinned again. "At least not right now."

Shannon met his eyes. She imagined she was wearing a seductive hint of a smile, alluring and coquettish. Unfortunately, the muscles around her mouth announced her lips were open too wide. She was saved from further looking like a fool when

Dee's arm shot across the table. "Okay, stop the bus. Back off, St. John. Shannon's married."

Peg pulled at Dee's back pocket. "You're making a scene."

St. John didn't seem to hear Dee because he remained facing Shannon. "Who's your husband? I might know him."

Shannon's lower lip disappeared between her teeth. She couldn't answer. She was too busy drinking in his aroma. White musk, cedar, a hint of pine. Earthy and intoxicating. And body melting. She felt like a marshmallow suddenly dropped into a mug of steaming hot chocolate.

"She's married to Justin Baldos. So leave her alone," Dee said.

"Baldos?" St. John scratched the gray-and-brown scruff on his chin and seemed to consider the information. "That's a shame." He added the last part as if he was disappointed.

Shannon found her voice. "Why is that?" She had no idea why he thought her marriage to Justin was a shame, but she could offer a few reasons for him to consider, starting with the fact that Justin sucked. She did, however, enjoy thinking St. John might be disappointed to learn she was married. Maybe he'd wanted to play pirate and wench too.

"He didn't mean anything," Dee said. "St. John, weren't you going to get us more coffee? We have to be in Salem soon."

"I have a class too, so please hurry up, Adam," Peg said. "Make mine an iced hazelnut."

"Mine too," Dee added.

"And what would you like me to give you, Shannon?"

"For crying out loud, St. John, stop it," Dee demanded. "She'll have the same as us. Now go."

"I'm on it." St. John hopped from the booth, but before walking away, he leaned in close to Shannon's ear and murmured, "Save my spot."

When he pulled away, the hot area of her face rapidly cooled, leaving her wanting more.

He needn't worry. She would save him any damn spot he desired.

Chapter 6

"Always believe that something wonderful is about to happen."
Unknown

Peg kicked Shannon's foot under the table and nodded in St. John's direction. "So, what do you think of my idea now?"

Shannon slid onto the spot St. John had just vacated and leaned out of the booth. She watched the movement of his ass and sighed, wondering if her original theory about the houses he built and his penis size was true.

"Stop it."

She turned and grinned at Dee. "I'm just admiring the view. Who knew St. John was so frigging sexy?"

"Everyone except you, and he knows it too, but that doesn't matter. Stay away from him."

"Why?"

"You're married."

"So? You're the one who said I should have an affair."

"No, that was Peg. I'm ordering you to forget any ideas about sleeping with Adam St. John. He's not for you."

"Again, I ask why?"

"Because he collects women like some men collect baseball cards, and you'll get hurt."

Peg came to St. John's defense once again. "Dee, you're overreacting. Adam's not a bad guy. He might be just what Shannon needs to get her groove back."

"She doesn't need a groove," Dee said, her face resembling the color of a beet. She wiped at her neck with a napkin. "What she needs is to fix her marriage."

Shannon pouted. "Whether I need a groove or not, you're not acting very nice. I thought you liked him."

"I do; he'd give anyone he meets the shirt off his back, but if it's a woman, he'd take off his pants too. Trust me, Shan, men like him use women and then dispose of them."

"Oh, phooey," Peg chimed in. "I tell you this is a good idea. It's obvious Adam's into her, and it's pretty clear she likes what she sees."

"St. John is into any female with a pulse," Dee said, casting Peg a disdainful look.

Shannon patted her friend's hand. "Don't worry, I'll be a good girl. Besides, I don't even like the man." She saw an opportunity to tease Dee, so she added, "However, if I do get divorced, I'll toss my thong at him and see where it leads."

Dee's looked up, and her face flushed bright red. "Shannon, stop talking."

Shannon giggled. "Why? He's hot."

"Please, close your mouth."

"You're no fun. I wonder if he's good in bed. Any idea?"

"Shannon," Peg said, "listen to Dee and stop."

"I'm just saying he looks like he'd be very good."

"Shannon, please be quiet," Dee begged.

"What? Maybe someday I'll get to take his face for a test drive."

Peg buried her face in her hands, and Dee said, "For the love of God, please stop."

"Why?" Shannon asked. A sudden awareness washed over her face. She peered to her left and met eyes the color of a cloudless summer sky.

St. John grinned at her and sat down. "Anytime you want a test drive, say the word."

He raked his hair off his forehead, but the renegade piece returned to hanging over his eyebrow, tempting her to twine it between her fingers and kiss him hard enough to rattle his cocky demeanor.

Regaining her composure, she thanked him, adding a cool, "I'll let you know when I get my driver's license."

"Touché." St. John tapped his glass to hers. "So, you're the witch, eh?"

"Guilty as charged," she said, giving him a narrowing of her brows. "So you're the developer who's leveling the forests of Wexford, eh?"

St. John raised his glass in a salute. "Guilty as charged." He drank some coffee and then asked, "What does a witch do for fun in a town like Wexford?"

She played with a drop of condensation slipping along her glass. "The typical stuff: I turn people into toadstools and howl at the moon."

"Any running naked through the woods?"

"Sometimes." She licked at her finger, glad that he'd insisted on staying to have coffee. She was enjoying herself very much.

Dee slammed her hand on the table. "I'm serious, you two. Stop it."

"Adam, how's Sadie?" Peg asked, her hand on Dee's arm.

"Not bad for an old girl, still full of piss and vinegar."

"Shannon has a Lab too, only Jasper is young. Hey, Shannon, maybe Jasper and Sadie could have a play date someday. I bet Chad would love that." Peg added a loud, "Ouch," and scowled at Dee. "That hurt."

St. John lowered his glass. "I'd love to come and play with you," he said to Shannon.

"Come on, St. John, we're leaving." Dee pulled at his shirt sleeve.

"Wait," Peg said. "We still haven't decided what Shannon is doing about the divorce."

Dee reacted with, "Why don't you just tell the whole fucking town?"

"Dee, it's okay," Shannon said. "I don't mind if Mr. St. John knows."

St. John drank some of his coffee, wiped his mouth, and said, "The only people who call me Mister St. John are the ones who owe me money or are suing me, and you don't fall into either of those categories. Who's Chad?"

"My five-year-old. Actually, he'll be six in two weeks."

"Divorce can be tough on young children," he said, a seriousness passing through his chiseled features.

"If you go through with this, Shan," Peg said, "you do know Justin's never going to let you have custody of Chad."

"I know it won't be easy, but I won't leave without Chad. If need be, I'll get help; Jimbo said he has a friend who knows a good divorce lawyer."

"That friend would be me." St. John pulled a pen and business card from his shirt pocket. He wrote a name and phone number on the back of the card, added a second number to the front, and handed it to her. "Call Marty. He's the best divorce attorney there is. Tell him you know me, and he'll work for short money."

"Thank you, I will." Shannon flipped the card and read the front. ASJ Development out of Manchester. "I'm still not sure what I'm going to do."

St. John nodded. "It's not easy walking away from a marriage."

Dee waded her napkin and threw it at St. John. "You should know; you've made it a hobby. We have to go, or we'll be late."

"Right."

St. John offered his hand, and Shannon took hold more quickly than the first time and allowed him to guide her from the booth. Dee inserted herself between them, muttering under her breath about them driving her crazy. Peg followed, giggling as she walked.

At the exit, St. John held the door for the women, and when Shannon passed, he bent close. "When you're ready for that test drive, my cell number is on the front of the card. I'll even shave for the occasion."

******

With the noise of the highway blocked out by the closed truck windows, St. John and Dee rode along Route 111, heading toward his new development in Salem. During the first leg of the trip he busied himself with mentally running through his to-do list. It was halfway into the drive when he returned his thoughts to Shannon and asked his question.

"What's Shannon's story?"

When Dee didn't answer, he asked again.

"I heard you, but I'm not going to answer."

"Why not?"

Dee's eyebrows rose several inches. "Why not?"

"Yeah, why not?"

"You know why not."

"Pretend I don't and enlighten me."

"One, because she's married, and two, because she's married. Want me to list reasons three and four?"

"For crying out loud, Denise, you're acting like an overprotective mother. I asked an innocent question. If I was anyone else, you'd have a hard time keeping your mouth shut."

He lifted his right knee and controlled the steering wheel, giving him the freedom to crack several of his knuckles. He'd known Denise since she was a kid, and a good portion of the time, she was bearable. But when she took it upon herself to try and run the lives of people around her, it irritated the crap out of him.

"You're not anyone else. Stay away from her, St. John. I mean it."

"And if I don't?"

By now she was facing him, her cheeks a radiant shade of red. "I'm not fooling around."

"Calm down, Denise. I'm not going to bang Justin Baldos' wife; I do have rules against things like that."

"Great, so drop it."

He refused to let it go. "I still don't see why I can't know something about her. For instance, how about this: what does she do for work? You can't say that isn't an innocent question."

"She's a stay-at-home mom and runs a cooking blog on the side. I'll let you have one more question, and then the conversation is over."

"What's the blog's name?"

"*The Grateful Earth.* There. Done."

"Oh, no, that was part two of my first question. My second question is why does she want to divorce Baldos?"

"You're kidding, right?"

"I'm deadly serious."

The corners of Dee's naturally downturned mouth dropped even further. "Too bad. I'm not gossiping about my friend."

The laughter he released caused her to give him a startled look. "You're a hoot. You and Chambers' wife, Leeann—the two of you need gossip like fish need water."

"Not true." Dee faced the windshield, her arms folded.

He let her fume in silence. In time she'd tell him what he wanted to know; she'd explode if she kept things to herself.

"There isn't much I can tell you," she eventually said. "This morning was the first time I've heard about a divorce."

"I thought the two of you were friends?"

"We are. What's your point?"

"Well, something this big doesn't just happen overnight. Wouldn't she have told you when she started thinking about it?"

"I would have thought so, but today was the first time she's brought it up."

He grinned and listened in silence. When Dee got started, she ran like a racehorse.

"Shannon doesn't share a lot of details about her life," Dee continued. "I do know that. Whenever Peg and I are complaining...talking about our lives...Shannon listens but never joins in. I've known her two years, and this morning I learned more about her than I have in that whole time. Anyway, I think she's being selfish. Justin bought her a big house. He pays the bills... So what if he's seeing someone else? Marriage is sacred; she should honor her vows."

"But Justin doesn't have to?"

"What?"

"You said she should honor her marriage vows, but what about Justin? He's diddling a woman half his age and doesn't even try to hide the fact. Shouldn't he have to honor the marriage vows?"

"It's not the same thing."

"Really?" He was blown away by what he was hearing. "You're saying because he's a guy he gets a pass?"

"In a way, yeah. God made woman in man's image, not the other way around."

"That's very Christian of you, Denise. Your friend is married to a jerk and needs help, and all you're willing to offer is some bull the Church fed you."

"It's not bull, and why is it okay for *you* to treat women like shit?"

"First off, I don't treat anyone like shit, and you know that, and second, how did this come back to me? We were talking about Shannon."

"Not anymore." Dee huffed and turned to face the passenger window.

"Good chat," St. John said and focused on the road.

What did he care about the witch? He wasn't planning on screwing her, and with all the projects he had going on, he didn't have the head space to devote to her.

Then why wasn't he trying to resist the thoughts of her setting up residence in his head?

Chapter 7

"When one holds her breath for too long,
she forgets how to breathe."
Unknown

Shannon poured melted chocolate into the depression she'd created and blended the dark velvet with the flour. She was on autopilot as she moved the spatula. Her mind was elsewhere, as it had been most of the evening. She'd tried to keep thoughts of St. John at bay, but her consciousness had other plans, and as soon as she kicked him from her head, he'd leak back in. Even reminding herself she had way too much to figure out didn't help. As soon as she let down her guard, he was there behind her eyes in all his sexy glory, sometimes wearing nothing but his lopsided grin.

"This is stupid," she sighed and added a cup of walnuts to the batter. When this batch of brownies was done baking, she'd finally be finished in the kitchen. The full moon was in Sagittarius, and she wanted to cast a circle, but she still had to give Chad his bath and take her own shower. It would be well after midnight before her head hit the pillow.

"Mama, may I lick the spoon?"

"Sure thing," she said. "Pull over a stool."

"I'm still hungry. Maybe I should lick the bowl too."

"Can't honey. You can only have a little bit. The batter contains raw eggs, remember?"

"Mama, I want you to bake with cooked eggs. Then I can lick all I want."

"Baking doesn't work that way. Here." She dipped a spoon in the batter and handed it to him with a dish towel. "Don't give Jasper any, though."

"I know. Jasper can't have choc-lit because his heart will stop."

"Good for you for remembering. I made some without nuts, so you can have a baked brownie with ice cream if you want."

"Yay."

Chad jumped off his stool and danced around the kitchen, the spoon held high in the air while he sang about having a brownie and ice cream.

She never tired of his little songs.

"Okay, the last pan is in the oven. Get the ice cream from the freezer, and we'll have our dessert."

"Is Daddy having brownies with us?"

"No, munchkin, Daddy has to work, but he'll kiss you when he gets home, don't you worry." The lie slipped out easily. One of these days, he was going to catch her; then what would she do?

He carried the ice cream to her and she prepared two bowls, topping his with rainbow sprinkles. "Want to eat outside on the deck? There's a full moon."

"Yay, I love full moons." A seriousness cast a shadow on his face, and he asked, "Mama, are you a good witch?"

"Yes, sweetie, you know I am." She covered the ice cream and walked to the freezer, stopped, and turned. "Wait, why are you asking me that?"

"Stevie said you're a bad witch and that you fly on a broom. Will you take me for a ride? I promise to hold on tight. Please?"

"Chad, slow down. Do you mean Stevie Chambers?"

"Ah-huh. Can I?"

"When did Stevie say I was a bad witch?"

"Today at recess. Can we go flying tonight?"

She set the ice cream in the freezer. "Yeah, sure." She realized her mistake when he danced and sang about going for a ride on her broom. "Chad, Mama meant... Oh... Let's just eat our ice cream." She carried the bowls out to the deck.

"But Mama, you said yes."

"Sweetie, I wasn't paying attention; I'm sorry. But this is silly. You know I don't have a broom that flies."

"But I want to fly to the moon."

"Oh, Chad, even if I did have a broom that could fly, the moon is too far away." She placed his bowl in front of him and scooted his chair close to the table. "Just say hello and eat your dessert."

"Hello," he yelled and shoved his spoon into his ice cream.

She was dying to ask more about what Leeann's son had said but didn't want to make too big a deal about it. Involving Chad in the petty feud in which she found herself wouldn't be fair. But she had to know one thing. "Did Stevie say where he heard that I'm a bad witch?"

"Ah-huh."

She waited for him to swallow the spoonful of ice cream in his mouth.

"Honey, before you take another mouthful, tell Mama who told Stevie I'm a bad witch."

Chad dug in his bowl and lifted a heaping mound of brownie. "His Mama."

"His Mama told him I'm a bad witch?"

"Ah-huh. I punched him."

"You what?" The story was going from bad to worse.

"I'm sorry I hit Stevie." He turned his ice cream-smudged face her way.

"I know you are, but you can't go around hitting people when they say something you don't like. Use your words."

"I did use my words. I said, 'You're a liar, Stevie,' and *then* I punched him."

Chad demonstrated how he'd hit Stevie, sending ice cream sailing through the air. Jasper, quick on his paws, dove for it.

"Okay, but next time stick with the words, okay?" She wiped and kissed his cheeks. "Finish up. It's time for your bath."

"Can I still go to Cannery Lake?"

"Canobie Lake, and of course you can. Tomorrow, I want you to apologize to Stevie. Do you hear me?"

He nodded and murmured, "I wish we could fly on your broom."

She licked at her spoon. "I do too."

"The next time I see that blond pipsqueak, I'm going to say something," Shannon fumed into her phone as she folded clothes. She started sorting Chad's socks.

"No, you won't," Dee said on the other end of the call.

"Maybe I will."

"Come on, Shan, you're not one for confrontation."

"Maybe I'll change. Anyway, I made your brownies."

"Thanks, and hey, I'm sorry about today; I acted like a bitch when you told Peg and me your news. It's just that you've never mentioned having problems, and suddenly you're divorcing or wanting to divorce Justin. Did you talk to him yet?"

"Hang on." Shannon carried the clothes basket into the adjoining bathroom and closed the door. "No, he's not home." She contemplated mentioning that he didn't come home at night but held her tongue.

"I still think if you talked to Father Hannity he could help."

"Please, just drop it." She twisted a pair of socks into a firm ball.

"If you don't want to listen to God's teaching, then listen to me, your friend. It's not easy being a single mother. How will you afford rent and food, and what about Chad's needs? School supplies and his clothes? I can't believe I'm saying this, but maybe you should consider Peg's suggestion and find someone to help distract you."

"Like St. John?" She didn't want to think about St. John...or his arms...hair...eyes...fingers. No, no, no. She threw the socks at the bathroom door.

"Mama, what was that?" The sound of feet hitting the floor in the bedroom preceded a knock on the door. "Do you have a ball? Can I play too?"

"Dee, hold on. Honey, it's not a ball. Go and pick out what toys you want in your bath and let Mama finish talking to Aunt Dee."

The doorknob turned, and Chad's face appeared. "I want to play."

"Mama isn't playing; she's folding clothes. Do what I asked, please. And no dilly-dallying."

The door closed, and a tune about dilly-dallying receded down the hallway.

"I really have to go, Dee."

"Shan, don't toy with the idea of sleeping with St. John."

"I'm not interested in him. I only said his name because you and Peg started this whole thing about an affair."

"That was all Peg. Anyway, if you see him again, be nice but don't flirt. It only encourages him."

"What will happen then? I'll succumb to his charms?" She sat on the edge of the tub, suddenly very tired. All she wanted to do was crawl under the covers and sleep, no thoughts of divorce or Justin...or St. John.

"Every woman succumbs to his charms."

"Did you?" she asked.

"He never tried them on me. I was the annoying little runt who followed him and my brother around. By the time I was old enough to realize St. John was hot, he was already divorced and had made a rule to stay away from Wexford women. That's rule number two."

"What's number one?"

"Never date a married woman, if he could call what he does dating. Rule number three: no second nights."

"How many rules does the guy have?"

"I've lost count. Hey, I have an idea, how about the three of us girls go out Saturday night? The guys are taking the kids to Water Country on Father's Day, and Jeff said they want to do a sleepover at the lodge the night before. It'll be fun. We've never gone out at night, just us. What do ya say?"

"I don't know."

"Think about it, okay? I gotta run. The twins are bugging Jeff. See you Friday."

Shannon left the bathroom and added the clothes on her bed to the basket. It might be fun to go out and kick up her heels. Maybe they'd run into St. John.

No, no, no. No.

She entered Chad's bedroom. He was naked, sitting on his floor and playing with an assortment of dinosaurs.

"Chad, what did I say about dilly-dallying?" She walked into his bathroom and opened the tub faucet.

"I wasn't. I want these for my tub." Hard plastic legs, beaks, wings, and tails sprouted from between his arms. "Mama, can I sleep with you tonight?"

"May you sleep with me?"

"Yes."

"No, sweetie, you ask *may I*, not *can I*."

"Why?"

"Um, it's... Just do Mama a favor and say it. I'll explain some other time."

"May I sleep with you?"

"Yes, you may. But first, take your bath."

After the bath and once Chad's teeth were brushed, they climbed onto the master bed. He reclined on her lap, his head rising and falling with the movements of her chest as she read to him. Sleep tugged at him, and with each passing page, when she asked him to read a few words, his voice would slur a little more. By the time the lost ducks had found their mother, his breathing was the steady rhythm of someone fast asleep.

She eased out from under him, covered him with the comforter, and kissed his temple. So small, he barely made a bump in the king-sized mattress. What thoughts did he carry with him while he walked in his dream-state?

How did he act?
Was he fearless?
She hoped so.
At least one of them should be.

Chapter 8

"Life is either a daring adventure or nothing at all."
Helen Keller

Shannon's robe slipped from her shoulders, and it pooled on the grass at her feet. She closed her eyes and inhaled the aromas surrounding her. Pungent cedar from the nearby conifers that formed the boundary of the backyard. And musk. A smiled formed on her lips. The fragrance reminded her of... Her eyelids flew open.

"No, no, no, I will not allow him to dominate my thoughts. No."

With steely determination, she vanquished the grinning face of St. John from her mind, took a long breath, and began again, this time focusing on the breeze playfully tickling her naked form and less on the scents riding the swirling air. When she felt centered, she removed a box of matches from her altar and walked to the northern cardinal point of the circle's perimeter. There she lit a green candle and said, "Spirits of earth, Guardians of the North, I call on you to bless this humble circle."

In the eastern side of the circle, she lit the yellow candle.

"Spirits of the air, Guardians of the East, I call on you to bless this humble circle."

At the southern spot, the wick of a red candle glowed under the flame of her match tip.

"Spirits of fire, Guardians of the South, I call on you to bless this humble circle."

In the western corner she stood at the blue candle and said, "Spirits of water, Guardians of the West, I call on you to bless this humble circle."

She returned to the altar and took hold of her athame and

held her arms out to the side. She envisioned white light flowing from the double-edged knife's tip. Spinning carefully three times in a clockwise circle, she announced, "Goddess of the Moon, please join me and bless this humble circle you have so lovingly taught me to cast; keep me protected within its boundaries that no unwanted entities may enter; only those who mean me no harm are welcome into this space."

With her feet firmly planted in the cool grass, she imagined her toes absorbing the energy of the earth. Up her legs it flowed and into her belly. With her arms held toward the night, she drew down the moon's glow and let it bathe her skin. In her mind's eye, she saw brilliant rays of blue, green, and yellow light radiating from every pore. She was one with the Universe.

"This circle is cast. So mote it be."

Satisfied with her magic, she spread a blanket, knelt, and lit one of two white candles in the center of her small altar.

"Goddess, on this night of the full moon, I call on you from within this humble circle I have built. I ask that you join me so that I may learn from your wisdom."

She removed two silver cups and a bottle of bourbon from a cloth sack, and after she served her goddess, she poured herself two fingers' worth of the amber liquid and raised her cup high.

"On this night, when the moon is full, I yield to its power; I feel its pull. Crone of the moon, as your light begins to wane, so too will my uncertainty and fears as you reveal my true way. So mote it be."

The whiskey burned the inside of her throat, but unlike some, who shied away from the woodsy liquid fire, she enjoyed the way it made her body come alive.

Etched into the wax of the unlit candle was the rune *Uruz*. She'd chosen that particular rune because it represented inner strength and wisdom: two things she would give her right arm to possess. It wasn't lost on her the rune also opened a path to increased sexual intimacy. She could have used a different rune, but the power of *Uruz* couldn't be denied; if it made her horny, so be it. Having to purchase a new vibrator and a bunch of batteries was a small price to pay for gaining the courage to stand up to Justin.

The candle flame danced, and she focused on its swaying movements and whispered, "I am ready, I am strong; reveal to me where I belong." She repeated the spell a second and third time and closed her eyes, willing her path to materialize in her mind.

"No." She lifted her eyelids. "Not him."

She took another sip of bourbon and readjusted herself from kneeling to sitting, her legs bent. "Let's try this again. My eyes are shrouded, my soul is blind; the weeds they cling, and to my feet, they bind. Clear them away to reveal the lane I must travel to breathe once again."

As before, she repeated the spell and closed her eyes, only to open them again and sigh.

After finishing her bourbon, she settled further into the blanket and said, "Now listen to me. Stop playing games. This is serious. My life and Chad's depend on this, so I'll spell it out as clearly as I can. Ready? Okay, I ask that you show me the path I should take to create a loving, safe, blessed life for Chad and myself." She added as punctuation for her request, "Always a blessing; it always works. Blessed be."

Lying back on the blanket, she stared up at the moon and waited. It didn't take long. A mist covered her mind, and in it, she saw a cozy house surrounded by colorful gardens. Chad played hide-and-seek with Jasper around the base of a massive beech tree while, in the vision, she stood on the front porch, smiling. There was a peaceful comfort to the scene. At the beep of a horn, she faced the driveway, and her smile widened. Chad ran over to the large, black truck coming to a stop. The driver's side door opened, and St. John appeared.

"Give me a break," she cried out and covered her face with her hands.

******

St. John watched the flames consume the new piece of oak he'd added to the fire pit and sipped his second glass of bourbon. Overhead, a beacon of a moon lit up the pines framing his land, and Sadie darted from shadow to shadow, chasing nocturnal creatures. For the past two hours, he'd read Shannon's blog and had learned a fair amount about her spiritual beliefs.

He'd always thought there were only two kinds of witches—black and white, something he'd learned from spending time over in Portsmouth. But, nope, there were dozens of different types of white witches. Shannon belonged to a category called hedge witches, which were different from kitchen witches which were different from earth witches which were different from... His head was spinning, and he still knew diddly-squat about the woman behind the green eyes, although he had discovered a new recipe for roast chicken.

Her face refused to leave his mind, as did her laughter. And her perfume. He'd once joked that the woman capable of unsealing his heart would be wearing Chanel No. 5, and here she was. Unfortunately, she lived in Wexford. And she was married to Baldos.

How'd she even end up with a jerk like Justin? The guy was a misogynistic, loud-mouthed prick. He treated everyone around him like dirt. What on earth could he possibly have offered Shannon to get her to marry him? Money?

She'd mentioned a divorce, but Peg had said Justin wouldn't let the kid go, and Shannon didn't come across as someone who would put up a fight. Yeah, there'd been a glimpse of a determined spirit in her eyes, but the flicker hadn't lasted long.

Maybe taking her to bed would provide the push she needed. Plus, screwing Baldos' wife would be an added perk.

Denise had been clear: stay away from Shannon.

"Yeah, stay away from Shannon, good advice. Thanks, Denise," he told his drink before emptying the glass. The best part had been what she'd said about him using women, which was a lie; he didn't use women—and if he did, they used him right back.

But he didn't.

Every woman knew the score before he even laid a hand on them. No second encounters. No attachments. No chance of a relationship. Clean and simple. Just like his life.

Denise couldn't say he hadn't tried to be in a relationship. Three times, to be exact. Three marriages and three divorces.

He chuckled and refilled his glass. Marty's advice after his last divorce had been priceless. 'Keep your dick on a leash and carry a prenup.'

Well, he didn't need any contracts, and he didn't need to control his sex drive. He'd learned his lesson—once burned, shrug it off; twice burned, shame on him; three times burned, he was a fucking idiot. It was after his first divorce that the romance rules had come into play. The first four were the most important: never sleep with a married woman; never sleep with a woman who lived in Wexford; never offer a second night; and above all, never, ever fall in love.

Love. It was nothing more than an excuse people used to inflict heartache.

All three of his wives had professed their love, and look what it had cost him: a ton of money and his pride.

Emotionally vacant.

That's what his second wife had written as her reason for the divorce. And his third hadn't offered much better, telling him he was 'dead inside.'

Ah, sweet, manipulative Victoria. That debacle of a marriage had been the most expensive mistake of his personal life. 'You're incapable of loving someone,' she'd said. His response of a signature on a hefty settlement had sure made her happy, though.

Yup, love was for suckers. Better to enjoy the pleasure of someone's company and walk away, which was exactly what he'd like to do with Shannon Baldos. Spend a little quality time with her, then say goodbye and live his life.

His lonely, isolated life.

No, he wasn't lonely; he was alone. There was a difference. Being lonely meant he was walking around wishing someone would come along to share his life. Being alone meant he didn't need anyone. He'd gotten very good at being alone.

So why was he suddenly—? Yeah, he knew.

"Fuck this," he growled into the shot glass before dumping the contents into his mouth.

Sadie ran over to his chair and placed her snout on his knee.

He scratched behind her ears.

"Don't worry, girl, I'm fine. I just need a distraction."

He removed his cell from his shirt pocket and pulled up the phone number he'd received that afternoon. The call was answered halfway through the first ring. Always a good sign.

"Hey, it's Adam St. John. Feel like some company?"

Chapter 9

"No act of kindness, no matter how small, is ever wasted."
Aesop

Even with the early morning temperature nearing eighty, the excitement in the Wexford Community School parking lot was undaunted. Students, aged five to fifteen ran, laughed, sang, and shouted. Leeann, two e's-two n's, stood in the middle of the chaos, a stack of manila envelopes held in her left arm and a bullhorn pressed to her mouth. Each time she let loose a command, kids, all wearing T-shirts of the same color, would freeze. Once the chaperons had their charges safely stowed in a designated bus, another group would receive their instructions. And so the boarding of the busses for the end-of-the-school-year field trip to Canobie Lake progressed, with Leeann confidently at the helm.

It was into this military zone that Shannon and Chad walked. "Munchkin, go put your lunch in the box by Miss Brewster's feet and get your T-shirt from Dylan's mom."

Chad looked as if he was considering his options when Dee arrived with her youngest and snarled, "Dylan, go with Chad and get your T-shirt and don't get into any trouble, or you'll spend the day at home, locked in your room."

"Tough morning, Dee?"

"What else is new? I had to do everything while Jeff went to the lodge for breakfast. I swear, that man is useless." Dee took out a tube of sunscreen and waved it in front of Shannon. "I figured you'd forget yours."

Shannon frowned at the offering. What a win it would have been if she'd been able to say she had her own, but sadly, it was sitting on the kitchen counter where she'd left it after slathering Chad. "Thanks, I did, but the good news is I got Chad done before we left."

"You'll need more if he goes in the water park. I brought a couple of tubes. Keep that one." Dee wiped at the sweat around her neck. "Christ, it's seven-thirty and already eighty. Wasn't it fifty last night? I can't stand this stinking weather." As if she'd just noticed Shannon's black-and-white skirt, white sleeveless blouse, and black-and-white, polka-dot headscarf, she snickered. "Only you would dress as if you're going to a garden party."

Shannon looked down and swished the skirt, making the flowing fabric swirl around her legs. "Is this your way of saying I look nice?"

"Yeah, if you're going to visit the Queen of England. This is Canobie we're heading to, a place known for its dust and filth."

"I think you're exaggerating," Shannon said. "And besides, I don't plan on rolling on the ground."

Peg joined them and distributed iced coffees. "Nice outfit, Shan. Oh, great." She claimed the sunscreen and called after her two sons, but they waved her off. "Fine," she shouted. "Get sunburned. See if I care."

Dee lifted her cup and chided, "Mother of the year."

"Bite me."

"Someone woke up on the wrong side of the bed," Dee said. "What, you didn't get a chance to do leaping frog or whatever move you do in the morning?"

Peg narrowed her perfectly shaped brows at Dee. "As I said, bite me."

Leeann screamed into her bullhorn, and Shannon winced. "I wish someone would take that thing away from her."

"I'll do it," Peg said. "Miss two e's, two fucking n's, better stay off my back today, or that bullhorn will be so far down her throat she'll have to poop to get it out."

"Peg." The coffee that had been in Shannon's mouth hit the pavement. "Wow, this is a side of you I've never seen. Are you okay?"

"It's Howard. I can't stand him, and I can't stand my witch—oh, sorry, bitch of a daughter either."

Shannon widened her eyes and gave Dee a look that asked if she knew what was going on.

Dee responded with a shrug. "Peg, you're gonna have to can it. Shannon, did you check in with the blond commandant?"

"Not yet. I'll see you two at the park. Thanks for the coffee, Peg."

"Do you want your sunscreen?"

"Oh, yeah, thanks." Shannon waved the tube and dragged her feet in the direction of their leader. "Hey, Leeann, I'm here," she called out and quickly changed direction for bus twelve, hoping one of the other chaperones had the roster.

"You can go home," Leeann said.

Shannon stared at the five-foot woman. "Excuse me?" She couldn't have heard correctly. As of yesterday, they were still looking for chaperones, and now she was being *dismissed*?

Leeann raised the bullhorn to her lips. "Go home. We don't need you. Go count toadstools or something." She made a shooing motion with her hand and returned to shouting orders.

Shannon glanced around, hoping no one had heard the dismissal. Who was she kidding? The bitch had used a frigging megaphone.

She wiped at the corners of her eyes and scanned the area near Chad's bus. He was giggling with his friends while they waited to board the bus. When he'd found out she was going to be a chaperone, he'd started singing one of his silly songs about how his mommy was sharpening him at Canary Park. Was she really going to let the Wicked Bitch of the East steal their memories?

She collected the folds of her skirt and strode back to where Leeann was playing commando. "Leeann, got a minute?"

Leeann spun, eyes wide with shock. "Shannon, I'm...I'm busy. Go away."

"This will only take a sec." Shannon grinned. "I'm thinking your comment about the toadstools is a reference to my being a witch. Am I correct?"

The suddenly pale blond looked as if she wanted to bolt. "W...what's your point?"

"You're not too bright, are you?"

Leeann's petite hands pressed the megaphone against her rib cage. "I..."

"Let me finish," Shannon said. "You see, I'm wondering why, since you know I'm a witch and you know what witches are capable of, you'd want to piss me off. I'll take that." A low snickering spread through a nearby cluster of mothers when she plucked from Leeann's hands the manila envelope with the number 12 printed on it. "Thanks." She added a sweet smile, turned, and strolled toward the bus. There she greeted the two other chaperones, who each discreetly gave her a thumbs up.

One hundred and thirty kids sat on towels in the shade of Canobie's picnic grove. They ate sandwiches, chips, and carrot sticks, and sipped their juice boxes while their voices carried through the tall trees. Only one boy, Raylan Griffin, sat crossed-legged, his head bent, silently crying. It was next to this young man that Shannon knelt. His mother had packed a peanut-butter-and-jelly sandwich, a carton of milk, along with a chocolate chip cookie wrapped in a napkin. And Leeann had confiscated it all.

'Your mother could have killed someone," Leeann said. "And it would have been your fault for bringing this into the park. Do you understand? I'm taking the whole bag because the cookie could have nuts, and the milk has been next to nuts.'

While listening to Leeann deliver her chilling malice with expert precision, Shannon had remained quiet, as had all the other parents and the children.

Raylan Griffin, along with five older siblings, lived with his parents in an apartment over the town's one gas station and liquor store. Raylan's mother cleaned the mansions St. John built, and the father, labeled the town drunk, performed odd jobs such as mucking horse stalls and repairing broken gutters. The town residents knew Harlan Griffin didn't drink. He'd been walking home late one night, and a car had hit him. The driver left the scene and the unconscious father of six was found the next morning. It was easier for the residents of Wexford to blame alcohol as the reason Harlan was no longer 'right' instead of admitting that one of their own had done a terrible thing.

"Hey, Raylan," Shannon said, "I packed two lunches for Chad, and he only wanted one of them. Would you like the other one?" The bag she held hadn't been prepared for Chad. She'd run to one of the food stands. She knew he'd never accept her offering if he knew the truth; the Griffins were a proud lot.

Raylan responded in a whisper, "No thank you, ma'am." Fat tears hit his ragged towel.

Shannon remained next to him. There was no pity in her heart. There was anger. White, hot anger. People like Leeann *and* Justin weren't just bullies; they were monsters, spewing their candy-coated toxicity at anyone they deemed too weak to fight back.

It was a fair contest when they chose adult targets; adults possessed the power to fight back although, like her, many didn't. But when self-serving assholes singled out children, it made her blood boil.

"Come on, Raylan, it will just go to waste. There's a burger, hot dog, and even brownies. You can share if you want. I don't mind at all."

She opened the bag and placed it near his scuffed knees,

the aroma of French fries escaping as she rejoined her companion chaperons and watched. Nearby boys came over, sniffing and wanting to know what was in the bag. Raylan inspected the contents. His tears stopped. Eventually, the only reminder they'd even existed were brown streaks along his cheeks.

"Are you gonna share, Ray?" a nearby boy asked.

"Sure." Raylan poured the food onto his towel and the kids converged like seagulls on a plate of fried clams. Soon they were grinning and laughing, and for one small moment in time, Raylan Griffin was on top of the world.

Leeann cooed, "Shannon, Chad left his towel in the water park. Would you mind going and getting it?"

"I could have sworn I saw him holding his towel." Shannon stood on the pavement next to bus 12 and checked the names of students against her roster while they boarded. "Give me a sec."

"There's no time." Leeann took possession of the clipboard. "He said it's near the gift shop?"

"But—"

"Go." Leeann made a shooing motion. "We'll wait."

Shannon nodded and ran to the park entrance. The busses were on a schedule, but of course they'd wait; they wouldn't leave her behind.

The cashier at the gift shop told her nothing had been left behind. "Ask the lifeguard," the elderly woman offered.

"Where's that?"

"Next to the carousel."

Shannon swore and went to find the lifeguard.

"Nope, not here. Try lost-and-found."

"Of all the stupid..." She ran on.

She raced inside the building and, gulping for air, asked for the lost-and-found.

No towel.

That was when the light dawned.

Not caring if she knocked over little old ladies, she rushed for the entrance. Just as she'd expected, the busses were gone.

She sat on a nearby bench and contemplated crying. Instead, she pulled herself together and started making phone calls.

When Dee answered, a din of chaos blasted through the phone. "Hey, Shan, what's—? Harry, drop that. Shan, are your kids having a meltdown too?"

"I'm not on the bus." Shannon scowled.

"What? Speak up. Harry, if you don't put that down, I will make sure you have detention until you graduate."

"I'm not on my bus," she shouted. "I got left behind. Can you come and get me?"

"I can't. Jeff and I have that thing tonight. Did you try Justin?"

"Yes, he's out of the office. Peg's phone went to voicemail."

"Sit tight, and I'll call you right back."

"Thank you."

She returned the phone to her bag and slammed her back against the bench, her arms crossed. How did she think she could handle being a single mother? She couldn't even get through one stinking field trip.

Chapter 10

*"Beware of missing chances; otherwise it may be altogether
too late someday."*
Franz Liszt

The crew was long gone when St. John did a walk-through of
the work site. He'd been in a foul mood all day, and it wasn't
getting any better. For some asinine reason, he'd thought Shannon would text him: maybe to thank him for the lawyer's
number.

He double-checked the machinery, picked up stray pieces
of trash, and swore when he found the keys left in one of the
Bobcats. He'd grown tired of the construction end of the business, and on days like the one he'd just had, he would gladly
pay someone to take his place. Thanks to the crap surveyor's
report, all the trees he'd designated to remain would need to
come down. When the development was finished, it would look
like one of MacMillan's, and that was seriously pissing him off.
He prided himself on the amount of natural vegetation his
neighborhoods retained. It cost him a pretty penny to build
this way, but it was worth it. Not this time though. If he worked
around the trees, he'd lose a bundle. It would be cheaper to
mow them down and plant new ones. He was getting too old
for this crap.

He'd been fifteen when he put on his first hard hat. Back
then, his job had been collecting the construction crew's empty
lunch wrappers, and here he was at fifty-one, still doing the
same damn thing. If it hadn't been for Merry, he'd have left
Wexford in his rear-view mirror as soon as he earned his driver's
license. She'd needed him, so he stayed, especially since his
half-brother had been useless—still was, for that matter. It
would have been nice if things had turned out differently with

Malcolm, but they hadn't, so why dwell on it?

St. John entered the office trailer and unlocked the cabinet behind his chair. He removed a bottle of whiskey, dropped into his desk chair, and rubbed his face. Meredith had died five years ago, so what was he still doing in Wexford? He could be sitting on a porch overlooking fat, white sheep dotting emerald slopes instead of muttering to himself about his fucking brother.

Thinking about his land in Scotland kicked up thoughts of Shannon. Her eyes were the same color as the grass the sheep grazed on—deep, vivid green. He'd like a chance to look into those eyes again. Talk to her, smell her...touch her. If he ever got his chance, the first thing he planned to do was bury his face and fingers in her hair and drown in the black waves. Then he'd kiss her lips. And the rest of her.

He emptied his glass and refilled it. What was he doing? Why was he torturing himself when nothing was going to happen with Shannon? Not with Denise and Justin in the way.

"Let it go," he mumbled as he bent and exchanged his steel-toed work boots for a cleaner pair of Timberlands and propped his feet on the two-drawer filing cabinet, and ignored the ringing of his cell.

"Not going to happen," he muttered. Whoever was calling would leave a message. It was Friday afternoon, and he was off the clock. After he finished his drink, he planned on going home, taking a shower, throwing a steak on the grill, and getting drunk. Maybe he'd walk Sadie, or he might just sit and toss a stick for her. That's one of the things he loved about his dog—she was grateful with what he had to give and understood that sometimes the well was empty, and it was useless begging for more.

Women never seemed to get things like that; they just didn't get there were times when a man didn't have anything to give. His last two wives had been like that. Great in bed but needy and whiny, always demanding more, like a couple of bottomless pits.

He raised his drink and saluted the air. He'd divorce them all over again if given the chance.

Was Shannon like his wives had been? Taking and taking until she bled Baldos dry, and that's why she was divorcing him?

St. John finished his whiskey and slammed the glass against the desk, the sound connecting with the metal surface echoing in the trailer. Whether she was or wasn't shouldn't concern him, but just for the record, he didn't think she was.

Goddamn it, he needed a way to push her out of his head for good this time. His date last night had worked for a few hours, but the effects had worn off by midmorning. He could try again. Skip the steak and head up to Manchester. Jimbo was on the schedule at the bar, but it couldn't hurt to check in. It was Friday night, and the place would be hopping, guaranteeing someone willing to help him forget the witch. As his father had always said, 'Women are like buses: every few minutes another one comes along.'

His father had been an asshole, and since he was quoting the asshole, that made him one too.

"Well, this asshole is out of here." He planted his boots on the floor and stood. Screw Manchester, he was going to stay home and get plastered.

After setting the trailer's alarm, he locked the door and headed for his truck. Nobody needed him, and then he remembered that someone had called him a few minutes earlier. Before starting the engine, he removed his cell. The call had come from Denise.

"Not tonight, Denise." He hooked the phone to the dashboard and drove out of the work site. Home sweet home, he was on his way.

He'd only driven a few feet when the Bluetooth connection

caught the new incoming call. He grumbled and stabbed the speaker button on the steering wheel. "What's up, Denise?"

Voices of screaming kids blasted the cab's interior. "St. John, can you hear me?"

"Yes, make it quick."

"Are you still in Salem?"

It would be easy to lie and say no, but that would make him a complete jerk and break one of his most cherished rules. "Just leaving the site now."

"I need a favor."

The words 'of course you do' were poised at the edge of his tongue and ready to take a swan dive out of his mouth. When did Denise not need a favor? "What is it?"

Her hesitation annoyed the piss out of him, especially since he had to listen to the high-pitched wail of a kid who must have been sucking on her phone.

"Can you swing by Canobie Lake?" she asked.

Did the tilt of the earth go off kilter? Denise Boyle was asking him to a family outing? "Thanks, I appreciate it, but I'm dog tired. Some other time."

"What are you talking about? Oh, no, I'm not inviting you over; I need you to pick up a stranded mom. She was on the field trip and got left at the park."

And there it was; the truth shall set him free. "I'm not a fucking taxi service, Denise. Call the woman's husband."

He held the phone away from his ear and let her finish screaming at a kid named Harry.

When she returned, she was out of breath. "You there?"

"Yes. Have you ever heard the phrase 'you can catch more flies with honey instead of vinegar'?"

"You try spending the day with a million eight-year-olds and see how you do. So, will you go?"

"Sorry, not tonight. Call somebody else."

"Come on, St. John. You'll be driving by the park anyway,

and she's heading to the same town as you. It will only add another five, maybe ten, minutes to your ride." She ended her request by yelling, "Leave her alone."

"Are you talking to me or the kids?"

"You. How about if I reduce my commission on the Lakeview property?"

"Nice try, but if Jesus Christ asked you to take a cut, you'd still say no."

"Fine, just do it because you're a great guy."

"My, how your tune has changed. The other day you compared me to a dog."

"Harry, what did I just say? Thanks, St. John, but here's the thing: I'm only asking you because there's no one else. If I learn you got cute with her, I'll be on you like flies on you-know-what. Harry, put that down."

The call dropped, and St. John slammed the steering wheel. What the fuck had that been about? Do what to who? So now she thought he'd hit on some random mother? He had a good mind to ignore the request and let whoever was waiting at the park figure out her own ride home.

"Aw, for fuck sake." He slammed the wheel again and cut the truck to the left.

In under six minutes, a series of side streets delivered him to the park's main gate and a line of cars. He turned and looked behind his truck. It wasn't too late; he could still get out and be on his way. He shifted into reverse.

"Of all the fucking..."

He shifted back into drive and merged with the line of cars.

The traffic moved at a snail's pace along the lot's perimeter road. Parking attendants barely out of diapers waved red flags for people needing to park. It amazed him. He couldn't get grown men to figure out how to use the porta-potty, so how did Canobie, with its arsenal of teenagers, run like a well-oiled machine? Life wasn't fair.

He had no intention of parking, only wanting to get whoever he was getting and get the hell out. If the woman wasn't at the front gate, good luck to her.

'I'm only asking you because there's no one else.' Those had been Denise's words. She was a peach. She'd called him as a last resort. Why? What mother would she rather he not be near?

He let a grin happen. Maybe he should park the truck after all.

He pulled out of the traffic and parked. He jumped from the driver's seat and sprinted in the direction of the entrance, allowing himself a minute to catch his breath while he scanned the faces of the people. He didn't see Shannon, and he let his grin drop as he tried to figure out who he was supposed to be getting. A family moved from in front of a bench, and somewhere in his mind, a chorus of angels sang.

He mouthed, 'Thank you, Denise,' and added a grin.

She didn't notice him at first, but when she did and smiled, his stomach flipped into a somersault. All the day's frustrations melted off his shoulders, and he widened his grin.

Then her smile faded, taking with it his jubilation.

Chapter 11

"It is obvious that we can no more explain a passion to a person who has never experienced it than we can explain light to the blind."
T. S. Eliot

Shannon removed the smile that had sprung to her lips at seeing St. John walking her way. Even in his plaster-stained jeans and soiled work shirt, he exuded the same bewitching draw as the other day. Her heart galloped. She nibbled on her bottom lip and let his blue eyes hold her. How was it that she was the witch, and yet he managed to cast a spell on her?

He arrived in front of her, his hand pushing the renegade strand of hair off his forehead, and nodded at the empty spot on the bench. "Is that seat taken?"

She shielded her eyes from the sun and shook her head. An aroma of sweat and musk compounded her confusion about his appearance at the park, but instead of posing that all-important question, she asked, "How are you?"

The lopsided grin returned, and he sat, spurring her heart to double its pace.

"I'm good, thanks." He swept his gaze over her outfit, hair, and back to her face. "You look really nice."

She fingered the scarf tied around her head, more to keep her fingers occupied than anything else. Otherwise, they'd have buried themselves in his hair. "I've just spent a whole day chasing first graders, so I doubt that, but thank you just the same. What are you doing here?"

"This is where I spend my Friday afternoons," he said and rested against the booth, his hands inside his jeans' front pockets. "Nothing gets me going like a woman dragging a screaming kid in tow."

One such woman passed in front of the bench, the red-faced toddler she pulled by the hand wailing.

Shannon nodded their way. "How'd that work for you?"

"Instant woody," St. John offered.

He laughed, and she joined in. She enjoyed his laugh—the rolling tone of it. It was a sound she could get used to hearing.

A fragment of her vision teased her mind: Chad running toward a black truck, St. John stepping into view. She drew in a breath and licked at a drop of perspiration on her upper lip. His mouth was dangerously close, and she smelled the whiskey on his breath. Just a taste. That was all she wanted. One long, sumptuous taste.

She shook her head and looked away and across the parking lot. She hadn't even begun to clean up her current mess of a life, and here she was, potentially adding more chaos into the mix.

"Seriously, St. John," she said, once again giving him her full attention. "Why are you here?"

His chuckle indicated her abruptness hadn't bothered him. "Denise called. Said you missed the bus because you were having too much fun in the arcade."

"You're a hoot, but get back to the part about Dee. Why would she send *you* to get me? Wasn't she the one who said you should leave me alone?"

"I think what she said was that *you* should stay away from *me*, but I gave up long ago trying to figure out how her mind works."

When he stared at her and added, "Maybe she realizes she can't stop the inevitable," the air flew from her lungs. She found her lower lip and tugged on it with her teeth. She didn't want to talk; she wanted to dip her toes in the blue pools that were his eyes and submerge herself.

Someone released an air horn and jarred her out of her

stupor. She shifted and adjusted the folds of her skirt, looking down at her lap. When she couldn't resist any longer she found his eyes again and said, "You're forgetting I'm a married woman."

"That's not something I'm likely to forget." He wiped at the bead of sweat slipping down the side of her neck. "You see that's my number one rule: Never get involved with a married woman. However..." He brought his finger to his lips and brushed it over his bottom lip. "For you I'll make an exception."

She chose to ignore the deafening alarm bells clanging in her head and focused on the warm sensation in her groin. "You're putting yourself on a slippery slope. First, it'll be rule number one, then others will follow. Before long, you'll have nothing but anarchy. Tell me, what's rule number two?"

His grin widened. "Never get involved with a woman who lives in Wexford, and, since you're asking, rule three is never, ever give a second night."

"Do all your conquests ask for second nights?"

He frowned but his blue eyes still held their playful sparkle. "You see, that's how rumors get started; I don't have conquests. Everyone's a willing participant."

She bet they were. "You're a cocky bastard, I'll give you that."

"Guilty as charged. Let's talk about your rules. Any I should know about?"

"Just one."

"And?" He arched an eyebrow in a way of punctuating the question.

"Never again allow anyone close enough to hurt me."

"Good rule. That's actually number four on my list."

He kept touching her arm, each pass of his fingers delivering electric pulses over her skin.

"It seems we're on the same page," he added, "Now what?"

"I tell you I'm flattered but you don't stand a snowball's chance in Hades at getting under my skirt."

"Challenge accepted."

The pirate grin flashed and in her mind she lay on the deck of a ship, the sunbaked planks scratching the bare skin of her back as he moved on top of her.

She stood abruptly, the movement releasing a thin stream of warmth onto the crotch of her thong. "I'd like to leave now."

"Then let's go." He jumped to his feet and took hold of her bag's straps. "Here, let me carry that."

"No thank you. I'm fine."

"I know you are."

For a moment they both stayed attached to the bag. He notched an eyebrow, and she let go.

In the truck, Shannon rested against the leather seat, and St. John thrummed the steering wheel, keeping time with a Garth Brooks song playing on the radio.

She cast a quick glance his way. What monsters taunted him and forced him to create his rules?

"You okay?" he asked.

"I'm fine. Thank you for coming to get me."

"My pleasure." He moved his hand as if to reach for hers but quickly pulled it away. "So, how'd you miss the bus? Aren't the chaperons supposed to be the ones watching the time?"

"You're full of jokes today, aren't you? For your information, I was about to get on the bus when Leeann, two e's-two n's, threw a grenade at me."

St. John's eyes widened. "Leeann what?"

"Two e's-two n's. That's how she introduces herself. Haven't you ever noticed? Shannon switched her voice into a syrupy-sounding trill. "'I'm Leeann—two e's-two n's—Chambers.'"

Robust laughter escaped St. John. "You're right. I've never thought about it. I admit she is unique."

"That's putting it mildly."

"She has her moments."

Shannon explained about Chad's missing towel, and she told St. John about Leeann's treatment of Raylan Griffin.

St. John's expression soured. "I know the Griffin family; they're good people. I also know there's more than a few residents who would like to run them out of Wexford."

"Why? They're not hurting anyone."

St. John switched off the radio. "You need to understand, Shannon, Wexford is a town of snobs. When people spend close to a million dollars for a house, they see families like the Griffins as eyesores on the landscape."

"I get that, but many of the residents who are behaving badly aren't new to town. They've been living here, alongside the Griffins, their entire lives."

"That doesn't matter. People would like nothing more than to run what they call the riffraff out of town."

Shannon folded her arms and added a sound of disgust. "Honestly, sometimes I can't stand people. When my divorce is final, I'm taking Chad and getting out of Wexford."

"Unless you move to Mars, you're still going to have to deal with assholes. That's just how life is. How did the conversation go, about the divorce? I'll wager Justin wasn't too keen on the idea."

"It didn't go as expected."

"Chickened out, eh."

She faced him with an angry glare. "I didn't chicken out," she inserted between his chuckles.

"You asked him?"

"No."

"So, you chickened out?"

"No."

"I'm confused."

"It's complicated, and it's none of your business." She tightened her already-crossed arms.

"Are you going to sleep with me?"

She shifted her position and gawked at him. "What's your deal, St. John?"

"What do you mean?"

"Is this how you operate—you just come out and ask a woman to sleep with you?"

"Usually."

"And does it work?"

"Completely foolproof. At least it was." He winked. "You don't want to go and ruin my perfect record now, do you?"

"Let's talk about you, for a change. Tell me more about your rules. For instance, why do you have them? What dark fears does the infamous Adam St. John possess that would force him to build a wall of rules to hide behind?"

He smiled at her, but she noticed it wasn't his usual jovial expression. Eventually, he said, "Everyone has fears, and we all deal with them in the best ways we can. What about you? What fears keep you cowering behind a lowlife like Baldos?"

She sniffed and raised her chin. Justin was a jerk, a stinking, abusive jerk, but St. John didn't get to throw insults when he himself was as big a jerk. "At least he doesn't cheat people out of their property."

"Excuse me?" St. John's eyebrows almost reached his hairline. "Where do you get this crap about me?"

"I've heard talk." Of course, she could have added, the talk was mostly done by Justin.

"Well, don't believe everything you hear. Unlike someone you know, and I'm referring to your husband, I happen to have integrity."

She snorted a chuckle. "That's rich."

"How so?"

"It's simple: you have no problem stealing land; plus, you

seem to think you're Paul Bunyan and have the right to chop down every tree in town."

"Ah, so we're back to this. Yeah, you mentioned that the other day, about how I'm destroying Wexford. As for the land thing, you need an education in my business practices." His expression turned devilish. "I'd be more than happy to educate you."

She straightened her back and stared down her nose at him. "I could care less about how you do business. If people are too stupid to see a wolf in their midst, so be it, but the woods can't defend themselves."

He'd slowed the truck and turned onto the street that would take them to the school but now pulled over to the side of the road and shifted into park. He swung his body in her direction. "Are you finished? Because I want to make sure you've had your say."

"Drop me off here. I can walk the rest of the way."

"I'm sure you can but nope, not going to happen. You've had your turn, and now I get mine."

She undid her seatbelt and reached for the door handle, but he hit the safety lock. She swung around and glared at him. "Now you're going to hold me prisoner?"

"Until I've had my say, yes."

"I mean it, St. John, let me out, or I'll..."

"You'll what?" He offered his signature grin.

The answer came to her suddenly, and she couldn't help but grin back. "I'll tell Dee." She hadn't been prepared for his enthusiastic laughter. So much for her secret weapon. "Fine, I'm giving you ten seconds to say what you want to say, and then if you don't open this door, I'll smash the window if I have to."

"Deal. Now listen carefully." The amusement his eyes had held evaporated. "You seem to be operating under the assumption that just because you don't want something to happen it won't. Wexford's population is growing, and the people moving here want houses. If I don't build them, someone else will. That's just the hard, cold truth. At least when I'm involved, there are trees left standing." He returned the shifter into drive. "Put your seatbelt back on," he said and pulled onto the road.

During the short distance to the school, the air between them crackled with tension. St. John pulled into the parking lot and stopped before they reached the location where kids were disembarking the busses. He unlocked the door. "You're free to go."

She clenched her jaw and yanked the straps of her bag. She was determined to leave without saying a word, but unfortunately, her pride had other ideas. "That was a pretty speech, but the argument that if you don't do something someone else will gets old pretty fast. A person with integrity would try and find a solution; a person without integrity offers excuses." She remained with her hand on the door. Even though he was infuriating, she was still interested in what his response would be.

He let out a slow stream of air from his nose before he spoke. "You get to throw stones at me when you stop offering excuses for your own life." He reached by her and gave the passenger door a shove. "Goodbye, Shannon."

She climbed from the truck. "Thank you for the ride," she said, not even interested in slamming the door. She hoped he was happy with the point he'd made. Yes, she did offer excuses.

But he was still a land-grabbing jerk.

Chapter 12

"What you are is what you have been. What you'll be is what you do now."
Buddha

"How many days, Mama?" Chad leapt onto the bed, his bare feet sinking into the comforter before he started jumping in place.

Shannon held open a bath towel. "How many days for what? And come here, you wet, naked boy."

"Tell me. Tell me. Tell me," he said, bouncing higher after each phrase.

"You're getting my bed all wet, and you're going to end up through the ceiling. Come here."

"Tell me. How many days?"

She swung the towel and missed him. "How many days for what? Until summer vacation?"

"No, silly Mama, how many till my birfday?"

Shannon reached for him, but Chad bounced off the bed and raced down the hallway and into his bedroom.

Not wanting to be left out, Jasper barked and followed.

"Come back here, my little wood sprite; I have to dry you," Shannon called out as she ran behind the two of them. "Where are you?" she asked when she entered his room.

A tiny voice came from within the closet's depths. "Find me, Mama."

"Where could he be, Jasper? Did he return to his woodland home?"

Jasper shook his head and whined, pawing at the rug near the closet.

"Don't worry, Jasper," she whispered. "I know he's in there."

Calling out, she said, "Chad, oh, Chad, where are you?" She wondered aloud, "I guess he's gone. Maybe he'll come to visit us again someday. Come on, Jasper, let's go have some ice cream."

Chad burst from the closet. "I want ice cream."

Shannon swooped in, but he managed to escape again, his butt cheeks jiggling as he returned to the master bedroom.

"Tell me, Mama," he said, climbing onto her mattress.

"Tell you what?"

"The many days till I'm six?"

"Oh, silly me, I thought you meant until school ended." She inched his way. "Let's see, I believe there are... Let me think. Tomorrow is Saturday, then comes... What day?"

"Sunday, Mama."

"Oh, right, Sunday. And then there will be the last five days of school, which will bring us to Saturday again, so that makes... carry the four, add the seven... Wow, I don't know. Let's see if I can count it out." She held up her hands and raised a finger for each day while Chad counted along.

Her fingers brushed against his legs as he skittered across the king-sized bed.

"Seven days, seven days, seven days," he sang and held his hands over his penis as he jumped around.

"I give up." Shannon sat on the edge of the bed and flopped next to his feet.

"Are you tired, Mama?"

She tucked onto her side and swung her arms around him. "Haha, you fell for my ploy, little sprite, and I'm going to eat your leggies." She nibbled at the smooth, warm skin of his thighs.

He gave it a valiant try, but he couldn't squirm away, mostly due to his bouts of laughter.

She kissed his legs and then lay facing the ceiling fan and rubbed her belly. "It's a good thing you stopped me. I might have eaten your whole body. Yum."

He crawled onto her and rested his head against her breasts. "Silly, Mama, you didn't eat me. It was pretend."

"Yes, munchkin, it was pretend." She smoothed his damp hair. "Do you know what isn't pretend?"

"Uh-uh."

"My love for you. I love you to the moon and back."

Keeping his face snuggled into the folds of her shirt, he said, "I love you to the moon and back a bazillion times."

"Mine is more. Mine is a gazillion-bazillion times."

Chad stared at her. "Mama, is Daddy taking me to tryouts tomorrow?"

It was a mother's bane to learn about important school functions the night before they occurred, and this little announcement insisted she sit up and pay attention. She swung her legs off the bed. "Tryouts? What tryouts?"

"Can you make cupcakes? I said you would make cupcakes."

"Munchkin, slow down. What are the tryouts for?"

"Baseball. Coach John said we haf to be there by seven."

"Did I miss a flyer?" She couldn't have; she checked his backpack every night and wouldn't have missed a notice about baseball tryouts. "Go and get your backpack, please."

Chad scampered from the bedroom and down the steps, and Shannon collected his pajamas from his bedroom and placed them on her bed.

"I got it." Chad skipped back into the room, holding his backpack in the air.

"Okay, while I look for the notice you get in your PJs, got it?" She unzipped the main compartment and dumped the contents onto her bed. Nothing. No flyer in the front or back pockets, and no flyer in the side pockets either. Basically, there was no flyer. "Chad, when did they give you the paper?"

"What paper, Mama?" His head was buried under the twisted pajama top.

She went to him. When his face appeared in the opening, she repeated, "The flyer about tryouts?"

"What flies?"

"No, honey, nothing flies. The flyer?"

"What's a flyer?"

"It's a paper that announces things. Do you remember when you got it?"

"It flies *and* talks?"

"No, sweetie, please answer the question, do you know where you put the flyer, I mean paper?"

"Coach John said the computer has it."

"The computer... The school's website? Be a good boy and run downstairs and get Mama's laptop, please."

He went to fetch her computer while she tapped her cell phone only to hit cancel. Dee and Jeff were busy. Next in line, Peg.

"Hi, what's up?" came Peg's cheery greeting.

"Hey, do you know anything about baseball tryouts tomorrow."

"Yeah, seven o'clock. Make sure you bring Chad's glove and plenty of water. It's going to be in the nineties again."

"Peg, wait a second. Was a notice sent home?"

"Shan, it's been posted on the school's website for the past two weeks. You were supposed to sign him up. You did register him, right?"

"No. Now, what do I do? Do you have the coach's phone number?"

"Yeah, you do too."

"What? How—?"

"Adam's the coach. By the way, I didn't get to ask you when you came by to get Chad: how was the ride from Canobie?"

"It was... I didn't know about the tryouts."

"Relax, I have a feeling Adam will make an exception for you," Peg offered. "I still can't believe Dee sent him to get you, especially after she lectured you two about leaving each other alone. Did you have fun? Did he ask you out?"

"I'm married, remember?" Shannon said. Did asking her to sleep with him count as being asked out?

"No biggie, we'll find you someone hot tomorrow night. I can't wait to hit Manchester and whoop it up a bit. Life in Wexford is getting boring. Just so you know, I'm going to dress like a slut. Anyway, I've got to run. Byy-ee."

Shannon filled her travel mug with coffee. The morning was a frantic rush to finish breakfast and get out the door and to the baseball field by seven o'clock. Any other morning, it would have been a simple task, but after a second night of fractured sleep, she was off her game. The night before last, there had been a dream of being with St. John which had given her a pleasant jolt, but last night's dream had been X-rated, to the point where she'd finally decided to stay awake and blog.

She'd packed everything Chad would need: water, sunscreen, bug repellent. The container of sugar cookie bars was already in the car. She hadn't had time to make cupcakes; that's why her freezer in the basement was such a necessity, and she would make sure she kept it if—no, when—she divorced Justin.

The only three things missing were Chad, his baseball glove, and her backbone. How was she going to face St. John after the way she'd acted when he'd dropped her off at the school? Maybe he'd be too busy with the kids to even bother with her.

If only Justin would get home; he could take Chad, and she could stay at the house and cower. The way she'd spoken to St. John had been uncalled for, even if she disagreed with his business practices. She had about as much chance of saving Wexford's remaining open space as she did at saving the rain forests. The best she could do was fix her own life and find a plot of land for her and Chad that was far away from bulldozers and property developers. They could let the rest of the world fend for itself.

It seemed like forever since a man had excited her as much as St. John did. Sure, men got her engine going but nothing like the way she felt when she was near the cocky developer. One night with him would most assuredly distract her from her daily woes, but she had a sneaking suspicion one night wouldn't be enough. If he was as good in bed as she imagined, she'd want a whole string of nights. And mornings too.

"Mama, I can't find my glove."

Chad's frantic shouting pulled her back to reality.

"Did you look under your bed?" she yelled out.

"No."

She ran to the bottom of the staircase. "Then look, and if it's not there, come down. We have to go."

"But, Mama..."

"Forget your glove. We'll figure something out when we get there; we're going to be late."

Chad ran down the steps with Jasper trotting behind, his leash dragging over the steps. "But, my glove."

"I said we'll deal with it when we get to the field, and Jasper stays here." She herded Chad into the kitchen.

"But Coach John said I can bring him."

"Fine, whatever. Go get into the car, please."

"But my glove."

The third whine about needing his glove was one whine too many. "Chad, I said forget your glove; now, go get in the car, or we're staying home."

His expression crushed her. It wasn't like she'd never scolded him; she did when necessary, but this shouldn't have been one of those times. He hadn't done anything wrong. Lately, more and more, she was letting her frustrations with her own inept behavior leak out and touch him.

"I'm sorry I snapped at you, sweetie. We really must leave."

"But *Mama.*"

"Chad, please stop, I'm begging you. We'll figure things out at the park. I bet Aunt Dee will have one. Or Coach John. Please get in the car and take Jasper."

"Is Daddy coming?"

"He might. He's still sleeping because he had a headache."

As easily as melted butter gliding over a hot pan, the lie slipped out. It wasn't often he caught her in a lie. Actually, she didn't think he ever had—until that moment. A sour taste filled her mouth. He didn't have to say a word; the way he cocked his head to the side and stared at her with his brows narrowed, she instinctively knew she'd been caught. She'd gotten so good at deceiving herself she never stopped to think her son might see through her.

"Honey, Daddy—"

He stopped her and said, "It's okay, Mama." Pulling Jasper's leash, he left her with the follow-up lie still in her mouth.

Time slowed to a crawl. She held both the cooler's handle and her car keys in a rigid grip.

How many lies would it take before the trust of a child was completely eroded? Two? Ten? A hundred? And when that trust was gone, could it ever be rebuilt?

Chapter 13

*"I want you to lie to me just as sweetly as you know how for
the rest of my life."*
F. Scott Fitzgerald

Shannon steered the car toward the back of the school parking lot, near where the baseball field was located. It had been a silent ride from the house—no singing, no chatter, nothing. She might as well have been alone. Even Jasper had sulked.

"Yay, we're here. Baseball time." She did her best to sound chipper, but from Chad's silent response, she realized she'd failed miserably. She opened the rear door and tried again, this time belting out a tune. "Take me out to the ball game, take me out to the park...' Honey, sing with me."

Chad refused to look at her. "I don't want to go," he said from under a serious pout.

"Ah, sweetie, come on, we'll have fun." She pointed at the field and the multicolored sea of T-shirts. "Look, the kids have their shirts already. I wonder what color you'll get."

"No." Chad kicked his legs and pushed her hand away when she reached for the buckle.

"Chad, talk to me. What's wrong?"

She'd have to be brain dead to think he wasn't still upset with her lie about Justin sleeping. What kid wouldn't have been? It wasn't every day you found out your mother was a lying sack of dog poo, on top of being a coward. "I'm sorry I didn't tell you that Daddy wasn't home. He had to go to work very early before you woke up." And like a top-forty list of hits, the lies just kept on coming.

Jasper lapped at the tears on Chad's cheek, but Chad pushed his muzzle away.

"Aw, Chad, please. I'm sure Daddy will be here very soon."

"No."

"Of course he will. He wouldn't miss seeing you play ball." What was she up to now? Fifty lies?

Chad kicked out his feet, slamming them against the seat's edge. "Mama, I don't care about Daddy."

"If you're still mad because I lied, I'm sorry."

He bore into her eyes with an irate glare. "I don't care about your lies."

'Hey, give me a break,' she almost replied. 'It was only one lie...okay, two...three tops,' but she ended up asking, "Then what's bothering you?"

"My glove." He pounded his leg.

She breathed a sigh of relief and almost whooped out loud. Emotional scarring was something she'd need more time to fix, but a missing baseball glove was a piece of cake. "Is that all? Well, if Dee doesn't have an extra glove, I seem to remember that Coach John keeps some for any player who forgets or loses his. You'll see."

"Is that true, Mama?" His brown eyes studied her face, giving her another chance at redemption.

"You bet your buttons it's true." The lies were burying her. She unbuckled the safety belt. "Run and tell Coach John we're here. I'll bring our stuff and Jasper."

She tried to smile as she watched him barreling through the grass. She caught her reflection in the window. Red Sox baseball cap and a nose about a foot long.

"Get a grip," she told the woman frowning back at her. "White lies don't count."

She adjusted the brim of her hat and slipped the strap of her bag over her shoulder. Gathering the cooler, cookie bin, and Jasper's leash, she trudged toward the field.

"You'd better behave, Jasper, that's all I can say."

Jasper seemed to understand her warning and heeled like a pro until they arrived at the refreshment table. An unleashed chocolate Lab ran over, giving him a reason to whine and jump.

"Jasper, heel." A fat lot of good her command did when the untethered dog was doing its best to sniff Jasper's tail. What moron would let a dog wander without a leash at a kids' baseball tryouts?

She managed to get the cookies on the refreshment table, but as the two dogs circled each other, Jasper's leash tethered her ankles together.

"Sadie, heel."

The unleashed dog snapped to attention and darted away.

Shannon sucked in a breath and her lower lip. Heat spread around her neck and up the back of her head as the baritone voice settled around her and called to mind the wonderful things he'd done to her in her dream. She wasn't ready to see him. Please, she silently pleaded, go away until I'm ready, like in twenty years.

"I thought I saw you." St. John stepped in front of her. "I take it this is your Lab." He crouched, petted Jasper, and then lifted her foot and untangled the leash.

His familiar scent headed for her knees, and she held onto his shoulder for support, not missing the thick muscles moving under his shirt. Nor did she miss the slide of his finger up her bare calf.

He straightened to his full height and grinned down at her. "There, now you're finally free."

"Thank you," she sputtered. She twisted Jasper's lead around her hand and tried to think of something. She went with, "You should really have your dog on a leash."

"You're right. My fault entirely." He snapped his fingers, and his dog ran back under the table. "On to more important business: is Chad checked in?"

She blinked at the sudden switch of topics. One second he was seducing her with his smile, and the next he was all business. No wonder women fell at his feet; they all dropped from the vertigo his behavior created. Well, she wasn't going to swoon. "Yes, all set," she said, her tone matter-of-fact.

He nodded and stroked his chin. "Really? You filled out the paperwork?"

"Yup," she said, tightly looping the leash through her fingers.

"May I see it?"

"No."

"No?" His right eyebrow arched.

"I meant to say I don't have it with me. I...I forgot it." She nibbled at her lip. Good goddess, he rattled her.

"No problem, I have extra copies. You're checked in, right?"

"Yes."

"Who checked you in?"

"I did."

"I mean, who helped you at the table?"

"Oh, I don't remember."

He stepped to the side, giving her a glimpse of the registration table and the woman sitting behind it.

She stared, her lower lip turning white under the pressure of her top teeth. Leeann, two e's-two n's, with her perfect timing, lifted her pixie face and smirked.

"I meant to say I haven't signed in," Shannon offered. "I just got here."

"Ah, but Chad *is* registered, right?"

"Yes."

St. John lifted his baseball cap and raked his fingers through his hair. He replaced the hat and said, "Really? Well, I checked this morning, and no boy with the last name Baldos is registered. But, more importantly, and by this point I've lost count at how many you've offered me, I don't like lies."

She ignored his comment. So she'd lied. Big deal; lying was her theme for the day.

"However," he continued, "that doesn't mean Chad won't get on the team."

"Don't do me any favors, St. John."

She tugged on the leash, but St. John touched her elbow, his hand lingering.

"Follow me." He petted Jasper again and walked over to a row of oversized cartons. There he greeted a skinny girl wearing a halter top, Daisy Dukes, and high-tops. "Meg, this is Mrs. Baldos. She needs a Pittsburgh T-shirt and cap. She'll tell you the size." He thanked the girl and addressed Shannon. "You still have to fill out paperwork, and for that, you're going to have to see Mrs. Chambers at the registration table. When you're finished here, give Chad his shirt and have a seat. I'll come find you at the end of practice. I want to talk to you."

"Whatever," she said, hoping it would convey her indifference.

St. John's response was a low chuckle. He inhaled deeply. "You smell good enough to eat."

The words reduced her to putty. Oh, dear goddess, he'd said the same thing to her in her dream, right before his mouth found her—

"What size shirt do you need?"

Shannon sputtered a quick "What?" and stared at the teenager holding a baseball cap. "Oh, medium, unless they run small."

The rail-thin girl held out a purple T-shirt. "We have dog-sitters over there."

To the side of the bleachers, a cluster of dogs sniffed one another while four teenagers munched donuts.

Shannon delivered Jasper and walked over to the line at the registration table. When it was her turn, she met the close-set eyes of her nemesis and spoke in as pleasant a tone as she could muster under the circumstances. "I'd like a registration packet, please."

Leeann fanned herself with a sheet of paper. "Excuse me?"

"I said I—"

"I heard you. Name, please?"

"What?"

"I said, name, please."

Shannon bent over the table and spoke so only Leeann would hear. "How about go fuck yourself? Does that name work for you?" She returned to a straight stance. "Would you like me to spell that?"

Undaunted, Leeann said, "I don't see your name on the list. Next, please."

Before Shannon could say a word, she was yanked from the line and pulled away from the table.

"Go home," Justin ordered.

She squirmed under his grip and dropped Chad's T-shirt and cap. It wasn't even eight o'clock in the morning, but from the stench of his breath and bloodshot eyes, it was clear he'd been drinking. She twisted, trying to break his hold on her arm. "You're hurting me."

Justin released her, and she rubbed her arm. She checked the stands, but Dee had her back to them, talking to another parent, and Peg was gone.

"Go home," Justin repeated.

"I don't want to. I want to see—"

He regained his hold on her arm and squeezed. "You're not too smart, are you? If you know what's best for you, you'll leave."

"Yoo-hoo, Justin, over here." Leeann stood by her seat and waved. "I need to speak to you."

"I'm busy, Leeann," Justin called out.

"It'll only take a minute."

Justin released Shannon and, through a tight jaw, said, "If you're still here when I'm done, you'll be sorry."

When his back was to her, she picked up the T-shirt and cap and sprinted to the field, calling out to Chad.

He ran over to her, his face streaked with sweat.

St. John came up behind him, his face filled with concern.

"Mama, you were right," Chad said. He held up his right hand buried inside a blue baseball glove. "But I don't haf a T-shirt."

St. John took the shirt from Shannon, put it on Chad, and set the cap in place. "You're all set, buddy. Go join the team and let me talk to your mom, okay?"

Shannon bent one knee and hugged Chad. "Mama has to go home, but Daddy is here."

"Okay, I love you."

"I love you too." She watched him run to join his teammates, and then she stood, ready to bolt.

"Whoa, wait a second. What was that all about, with Justin?" St. John gave the red welt around her forearm a frown.

"Justin wants me to go home," she said.

"Why?"

They both turned at the sound of Justin calling Shannon's name.

"Don't let him bully you," St. John said.

She couldn't help but snicker. Bully her? Oh, if he only knew. "Save your advice."

"Shannon."

"St. John, please," she pleaded. "Just stay out of this."

"It's too late for that." The brim of his baseball cap cast a shadow over his face. "Go. I'll talk to you later."

She watched him move quickly to intersect Justin, who was walking their way, and then she ran to the parking lot.

"Shan?" Peg walked over to the SUV, a take-out tray of iced coffees in her hand. "I went and got us... What's going on?"

"Justin came." Shannon unlocked the car and placed her

hand on the door handle. "He told me to go home, and now he and St. John are..."

They watched as Justin shoved his finger toward St. John's face. St. John stood with his arms folded, seemingly unimpressed by the intimidating move. When Justin's shouting lost steam, St. John stepped forward so their belt buckles nearly touched. Whatever he said ended with his arm raised, finger pointing at the stands. Justin sulked away.

"Wow, and to think I almost missed the show by going to get coffee. Here." Peg held out the tray. "Want yours?"

"Thanks. I left my cooler and cookie container. Would you—?"

"Say no more. Want me to take Chad to my place, too?"

"No, thanks. Justin will bring him home. Oh, but Jasper is still with the dog-sitters. If Justin doesn't—?"

"No problem. You sure you're okay?"

Shannon nodded. She was as okay as any woman could be who lived with a bully. "Yeah, I'm fine." She said goodbye to Peg and got in the car.

On the ride home, St. John's quip about her being a chicken pecked at her brain. Yup, she was—so much, in fact, that she should lay eggs. She'd be a whole lot braver with someone to help her, though, someone like Adam St. John. He'd swoop down and deal with Justin while she baked scones.

That could even be a new rule: always let someone else do her dirty work for her.

Chapter 14

"Knowing yourself is the beginning of wisdom."
Aristotle

The door leading into the kitchen slammed against the wall as if a rhinoceros had charged through. A pleading shriek of "Mama" followed.

Shannon pushed from her desk and stood up. Chad's outcry could only mean one thing—he was missing a limb. "What's wrong?"

He came barreling into her office and buried himself against her legs.

"Are you hurt?"

Justin yelled, "Get upstairs." He entered the room, dragging Jasper and carrying the cooler and cookie container. "Next time," he said, "I'm leaving the dog." He tossed the items to the floor, along with the leash, and reached for Chad. "I said upstairs, now."

Chad scooted around behind Shannon's legs. She placed her arms behind her while Justin tried to grab hold of him. "Justin, stop. What is your problem?"

Jasper snapped at Justin, who was trying to extract Chad from the folds of Shannon's skirt.

"That's it." Justin pulled Jasper from the room. Shannon could hear him slam the kitchen door while Jasper barked from inside the garage as she tried to console Chad. When Justin returned to her office, he grabbed for Chad. "What did I say? Go to your room."

Shannon lifted Chad and hugged him to her breast, his legs and arms wrapped tightly around her.

Across from her, Justin glared, his body shaking.

"You're out of control lately, Justin, and unless you want

the police here, you'd better stop because, I'm warning you, I *will* call them."

With Chad still in her arms, softly sobbing against her shoulder, Shannon entered the kitchen where she sat him on one of the center island stools. Justin followed and removed a beer from the refrigerator. Jasper provided background noise by continuing to bark.

"Are you going to tell me what happened?" Shannon asked Justin, her back to him as she gently wiped Chad's face with a wet dish towel.

"First," Justin said, "I want him upstairs."

"Why? What could he have possibly done?"

"Don't make me say it again. Just do it, or you'll be sorry."

Shannon faced Justin but kept her arm around Chad's shoulder, supporting him with her hip. Odd as it seemed, she wasn't scared. The 'you'll be sorry' threat had been thrown at her so many times that it had lost its edge. "I've been sorry for eight years," she replied.

Justin's mouth opened and closed, and then opened again, reminding her of a fish—a wide-mouthed bass. If she'd had a few flies, she'd have tossed them at him.

For eight years she's been unhappy, not just with him but with herself. She'd done her best to distance herself and Chad from him. He was seldom in the house and when he was, it was to shower, watch TV, or sleep—in the third bedroom. Any warmth that had once existed between her and the man now gaping at her had long ago evaporated, leaving in its wake a nauseating stench. She'd fantasized about divorcing him, even researched the laws in New Hampshire; all that was left for her to do was to say the words.

She bent close to Chad. "Sweetie, go upstairs so Mama and Daddy can talk, okay?"

"No, Mama."

Caught off guard, she stumbled when Chad flung himself at her and clung to her neck. "Chad, you're choking me. I want you to do what I said. Now go." When Chad was safely upstairs, she faced Justin. It was time to do what she had... No, absolutely needed to do. "Justin, I'm l—"

"Stifle it."

His seething anger startled her.

"Nothing's good enough for you," he said, twisting off the cap from the beer bottle and flicking it in her direction where it skittered to a stop near the edge of the island's surface.

His tone, though eerily subdued, possessed a raw hatred that matched the poisonous look he was giving her, and she stepped back.

He took a step forward. "After everything I do for you, you and that brat are still determined to embarrass me."

As much as she wanted to avert her eyes, she couldn't.

He slammed the bottle on the island, sending a volcano of froth shooting in the air. "That asshole is going to pay. I have as much right to be on that field as he does, telling me to go sit in the stands like he owned the fucking place. Let me tell you something," he said, angling the neck of the bottle at her. "Chad will not be playing baseball."

Justin sucked on the beer bottle until he'd emptied it, then tossed it into the sink, his rant continuing. "Fucking kid couldn't even hit the ball with it two inches from his nose. It was sitting right there on the tee. And throwing. He'd be better off knitting, which I'm sure you've taught him. It was a good thing I got him the hell away from there before he made me look worse."

"Hold on..." Shannon shook her head. Here she was thinking his anger had to do with her being at the field when the real reason was Chad's inability to throw? "You mean to tell me you're mad because a six-year-old can't toss a baseball?"

"This is your fault," he said.

"In what way?" If he told her because she'd stayed married to him, she'd agree.

"You pander to him. You might as well put a dress on him and call him Candy." He removed another bottle from the fridge and said, "I'm outta here. The other pain in my ass wants me to take her furniture shopping. I should kick both of you to the curb."

She let the comment pass. She would have liked to raise her hand and volunteer to be the first to get the boot. "Will you be coming back to get Chad?" she asked.

"Why would I do that?" he spat back.

"You and Jeff and Howard are taking the kids to Water Country, remember? Tonight there's a sleepover at the lodge."

"Forget it. I'm not spending another minute with that brat."

She'd rather have kept Chad home and as far away from Justin as possible, but all Chad's friends would be there, and being left out would crush him. She could ask Dee to tell Jeff to keep an eye on Justin to make sure he didn't yell at Chad.

"Fine, go," she said. "You're so concerned with your reputation, I'm surprised you don't mind looking bad in front of the other dads."

"What the fuck are you babbling about?"

"Tomorrow's Father's Day, or have you forgotten? How will it look if Chad is banished to his bedroom while you play house with your mistress?"

The muscles on the sides of his jaw twitched, and she cautiously added, "I'm just trying to help."

"Shut up and let me think." A sinister look spread over his face. "I get it: you want Chad out of the house so you can fuck your boyfriend." When she didn't offer a response, he continued by saying, "Did you think I wouldn't find out?"

She released an uneasy snicker. "You're not making any sense."

"You see, that's where you're wrong, Shannon. I'm making perfect sense. Chambers told me everything, like how you spent yesterday afternoon fucking St. John."

"What? Leeann made me miss the bus. Dee sent—"

Justin came her way, reached out, and squeezed her jaw. "Why do you lie to me?"

The way she saw it she had two choices: take Chad and leave the house and never come back or buy herself some more time. While a barnyard full of chickens clucked madly in her ears, she cast her eyes down and said, "I'm sorry."

"So, you admit you slept with St. John."

He released her, and she nodded quickly. "I'm sorry. Yes, I did. Please forgive me."

"That's my girl." He held her in a tight embrace, pinning her arms to her sides.

She held her body rigid and suppressed the scream lodged in her throat as he whispered, "You know I always find out if you're lying."

"Drop Chad at the lodge," he said, releasing her, and removed a hundred-dollar bill from his wallet. "Peg said you girls might go out tonight; buy them a round of drinks on me." He swiped his keys off the counter. Before leaving, he added, "I want to make something crystal clear: I don't care if you fuck the entire town, but if I find out you've been with St. John again, I'll destroy you. Have a good night."

She stared at the closed door. "But you have destroyed me, Justin. You have."

The climb up the steps seemed to take forever, but she eventually reached Chad's bedroom, where she found him face down, his pillow pulled over his head.

"Munchkin?" She sat and rubbed his back. "Are you okay?"

She wanted to slap herself for asking the question. What kid would be okay after the day he'd had so far? In a few short hours, his mother had lied to him and abandoned him— leaving him at the baseball field—and then he'd had to witness his father's wrath. It would take most people years of therapy to get over that kind of stuff.

"Sit up, Chad, so I can look at you."

He did as he was told and wiped at his eyes. "I hate Daddy."

"Don't say that, Chad. You love him."

"No, I don't," he said, shaking his head. "He baressed me."

"He what? Oh, embarrassed you. Yeah, there's a lot of that going around." She dipped her head and kissed his grimy brow. "How about if I take out the sprinkler? You can invite some friends over."

"No," he said through a pout. "They're at the party."

"What party?

"For pizza." He slipped from her arms and stood and faced her, his face eager. "Can I go, please, can I?"

She smoothed his bangs to the side of his forehead. "Slow down. When? Where?"

"The Stone Pizza."

"The Pizza Stone? When?"

"Today. Every guy is there. All my friends. Coach John took them."

"Coach John had a pizza party? Sweetie, it's probably over by now."

"No, Mama, he said to come. He told me."

"Who, Coach John?" She did a quick assessment. Why not go? She'd showered when she came home from the field, so she was ready, and Chad could get by with only a face washing and change of clothes. Dee and Peg would be there and...and she'd get to see St. John. Only to get the baseball paperwork. She added the lie just in case the universe was listening.

Chad pulled at her hands and pleaded, "Please, Mama, please can I go?"

"Let's do it. Change into clean clothes and come into my bath-room so I can wash your face. Ready... Set..."

"Go," Chad shouted and tore at his clothes.

In the master bath, Shannon applied her makeup. An image flickered in the mirror. She held the tube of mascara and blinked. The small house from her vision appeared. Again she saw Chad happily playing in the front yard and then running over to the black truck arriving in the driveway.

She released the image and grinned.

Maybe there was hope for her after all.

Chapter 15

"Trust yourself and your instincts."
R. M. Rilke

In the back seat of the SUV, Chad sang quietly about baseball and pizza. Shannon hummed along with his little tune, content in her happiness that, after his emotional morning, he'd found a reason to sing.

At the Pizza Stone, she parked in the rear of the lot, off toward the side, near where MacMillan Development's eighty-unit condo project was underway. Last year an expansive field of feathery corn stalks had filled the land. Today, in its place yawned a gaping hole with steel rods protruding from the rocky subterrain like tentacles from some futuristic octopus.

The sign advertising the project stated the condos were *The Future of Wexford*. And what a glorious future it will be—each unit had its own balcony, the lower floors looking out at Stone Pizza's parking lot and for the residents lucky enough to afford the units on the upper floors, the town dump across the road.

At least St. John wasn't involved in this scar on the land-scape. Still, he had his name on plenty of others, although not condos. Nope, no high-rise buildings for him, only houses the size of small mountains suited his taste. It was quite possible he built the humongous homes as a way of compensating for a small penis. Hopefully, she was wrong.

As she walked toward the building, Chad pulled on her skirt. "Mama, hurry up, all the fun will be gone."

"I don't think you have to worry about that munchkin."

He urged her to keep up and only relaxed when they passed through the door. Once inside he became completely dejected. "They're gone."

"Check again." She pointed to a wall of windows looking

into a large room on the opposite side of the dining room.

"Come on." Chad leapt away, knocking into a waitress carrying a pizza tray.

"Hey, little buddy, watch where you're going."

Shannon took hold of his hand. "Apologize, please."

"I'm sorry. Now can we go, Mama?"

"Yes, but slow down and walk nice. We don't need you destroying the place."

"Fine." He solemnly walked beside her. When they reached the door, he huffed a loud "Finally" and burst into the room, his face lighting up when his teammates called out his name.

Shannon scanned the crowd around the long table. Kids at one end, adults at the other. Dee and Peg were close to the door but no St. John. She came up behind her friends and hugged both women. "Hey, ladies."

Peg swung around and shouted, "You made it," and nudged her chair to the left. "Grab that chair."

Shannon shoved the chair into the spot Peg opened up. Shannon tried to sound innocent as she asked, "Where's the coach?"

"He had to leave," Dee said. "Hot date. So, tell us, everything okay with Justin? He was pretty angry when he left the field."

"Yeah, he's fine." Shannon had given up trying to keep count of her lies. "He even gave me a hundred dollars to buy you guys drinks tonight." At least that part was true. Did a truth cancel out a lie?

"Yippee for Justin," Peg yelled.

Shannon scanned the pizza choices. "I need to get Chad's T-shirt back and his cap. Also, I need the papers. Can one of you reach me a slice of veggie?"

"Adam has everything in the back of his truck," Peg said, tapping the woman next to her to reach for Shannon's slice. "I don't think he's coming back. Right, Dee? He looked pretty eager to go and meet his friend." She emphasized the word friend with air quotes before accepting the plate with pizza the other woman offered.

"I get the picture." Shannon studied her food. She didn't like that she was feeling a teensy bit jealous about him being on a date. What had she thought—he'd forgo his lifestyle until she lay down for him? "When is the first practice?" she said.

"Check the school website. All the practice and game times and dates will be posted there. St. John had to shuffle things a bit and add two more teams," Dee said. "Seems you weren't the only one who didn't register."

"Leeann was flipping out," Peg added. "Shouting at people to go away until Adam reined her in. Do you think they've slept together?" Peg looked at Dee across Shannon's chest.

"Are you kidding me?" Dee cleared her throat and said in a gruff voice, "I never sleep with married women or women from Wexford."

"Good impersonation," Peg said.

Dee stood and reached for a bottle of water. "Shan, want something to drink?"

"Water, please. Does he ever break his rules?"

"St. John?" Dee replied. "Nope, never, so get the idea out of your head."

"Maybe he has, and you just don't know it," Peg piped in.

"It's possible, but at least I know he hasn't broken the rule about not falling in love or something silly like that." Dee placed her hand over her heart and pretended to sob. "The poor baby's been hurt."

"He's been cheated on, Dee," Peg reminded her.

Peg described to Shannon how St. John's first wife had cheated on him with his best friend and that his second and third wives had cheated on him too. At the end of her story, Peg asked, "So, now that you've met him, do you still think Adam is some mean ol' developer?"

Shannon stretched for the nearest pizza pan and snatched a slice with mushrooms on it. "Business practices aside, he seems like a nice guy. It's too bad about the marriages."

Dee scowled. "His failed marriages are his own fault."

"Aw, come on, Dee, he loved Coleen." Peg added, "If she hadn't lost the baby, they'd probably still be married."

"What baby?" Shannon switched her gaze from Dee to Peg. "Who's Coleen?"

Eager to share what she knew, Peg explained, "She was St. John's girlfriend in high school. They were like this fairy-tale couple, even the king and queen of the senior prom. She became pregnant, and they got married. When she lost the baby, it shattered her and St. John too."

"Coleen started spending time with St. John's friend, and the rest is history," Dee included. "The bottom line is Adam St. John is an emotional train wreck."

"Yeah, it's too bad." Peg sighed. "He's the kind of guy who'd run into a burning building to save the woman he loves. Unfortunately, he was the one who set the place on fire."

"That's sad," Shannon said.

Dee gave her a suspicious look. "This is a big turnaround for you, Shan. You used to think he was ruthless."

"I never called him ruthless, and all I meant was it's too bad he's had such bad luck with his marriages, which it is. I can barely accomplish one divorce, and he's been through three. I didn't say I wanted to marry the guy." Shannon tapped Dee's hand. "Let's not forget, young lady, who sent him to rescue me yesterday. Did you want to tease me by dangling the carrot I can't eat?"

Peg snorted and grabbed a napkin. "I couldn't believe it when I found out. Way to let the wolf loose in the sheep's pen, Dee. You're lucky Shannon's still in one piece."

"He promised he'd behave. He did, right?" Dee watched Shannon. "Did he behave?"

"He was a perfect gentleman. So, where are we going to-night?" Shannon said. It was time to change the subject before she said something that would get St. John or her in trouble with Dee.

"I think we should stop at Adam's nightclub," Peg said. "He's very generous about providing free drinks, and the chicken wings aren't half bad."

Shannon held up her hand. "Wait a minute. St. John owns a nightclub?"

"More like a pick-up dive," Dee said. "He owns it with Jimbo and his lawyer. We'll start at *Elements* and figure out the rest as we go."

"You three look like you're plotting the takeover of the world."

Three sets of eyes focused on the owner of the deep voice. St. John stood behind them, looking dashing in a tailored blue suit. He'd slicked back his dark blond hair, and even the way-ward strand was behaving.

Shannon managed a discreet sniff. Dear goddess, she'd love to wear him on her skin. Since Justin already thought St. John was her lover, she wouldn't be cheating, technically, if she slept with him—she'd just be tying up loose ends, that's all.

Peg let loose a catcall. "Wow, Adam, she must be pretty special to get you all dolled up. What are you doing here?"

St. John adjusted a gold watch under his left cuff. "Contrary to popular belief, I'm not a complete hick, and I'm here because I wanted to check on things."

"Every thing's under control," Dee announced. "The kids are soaring high on sugar, pizza, and more sugar, and *we're* planning a girls' night out for tonight."

"Really? Tell me where you're going, and I'll catch up with you. My meeting shouldn't last long."

"Screw 'em and lose 'em," Dee snickered. "That's your motto, eh, St. John?"

"For your information, Denise, this is a business dinner about the Hancock farm. I have no plans on hitting on the woman, or her husband." He offered his devilish grin and added, "However, that doesn't mean I won't find someone for later."

Shannon sucked in her bottom lip when he settled his blue eyes on her.

"I'm glad to see you made it," he said. "I have Chad's stuff in my trunk. Got a minute?"

Peg nudged Shannon. "Go. We'll watch Chad."

St. John held up his index finger. "In a minute." He walked over and stood by his assistant coach and clapped to get the kids' attention. "Give me a sec, will you guys?" he said. "And ladies," he added, smiling at the team's female players. "Coach Enders and I couldn't be happier with how hard you all worked today during the tryouts. One thing we want to know is, did you have fun?"

Most of the parents covered their ears at the volume of the chaos he'd unleashed. Dee shouted to Peg and Shannon, "He sure knows how to work a crowd."

Shannon spoke into Peg's ear. "I don't understand. Why does he act like he's in charge?"

"Because he is. It's his money that's paying for everything. The town cut baseball for six- and seven-year-olds."

"Oh, wow." Shannon clapped along with the rest of the adults. The more she learned about St. John, the more confused she became. She wanted to dislike him. Be attracted to him, yes, sleep with him, double yes, but dislike him none the less. Yet, he really seemed to be a decent man.

St. John stopped to talk with a few parents and eventually stood by Shannon. "Ready?" When they reached the exit, he held the door and said, "I'm parked in the back, next to you."

She entered the steamy heat of the afternoon, enjoying the feel of it wrapping around her bare arms and legs. She gave him a quick smile. What would he say if she asked him to take her away, someplace far removed from the town? A remote beach house perhaps, someplace where two people who'd been beaten up by love could pretend nothing existed except for the two them.

"Are you okay?" He lightly touched the bruise on her arm.

"What?" she said, surprised by his expression of genuine concern.

"Justin did this."

It wasn't a question but a statement of fact. She shook her head, however. "Yes. No— I mean, I have something I need to talk to you about."

"Gee." He grinned. "I wonder if we both want to talk about the same thing. Does it have anything to do with us having an affair?"

Chapter 16

"The only way to get rid of temptation is to yield to it."
Oscar Wilde

St. John noted Shannon had changed into a white, flowing skirt. In the few days since he'd met her, he'd seen three such skirts, and he was enjoying this one more than the others thanks to the way the sun filtered through the sheer gauze. A slip or something blocked the view of the tops of her legs, but that was fine. He was quite capable of filling in the missing pieces. She wasn't a cluttered witch, like the ones that hung around Portsmouth, and he liked that. Christ, with all the bells and jangly stuff, you could hear them a mile away. Except for the silver pentagram earrings she wore, he'd never seen any other type of jewelry on her. Not even a watch. He also liked that her hair wasn't blue or purple. Midnight black was fast becoming his favorite color.

They reached his car, and he walked around to the driver's side. "I heard a rumor today. Want to know what it is?" he called out.

Shannon didn't respond at first. Instead, she unlocked the front passenger door of her SUV and leaned in to insert her key in the ignition. The way she was bent over the seat gave him all sorts of ideas, each one ending the same way—her calling out his name as she climaxed.

His crotch tightened, something he relieved with a discreet adjustment.

She lowered her passenger window before facing him. She still didn't respond to what he'd asked, so he kept talking while he opened his own car and hung his suit coat on the hook behind the driver's seat.

"You and I are sleeping together."

"Don't believe everything you hear," she said, a half-smile on her lips.

"Usually I don't, but this one came from the horse's ass, so it must be true. Although..." He rubbed at his chin and slipped on a confused expression. "I'm really disappointed I can't remember any of it. How was I?"

"Fair." She crossed her arms.

She didn't miss a beat, and he enjoyed that about her. "Hmm, that sounds about right. You must have been lacking too, or else I'd remember *something* about you."

She angled her head to the side. "I guess we're both duds."

"I don't think so. In fact, I'm convinced we'll be great together." He moved around to her side of the car and lightly touched the bruise on her arm. "Has Justin done this kind of stuff before?"

She swung away from his hand. "Just so we're clear: what Justin does or doesn't do isn't your business."

"I'm making it my business."

"Well, don't. If you feel like pretending you're a white knight, go rescue some other damsel in distress."

"Are you admitting you're in distress?"

"Just drop it, okay, St. John?"

He had no intention of fulfilling her request. Either she'd tell him, or he'd get the information out of Justin. One way or another, he would find out the truth, and if it was as he suspected, Justin would pay. First, St. John needed to deal with her shutting him out. "Want to hear another one of my rules?"

"Does it come before or after the one about love?"

"After."

"How many rules do you have?" Shannon asked.

St. John ran his hand through his hair and sighed. "Enough to keep me out of trouble. Do you want to hear the rule or not?"

"Fine, enlighten me."

"Don't shut me out; I might never come back." He enjoyed

her chewing on the corner of her lip. "Any questions?"

"I don't get how that's a rule; it's more like a command."

"Forget whether it's a rule or not. Do you understand what I'm saying?"

Shannon hardened her gaze. "Who said I would want you to come back? I didn't even ask you to be here in the first place."

"You're doing it again. If I'm bothering you, just say the word, and I'll go away."

"Ha, you keep saying that, but you're still here."

He hoped the look he was giving her said he didn't want to go anywhere.

She held out her hand. "Can you just give me the papers, so I can get back inside where it's cool?"

He reached onto the back seat and brought out a manila envelope, Chad's T-shirt, and hat. "Bring them with you Monday night. By the way, you have a great kid. Are you going to do the right thing by him?" The last question hadn't been planned; it sort of popped out, but he was glad it had.

"What?"

He could have sworn he saw sparks flash in her green eyes. There was no way she would be a dud in bed, not with that emerald fire burning inside of her. "I said—"

"I heard you."

"Then, why did you ask—?"

Shannon tore the envelope from his hand. "I asked because I couldn't believe what I heard."

"Then you should have said *that* instead of what?"

"What?"

"Exactly."

"Oh, for...give me those." She swiped the shirt and hat away from him. "I swear, you seem to enjoy rattling my cage."

"What I'm trying to do is give you the combination to the lock, so you can set yourself free."

"Skip the metaphors." She threw the items into her car and

slammed the door.

"You're the one who uses metaphors. I was just joining in the fun."

He expected her to walk away. He'd pushed as many buttons as he could while they were out in public, and he'd given her Chad's stuff, so there was no reason for her to stay out in the oppressive heat. But he wanted her to. No, what he wanted was to take her someplace isolated where they could pretend they cared about each other.

"Have dinner with me tonight."

Her nasal chuckle failed to sway him.

"Why not?"

"Are you kidding? First off, you know I have plans with my friends. And second, I'm done with men ordering me around." She stepped close, her chin raised. "Here's one of my rules, St. John, and you'd be wise to remember it: if you can't ask me nicely, don't ask me at all."

He couldn't contain his grin, which seemed to enrage her even more. "Sorry, it's just that you're becoming as much a rule person as I am. Okay, here goes: please, will you have dinner with me tonight?"

"I can't, but thanks for asking. And thank you for Chad's things. We'll be at practice Monday night. Have fun on your date."

"It's not a date. It's a meeting."

"Whatever. Have fun."

"I might be in Manchester later. Maybe I'll run into you." Begging wasn't his style, but here he was, on the verge of dropping to his knees.

"What's up with your bar?" she asked. "Dee said it's a dive?"

He laughed. "She would. Jimbo, Marty, and I own it. We bought it about ten years ago. The city was going to tear down the building, which would have been a shame. It's a historic landmark.'"

She raised the corner of her mouth. "So it *is* a hookup place?"

"You could call it that. Let's just say nobody goes there for the chicken wings. It's certainly not a place for you if that's what you're thinking."

"You have no idea what I'm thinking, St. John."

"But I want to." To hell with trying to decipher her thoughts. He wanted her, maybe even needed her. "Sleep with me, Shannon." When her eyes widened, he said, "Will you sleep with me, please?" Obviously, begging wasn't off the table. "For Justin's sake," he quickly added. He could tell he'd piqued her interest.

"Justin?" she said. "Let me get this straight. When asking a woman to sleep with you doesn't work—"

"It always works," he interjected.

"Not this time it isn't."

"Not yet, but I have faith. And, yes, I'm asking for Justin's sake if that will get you into my arms."

She didn't say anything, and he held his silence, choosing instead to watch as a bead of sweat eased down the side of her neck. He'd love to be doing the same thing with his tongue. When the drop pooled near her collar bone, he licked his lips and said, "I bet he's already told the whole town about us, so why not make him an honest man? I mean, we've been standing out here for God knows how long, and people *have* been walking by, and wouldn't you like to find out if we are duds together?"

Her laughter stirred his blood.

"I wasn't joking."

"Are you trying to save my husband's reputation or your own?"

He closed what little distance remained between them. "Neither. I'm asking because I want to feel you under me. I'm asking because I want to taste you." He grinned as she nibbled on her lip. Hopefully, he'd be doing same exact thing very soon. "I'm asking because if I don't make love to you, I'll go crazy. Plus, you told me if I asked nicely I'd get my way."

She thanked him again for Chad's things and strolled across the lot.

Watching her hips sway made him groan. This wasn't going at all like it usually went. Typically, he'd find someone who sparked an interest and be done with it. He never had a desire to talk to any of them, outside of ordering drinks or asking for a name. So why, for fuck sake, did he want to spend time with this confused woman?

He got in his car and started the engine, directing all the air-conditioning vents his way. His shirt was soaked through, but he didn't have time to go home and change. As it was, he was going to be late for his meeting—which made him sitting in his car with the gear shift in park all the more peculiar. Just because Baldos was an ass didn't mean she wasn't still his wife. There were plenty of other women he could bed, women who didn't come with a load of baggage. He would be smart to avoid her.

What he needed was a stiff drink and to get laid. Maybe get hit in the head with a brick. Anything to clean her out of his system.

His phone vibrated, and he glanced at the text.

Dee, Peg, and I are starting at Elements. We'll be arriving around 8. Game on.

Good thing he didn't pass anyone as he was pulling out of the parking lot, or they'd have thought he'd gone insane from the goofy grin he was sporting.

Chapter 17

"Love demands all, and has a right to all."
Beethoven

Barefoot, with her shoes dangling from her fingers, Shannon slowly ascended the steps leading to the second floor of her house. She entered her bedroom and tossed the sandals into the back of the closet. After peeling off the confining jeans, she threw them down the laundry chute. If only she could toss away the night as easily. The ride home had soured the whole evening, courtesy of Dee's lecture about the divorce, shouted over Peg's drunken singing from the backseat of the car.

'There are worse things than staying in a loveless marriage,' Dee had started without warning. 'When Chad is having trouble in school or starts taking drugs, you'll wish you'd stayed with Justin.'

'Are you kidding me?' she'd shot back. 'Now you have Chad shooting up in some dark alley in Manchester? What's next—he'll turn to prostitution?'

Since their referee was inebriated, they'd shot barbs and accusations back and forth until Dee had pulled into the driveway and summed up her real feelings. 'I'm scared for you and Chad.'

"I'm scared for me and Chad too," Shannon whispered now as she removed her makeup.

Jasper jumped on the bed and did his usual routine of circling around before curling up. He settled himself in the spot near the second pillow, rested his head between his paws, and sighed.

Shannon sighed as well. "My feelings exactly." Once under the comforter, she lifted her phone to reread the text Justin had sent after she'd called to say goodnight to Chad.

Kids watching a movie. Your boyfriend is here slobbering over the new bartender. I made sure he won't be bothering you anymore. You can thank me tomorrow.

She double sighed. The night had worked out as it should: she and Chad got to be with their friends, and St. John got to charm someone into his bed. All was right with the Universe.

Things would have been so much easier if St. John hadn't blown her off. She'd be lying in his arms, the glow of sexual bliss on her face, happy that she'd found a safe haven to hide from Justin. But, nope, she was in her king-sized bed with her dog, and St. John was snoring with his face planted on the woman's Brazilian-waxed crotch. Good for him.

She didn't need him. She didn't need any man. She just needed to make a stinking decision about her marriage.

The rich timbre of St. John's voice penetrated her thoughts. 'Are you going to do the right thing by him?'

She grumbled at the intrusion. "You don't get to have an opinion because you blew me off for a hot bartender."

She checked her cell phone, frowned, and dropped it on the nightstand before switching off the light. Soon—hopefully, please make it so—she'd be sleeping in a different bedroom. Oh, please goddess, not a condo. A house. Like the one in her vision. Small enough to keep her from getting lost in its rooms... and her fears.

Divorce Justin, don't divorce Justin, leave, stay—her brain was a ping-pong ball. She threw back the comforter, sweeping Jasper along with it, and entered the bathroom.

"Make a decision," she scolded her reflection. "But know one thing: if you stay with Justin, you're a fucking coward."

The bluish mark encircling her arm was one of a million reasons to leave, but walking away was so stinking hard. Why?

A noise outside caught Jasper's interest, and he took off down the steps.

She yawned and crawled back into bed; he'd let her know

if she needed to get involved. It was most likely a raccoon scratching around the deck.

In bed, she allowed her vision to fill her mind. The quaint house looked perfectly suited for the life she imagined for her and Chad. She knew the black truck would soon appear, and St. John would step from it. The whole scene played like the end of some romantic movie, but it didn't answer the questions she had, like how the frig had she gotten away from Justin? Had she walked out? If so, what had been the proverbial straw to push her over the edge?

Maybe her vision was nothing more than wishful thinking. Her conscious playing tricks on her subconscious.

Shrugging under the comforter, she let the vision play out. The black truck arrived, and St. John emerged. He came to her and opened his arms; she entered them and allowed his lips to find hers.

The rattling of her cell phone against the bedside table burst through the scene, her first thought going to Chad.

Are you still awake?

With her heart beating inside her eardrums, she scowled at the screen. Who did he think he was, texting her at midnight? She had a good mind to turn the phone onto mute and... But then if something happened to Chad... Oh, for crying out loud.

Yes, she texted back.

Want some company?

The guy was definitely one of a kind. He'd just screwed one woman and was now hoping to get laid again. He gave double dates a whole new meaning, although she'd had a few of the same back in her day. But that wasn't the point. She'd been in her twenties and he was almost—what? How old was he? Forty? Fifty? Anyway, that didn't matter. She would be damned before she became St. John's second conquest of the night.

No, she typed.

We need to talk. I promise to keep my hands in my pockets.

She responded with a loud, "Yeah, right, talk my ass." It wouldn't matter if his hands were tied behind his back; if he came into the house he wouldn't stand a chance. *We can talk via texts.*

Not a good idea and delete this text when we're done.

What's the magic word?

Please.

Why?

Because your husband is out for blood.

What else is new?

Not much, except he and I had an interesting conversation tonight.

Where?

At the lodge. I'm sorry I didn't meet you. After giving it some thought, I've decided to stay away.

You're funny. You pursue me like a dog in heat and when you might have a chance you back down.

Funny, and correction, you would be the one in heat.

Excuse me?

Female dogs go into heat, male dogs are just horny.

I guess that makes you a male dog.

Guilty as charged. Can I come over?

I don't know, can you?

Are you always so difficult to get along with?

Guilty as charged. Why bother? You blew me off. Face it, you lost what little chance you had.

I'd like to explain my reason for not showing up.

Save it. You think you can get whatever you want.

Not true. I try my damnedest but sometimes I fail.

I doubt that.

It's true.

Name one time.

I want to make love to you but I'm afraid that's not going to happen.

The pulsing of her blood moved from her ears to her groin as she reread his last string of words. There was a reason he hadn't met her at Elements that went beyond him physically not driving there. Even if she was disappointed, she shouldn't alter the course of fate. *Go home, St. John. Chad is here.*

You're doing it again.

What?

Lying? I get lied to all the time. It's part of doing business and dealing with people. I'd like to know one person who doesn't lie to me. Could you be that person?

I'm not lying.

Still lying.

No, I'm not.

Still lying. You're not paying attention.

Excuse me?

I already told you I saw Justin at the lodge. In fact, I played several games of pool with him. He's not very good. I won a ton. And, before you give me another excuse, I saw Chad too.

Okay, so he'd caught her. Big deal. She still wasn't giving in.

Please, can...may I come over, he continued. *I'd really like to talk to you and I don't want to do it through a string of texts. And, again, delete everything when we're finished.*

No.

Shannon.

Fine, but you can't park in the driveway.

I'll park at the entrance to the development and walk down.

Fine.

She jumped from the bed and swung on her robe. A soft tapping filtered through the open bathroom windows. What'd the guy do, fly? Or had he been outside the whole time? She ran to the Great Room where Jasper stood at the sliding door, his tail wagging.

"Some attack dog you are." She held Jasper's collar and unlocked the door, stepping back to put distance between her and the man she wanted to ravage.

St. John entered, closed the door, and remained in place. He still wore the suit pants and white shirt—gold watch too. But instead of the slicked hair of earlier, the dark blond strands were strewn every which way, and his eyes revealed an exhaustion she'd yet to see in him. And his leg-weakening grin was gone.

She wanted to run to him, give him a reason to smile again. Take him to her bed and make him forget whatever had darkened his blue eyes. But, like some Mexican standoff, they remained in their respective spots, neither speaking, both staring.

One of them had to break the stalemate, so it might as well be her. "Go ahead. Talk."

He bent and scratched Jasper's head before he said, "I'm sorry."

"I don't understand." She moved to the couch.

"I shouldn't have talked to you as I did," he said, remaining by the door, Jasper at his feet. "I should have said no to Denise the other day when she asked if I would pick you up. But in my defense, I didn't know it was you at the park."

"So, if you had known it was me, you would have said no?" She hugged one of the pillows on the couch. She wasn't sure where his remorse was coming from, but she had a sneaking suspicion her soon-to-be-goddess-please-ex-husband was at the heart of it.

His chuckle lightened the mood a fraction. "No, I would have still said yes."

"Then what is all this about, St. John?"

"Look, Shannon, you're married, and I don't... Listen, name something, and I'm sorry for it."

"I get it. You can stop with the apologies. Does this sudden wave of guilt have to do with you seeing Justin tonight?"

"In part. May I have something to drink? Water, anything?"

"I don't think so. I kind of like watching you suffer." She'd been ready to grin, but when he didn't, she shrugged. "Fine, what would you like?"

"A shot of whiskey would be great, thanks."

She left to get his drink and returned with a shot glass in each hand. Standing in the doorway, she said, "This room is like a cavern. Let's sit in my reading room."

He took the glasses from her and, since he was the person who'd built the house, found his own way, and she followed.

"Most people don't call these rooms reading rooms," he said. "They become game rooms, TV rooms, second offices, but nothing to do with reading. It's a shame too; reading is a great way to escape the bleakness of life."

He hadn't seemed to be speaking directly to her more than thinking out loud, so when he finished, she let the topic drop though she would have liked to agree. Life did have its bleak moments.

Her seat selection was limited. Since he'd made himself comfortable on the overstuffed love seat, she could sit next to him or across the room on the recliner. One seemed a bit too close and the other too far away.

"Chose a seat, Shannon, please. The suspense is killing me."

She was still deciding when he grabbed her hand and pulled her onto the love seat. He handed her one of the glasses.

"Drink up," he said, tapping his glass to hers. "We've got a few things to discuss. As I was saying, I'm sorry for getting you into a pickle with Justin. I was only thinking of myself and not how my behavior would affect you."

She scooted into the corner of the love seat and tucked her legs under her bum. "Supposedly, some English king once said to never offer an apology until you're accused of something. You've done nothing wrong, St. John. I played the game as enthusiastically as you did. And, besides, we didn't do anything." She took a sip of her drink. "The flirting was fun."

"Yes, it was." He downed his whiskey and then took her glass and finished hers as well.

"I wasn't done with that."

"Too late." He set the glasses on the coffee table and resumed looking at her. "This might have been a big mistake." He reached out his hand and placed a finger on her bottom lip.

Her breathing became erratic under the power of his touch, and she pushed his hand away. "Fine, leave. You're the one who insisted on coming in."

"No, I'm not talking about... I meant this..." He waved his hand. "Us."

She stood and walked from the room, coming back with a bottle of Maker's Mark. "You're delusional, St. John. There is no us. There's me, Chad, and Justin, and then there's you with whomever... The bartender at the lodge, for all I know."

"The who?" He took the bottle and filled both their glasses. "You think I slept with the bartender? Where did you get—? Oh, right, Justin. He really is an asshole."

"Yes, he is." As are you, she wanted to add. Since he had no intention of screwing her, why was he even in her house drinking her booze? "What did Justin say to make you change your mind about this?" She waved her hand as he had.

"That he'll make your life difficult."

"So what else is new? My life has been difficult with him ever since Chad was born. What more can he do?"

St. John reached for her hand and lifted the sleeve of her robe, exposing the bruise. "I don't want you or Chad getting hurt, so, I'm backing off."

"Good for you." She yanked her arm away, claimed the two glasses, and downed both drinks. "It's not as if you changing your mind is creating a hole in my life. So, please go home and cry in your own whiskey." She kept her composure as she carried the bottle and glasses to the kitchen.

The click of the patio door locking in place told her he'd taken her at her word.

Chapter 18

"She was the dawn to his night."
Anonymous

Shannon slammed the glasses into the sink. Of all the self-important jerks in the world, he was at the top of the pile. Good riddance to him. She didn't need him to get her out of her marriage; she didn't need him period. Seriously, what had he wanted, anyway, coming over in the dead of night? To apologize, her ass. He'd expected her to beg him to screw her that was why. He'd wanted her to become the damsel in distress and plead for him to save her so his ego could get a testosterone rush and his puny penis a boost. Well, she was way past pleading with any man, and she refused to shed one teardrop over him.

And he'd called Justin an asshole.

"Takes one to know one," she told the sponge being squeezed to death by her fingers.

She rinsed the glasses and then dried and put them away, each movement bringing the tears burning the edges of her eyes a little closer to reality. She returned the whiskey bottle to its home in the bottom cabinet and slammed the door, catching her finger in the process.

"You piece of... Ow!"

The tears came.

And they stayed with her as she turned off the kitchen light and were still falling when a soft knock echoed into the hallway.

She raced forward and flung open the front door.

And met a pair of blue eyes and a leg-melting pirate grin.

Before he had a chance to speak, she crushed her mouth to his. His saliva tasted of bourbon, and like a woman dying of thirst, she drank, unwilling to let him go until she'd had her fill.

St. John surrounded her with his arms and lifted her feet off the floor. They entered the house entwined, and then he kicked the door closed and forced her against the wooden surface. His kisses were those of a starving man, and she matched his hunger with her own. But when she flinched, he pulled away, a look of worry on his face. "What's wrong?"

She choked out the words "doorknob" between her rapid breaths.

"Sorry." He moved her to the right. "Better?"

"Yes." She met his gaze straight on and whispered, "Say my name."

His right eyebrow lifted, and he grinned. "Shannon."

"Again."

"Shannon."

The look in his eyes was the same he'd worn that first morning they'd met. He was the predator, and she was his prey. She clutched his shirt and flipped their positions. He would soon learn sometimes things weren't always what they seemed. While maintaining eye contact with him, she unbuckled his belt and opened the zipper of his pants. She reached in, wrapped her hand around him, and grinned. Her whole big-houses-small-dick theory was shot to hell.

"Again."

"Shannon," he growled low and buried his hands in her hair. "Shannon."

"Perfect," she cooed and knelt in front of him.

That the doormat needed a vacuuming registered for a brief second, soon replaced by what she was about to do. The hunted was about to become dinner.

She took him in her mouth and heard the sound of his head when it hit the door as he gasped her name.

Hearing him call out to her in the darkened hallway thrilled her. She was making love to a man: a viral, sexy, powerful man. She'd been wrong—Justin hadn't destroyed her. She was alive after all.

She traveled her tongue along the shaft, enjoying the way he moaned with each pass. Some men liked having their testicles squeezed and some didn't. There was no way to know except to try. As she slid her mouth around him, she cupped his balls in her hands and applied a slight pressure. His long moan indicated he belonged in the first group.

The revelation heightened her passion, and she worked his balls and scraped her teeth against the soft skin of his penis. That was all he needed, and soon she tasted the salty warmth she hadn't realized she been craving.

He helped her up from her knees and held her. "You certainly come out swinging," he said, his breaths coming fast as if he'd run a marathon.

She pressed her toes into the floor and brought her lips near his ear. "Need a drink?"

He returned his hands to her hair and placed a slow kiss on her mouth. "Make it a double."

"Be right back."

Her feet obeyed her brain's instructions and remained steady, allowing her to walk to the kitchen. It didn't seem right to invite him up to her bedroom, which was still Justin's even though he didn't sleep in there anymore. Still, some rules were better left intact and the sanctity of the marriage bed was one of them.

She removed the bottle from the lower cabinet, being careful not to catch her finger again. The throbbing had stopped, which wasn't a surprise—all her blood was in her groin.

Sanctity of the marriage bed. What an archaic thought. Her grandmother must be channeling into her. She didn't have to think too hard about what her grandmother would say regarding her present activity. "You're going to burn in hell's fires," she said out loud.

"Let's burn together."

St. John stood behind her and placed his hands on her shoulders.

She arched her neck, her fingers remaining firm around the bottle, and allowed her head to rest against his chest.

He moved his fingers over her, following the swell of her breasts and the soft mound of her belly. As quickly as the image of her out-of-shape body entered her mind, it vanished, replaced by a new and delicious realization—she was in St. John's arms.

He untied the sash of her bathrobe and returned his hands to her breasts. The cotton nightgown offered no protection from his searing fingertips as he moved them in circles over the hard nipples.

She arched her head and moaned. The flames inside her raged. Glorious goddess, if he didn't take her soon, she would melt under the intensity, becoming nothing more than a puddle at his feet.

He removed her bathrobe and placed it on the counter. Next, he slipped the straps of her nightgown from her shoulders and, helping her step free, he added it to the robe. He then cupped her breasts.

She covered his hands with her own and forced him to squeeze. He followed her lead until she couldn't stand waiting. "Fuck me, St. John," she said, forcing the words out between her rapid breaths.

He kissed the tender spot behind her ear. "Don't worry. I plan on it."

His hot breath opened the dam and warmth spilled from the lips of her groin, moistening the surrounding skin. Even her upper thighs didn't escape the flow.

Wet fingertips played with her nipples, the skin becoming taut from his cooling saliva. When she trembled, he said, "Say my name."

"St. John," she moaned as he squeezed the erect tips.

He looped his left arm around her waist and kissed the spot where her neck and shoulder joined. "Perfect," he said, moving his free hand between her legs.

"Again."

She closed her eyes and let her head fall against his shoulder. "St. John."

The hunter was in charge once again.

He found her center and stroked, slowly, as if to tease her. Like the waves under the moon, his finger controlled the ebb and flow of her orgasm. He brought her to the edge and then let her fall back. Her breaths were coming too fast. She was going to pass out. All she could do was hold his arm and gasp for air.

More fluid leaked from her, and he used it, extending her pleasure. He was the puppet master, and she was about to faint. Dear goddess, her heart was going to fly out of her chest.

"I can't..." she gasped.

"Can't what?" He continued driving her to a frenzy. "Do you want me to stop?"

"No, no."

She couldn't imagine having anything left to give since what he'd just said sent a tsunami down her inner thighs.

"Please, please, please," she whispered. "Please."

His arm muscles locked, and he held her tight as his finger picked up speed.

She cried out, and he slowed his momentum but not to a full stop, keeping her prisoner as her body shook with each additional pass of his fingers.

She slumped against him, her skin covered in perspiration. When her breathing returned to normal, he circled the tip again, sending her over the edge again. Their roles had switched; he, once again, was the hunter.

He turned her and drove his tongue into her mouth. "Can you handle more?" he asked, his lips on hers.

"More?"

"Yes, more."

Her groin pulsed, keeping time with her heartbeats. "Yes please."

"Good, because I am far from finished with you," came his reply, ending with him stepping away.

He removed a foil packet from his back pants pocket and handed it to her. While he unzipped his pants, she removed the latex coil and, marveling again at his prowess, rolled the condom down the shaft. He lifted her onto the counter and opened her legs. Supporting the back of her head with his hand, he entered her.

The tight muscles of her vagina, long gone unused, pressed against him, threatening to bar entry. She opened her legs wider. She wanted every inch of him.

The rapid flow of his breath against her neck singed the tender skin, and she clutched his sweat-soaked shirt. A surge of electricity filled her lower abdomen, and she cried out.

He finished with a final thrust. His hand remained between the back of her head and the cabinet door and she held him, her legs wrapped around his hips, ankles linked.

"Damn," she exhaled.

"I couldn't have said it better myself."

He motioned to withdraw, but she shook her head. "Don't."

They remained in their embrace until Jasper decided enough was enough and whined.

"I think your dog is trying to tell us something," St. John mumbled against her neck.

He pulled out, and she whined along with Jasper. When she saw his grin, she said, "Do you know your grin is lopsided?"

"So I've been told. Now stop talking and kiss me."

She parted her lips for him, inwardly jumping for joy as her desire ramped up again.

"Your lips taste like a ripe peach," he said. "I don't think I'll ever get tired of kissing them."

He helped her down from the counter and held her robe open for her. While he closed the front, he swept his fingertips over her nipples, and her body responded with a delicious quiver. He grinned again and, taking hold of her right breast, surrounded the nipple with his mouth.

Each time his tongue tickled the tip, she moaned. He straightened and gripped her wrists over her head and moved his right hand between her legs. He toyed with the still-erect tip

"Tell me to stop," he whispered into her mouth. "Beg me to stop."

"I don't want you to stop," came her breathy response.

He released a stream of hot breath and insisted. "Beg me."

She grinned. Someday, if she had the chance, he'd be the one begging, but she was more than happy to play it his way. "Please, St. John, I can't take any more. Please, stop, please."

"Again."

He pressed three fingers against the swollen skin and rubbed.

"Please, I'm begging you. I...can't—"

His kiss silenced her but didn't prevent a rainbow of colors from exploding in her head—and body.

His arms still held her, not seeming to want to release their hold. Eventually, he asked, "Mind if I use your bathroom?"

She kept her head against him and moved it in an affirmative motion. "Yes. No. Whatever. Fine, use it. You know where it is. Help yourself."

"You okay to stand on your own, or would you like me to carry you to the chair?"

"I'm fine." She waved him away, closing her bathrobe in

the process. With him out of the room, she removed a spray bottle from under the sink and spritzed the counter. After she finished, she placed two glasses on the clean surface and filled them with bourbon. Her nipples were still hard, as was the spot between her legs. The most time she'd ever climaxed in a row had been two, and St. John had gotten her there... How many times? She'd lost count. She prayed a whole many more were in their future.

If there was a future.

Was this all she was going to get?

St. John walked back into the room, a wad of tissues in his hand.

Wearing a quizzical look, she asked, "Do you always keep your used condoms?"

He held up the wadded tissue and nodded. "How else do you think I hold onto my money? I'll rinse this one out and use it again."

"How about I supply next time?"

His silence told her everything she needed to know. She handed him one of the glasses and tapped it with hers. "Toast to a romping good time."

St. John rubbed the back of his neck. "Shannon, this didn't change anything. I'm not going to make your life with Justin more difficult. That bruise on your arm is an indication of what he's capable of." He sipped his drink, his grin long gone, and looked out the kitchen window and then at his watch. "It's late, or should I say early? We should both get some sleep."

"I'm going to divorce Justin," she announced, maybe a little too loudly. Hopefully, she hadn't woken her neighbors.

He sighed, long and slow, and then finished his drink.

She prepared herself for what was coming.

"Don't divorce Justin because of me, Shannon." He continued, adding words as hard as his expression. "Let's get something clear: I don't need a relationship nor do I want one.

This—" He spread his hands. "—was just sex. Don't go turning it into something it won't ever be."

She snorted and shook her head. "You're a cocky prick, you know that?"

"I'm just saying—"

"Save it, St. John." She folded her arms. "You can go now."

He didn't look like he intended on moving.

"What are you waiting for? Go," she challenged.

He scratched at his chin. "Let me ask you something. Why is it you cower when it comes to Justin, but with me your claws come out?"

"My claws? You bastard. How I act around my husband is none of your business." She softened her tone and added, "Please, leave. Is that better for you? I even said please."

"Yeah, you're big on politeness. Why are you so angry all of a sudden?"

She repeated in a falsetto voice, "Don't divorce Justin because of me." Then she returned her voice to normal and continued. "Listen up, St. John, I don't give a flying fuck about you; I'm divorcing Justin for my own reasons, and you don't fit into the equation at all. If you ceased to exist, I'd still divorce him." She took a step nearer to him. His scent defied her to kiss him. She ignored the challenge and drew out her statement. "Please leave, St. John, so I can get on with my life."

He claimed her glass and tossed the contents into his mouth. Then he bent and scratched behind one of Jasper's ears. When he looked at her again, his eyes lacked emotion. "Thanks for the fuck." He walked out of the room and out of the house.

She stomped up the stairs and into the master bath. "Don't divorce him because of me," she mimicked. She stepped out of her robe and into the shower stall. She couldn't get his scent off her skin fast enough. The water ran while she inhaled the skin on her arm. She turned off the water, got into bed, and buried her head under her pillow.

Adam St. John possessed the skill to make a woman feel like she was floating on air one minute and spiraling to her death the next.

He *was* an emotional train wreck.

And he'd just run her over.

Chapter 19

"A man wrapped up in himself makes a very small bundle."
Benjamin Franklin

"Cool your jets." St. John directed his canoe toward the sandy beach, and Sadie let him know he was moving too slowly, her tail wagging as she stood at the bow and barked at the water.

He jumped into the few inches of water and pulled the canoe onto the beach, where he'd parked his truck at five that morning. They'd spent the past three hours on the still surface of Massabesic Lake, and they both needed to stretch their legs and empty their bladders.

Sadie hopped from the boat, and ran and peed on a log. St. John did the same, only his chosen location was more secluded. With business taken care of, he collected their gear, making sure to swap the empty canteen for a full one. He clicked Sadie's leash in place and started the four-mile hiking loop through the woods. He couldn't ask for better weather: mid-eighties, no humidity, and his knees were cooperating. Playing football had been fun in its time, but it had taken a toll on his body, and with each bend of his knees, he paid for every tackle he'd made at a younger age. But today was great—no pain, no tightness.

Everything about the day was perfect. Too bad he couldn't say the same about his head. He didn't regret what he and Shannon had done—far from it. He'd be with her again if given the chance. The only thing gnawing at him was what he'd said before leaving her house. When she'd told him she was finally going through with her divorce, he'd wanted to celebrate by taking her upstairs. Instead, he'd acted like a prick.

He'd never treated any of the women he screwed like they were disposable. Sure, he never slept with them a second time, but he'd always been respectful, making sure they understood where he was coming from before the first kiss even happened. But last night, he'd gone out of his way to hurt her. He supposed he could have been worse, though telling her thanks for the fuck had been pretty goddamn bad. Obviously, Justin wasn't the only asshole in her life.

Now what? He was going to see her at the field for practice. How the hell was he supposed to make small talk with her after the way he'd acted? And why had he even done anything with her in the first place? He'd honestly meant it when he'd told her his decision not to have sex with her. Say it and leave; that had been his plan—which he'd done, more or less. Being thrown out was close to leaving. Whatever. The reason he'd left wasn't important; he'd gotten out the house without touching her. But, like an idiot, he'd come back. All it took was one taste of her lips, and his dick had taken over.

Before heading out that morning, he'd had several shots of bourbon and a gallon of coffee to help clear the fog from his early-morning brain and, since then, a whole canteen of water and a protein bar, but the taste of her still lingered on his tongue. And her scent. Of all the perfumes she had at her fingertips to buy, why did she have to wear Chanel?

The trail split, and St. John tugged off his backpack and sat on a wooden bench located at the signpost. It was a waste of time to continue walking. He couldn't clear his head, and he was exhausted, which tended to happen when a person was running on only two hours' sleep. He filled Sadie's water pouch and had a drink himself. So far, his plan of sweating Shannon out of his pores wasn't working. It was time to try a different tactic: he'd go back home, get cleaned up, and head to the office where he could bury his head in the stack of papers on his desk. From there, he'd head to the bar. It was his night to work. Sunday nights were nothing but a desperate scramble of people looking to get laid before the weekend ended and they had to return to their lonely lives, so he was sure to find a willing partner who'd help take the taste of Shannon out of his mouth.

"Keep telling yourself that, asshole." He'd have to sleep with a hundred different women to clean her out of his system.

He drained the remainder of the water. Rules number one and two, firmly upheld for close to thirty years, shattered to pieces with Shannon's smile. He stared into the trees. It wasn't her perfume, although that hadn't helped matters; it was the whole package. Green eyes the color of a Colombian emerald, hair the color of ink, and the feel...satin, pure satin, and her lips... He'd never get enough of her lips. He'd have liked his interest in her to end with her physical attributes, of which she had many more he could list, but his attraction to her went beyond her skin. She intrigued him like no woman ever had. Spirited, withdrawn; at times, when he looked at her, her eyes seemed to plead for safety. Other times... Those were the times when he should be the one taking guard.

St. John removed his baseball cap and ran his hands through his seat-soaked hair. If he didn't stop himself, and soon, he'd end up breaking another rule—allowing someone close enough to hurt him, and that wasn't something he wanted to do.

When his cell vibrated from within the holder strapped to his belt, he hesitated before removing the phone and allowed the prospect it might be Shannon to solidify in his skull. Should he act happy to hear from her? If it was her, he *would* be happy—no act. Maybe he should behave disinterested, as if her calling wasn't a big deal.

His moment of elation ended when he checked the number. *Now,* what the fuck did she want? It was never a good thing when Denise called on a Sunday, especially this early.

"St. John, I'm at your house. Where are you?"

What was she doing at his house? The rock dropping into the pit of his gut told him the answer; she'd found out about last night.

It shocked him that Shannon had said something about what they'd done. Especially to Denise. But women talked, and now he'd have to deal with the repercussions. Well, Denise would have to wait; he was in no mood for a scolding, even if he deserved it.

He launched right into an apology. "Before you even start, I'm sorry, okay?"

"I brought over coffee and donuts, but you're not here. What did you do now?"

She seemed uncharacteristically chipper for someone about to chew him a new asshole. "Nothing," he said. "Did we have an appointment?"

"Since when do I need an appointment to visit you?"

He grumbled, "Since you've never dropped by without telling me first, I can't really answer that question."

"Wow. What has you in such a shit mood this morning? Where are you?"

Either she didn't know he'd slept with Shannon, or she was dicking with him. "I'm on the moon. What can I do for you?"

"I'd rather not discuss it over the phone. I'll wait."

"You'll wait where? At my house?" His response came out too gruff. For a man who'd been granted a stay of execution, he didn't sound very thrilled.

"Where are you?"

"For Christ sake, Denise, I'm over in Auburn hiking with Sadie."

"When will you be back? I can't wait too long, I have to go food shopping before Jeff gets home with the kids. We're all meeting at Shannon's for a cookout, and I'm bringing my potato salad."

Denise was one of the few people he knew who got right to the point; vague wasn't even in her vocabulary. If she did know about him and Shannon, there was no way she'd hold in her anger, so what could she want to discuss that was so urgent?

"I'm sick of playing twenty questions," he snarled. "Say what you have to say, or I'm hanging up."

"Never mind. I'll leave your coffee and the donuts on the back deck. Bye."

He was behaving like an ass, just as he'd behaved last night. He was disappointed the call hadn't been from Shannon, and he was taking it out on Denise. Not cool; she was an innocent, albeit opinionated, bystander.

"Tell you what," he offered, returning his tone to a somewhat more easygoing sound. He picked up a long stick and tapped at the ground. "I'm in the office all day tomorrow. If you get a chance, drive up around eleven, and I'll buy you lunch. You can tell me what's on your mind."

He returned his phone to the holder and tried to direct his thoughts back to sorting the rest of the day. Things would certainly get interesting if he showed up at Shannon's during the barbecue. Real interesting.

He took the long stick with him and continued walking. His pool game with Baldos had been far from friendly. Caused by the loss of a great deal of money and consuming several bottles of beer, Justin's mood had morphed from basic hostility to outright threatening.

'Touch my wife again, St. John, and she'll be sorry.'

He swung the stick, smashing it against the trunk of a nearby tree.

"Over my dead body."

******

Shannon took Jasper and walked the length of Bebe Pond Road until she came to where the road forked. She'd decided exercise would help her sort through the complicated emotions she was feeling but had gone much further than she'd planned. From where she stood, her house was three miles away. She veered to the left and pushed onward.

They reached Mockingbird Lane, one of St. John's developments. She stopped in front of the large, billboard-style sign. ASJ Development, the bank's name, and Dee's were all listed, along with a detailed map of the layout, each plot sporting a bright red 'sold' sticker.

"Come on, Jasper, let's take a look."

As with the development she lived in, one road led both in and out, and at the distal end, the street looped around a cluster of trees, dense enough to offer privacy for the houses located on either side. The foundations of all the homes were already poured. She stopped and looked around, aware of her ignorance. Each plot was surrounded by trees, and woods framed the backyards, just like in her neighborhood. Somehow St. John managed to build *and* keep a good deal of the natural vegetation.

"Fine, he's a pillar among men, but he's still a jerk."

The acidic tone in her voice dripped easily off her tongue. She fully expected bubbling and spitting on the surface of the road where she stood.

The memory of him touching her hadn't finished forming in her brain before her groin pulsed. She'd love to have him touch her just one more time.

"No. No. No."

She removed a red stone from her fanny pouch, held it in her right hand, and concentrated. When she'd woken up after what could only have amounted to fifteen minutes of sleep, she'd invoked the protective crystal to keep thoughts of him at bay. And it had worked. Mostly. Sure, his face peeked under the veil of the spell now and then; and, okay, she admitted that, even though she'd showered, she could still smell him on her skin; and, fine, the press of his mouth on hers lingered... Obviously, she'd done a lousy job with the spell. And now she had to pee.

Jasper insisted on stopping in front of one of the completed but unoccupied houses and used as his toilet the dirt where a lawn would eventually grow. With a plastic bag filled with poop in hand, Shannon walked around back, looking for a dumpster. She found exactly what she needed near the tree line. She frowned at the trees and walked back to the front door. It was locked. She had to pee. She headed to the back again and tried the slider on the deck. Pay dirt.

"No one ever thinks of locking the slider," she chuckled and walked in.

She sauntered upstairs and along the hallway until she entered the palatial master bath, complete with a sunken whirlpool tub and a triple-sized shower stall lined with tiles depicting a Tuscan hillside. Obviously, the new owners liked Italy.

There was a bidet next to the toilet and a vanity long enough to double as a landing strip if Manchester airport ever needed an additional runway.

The finishing touch was the private dressing room. She and Chad could live in there, and the new owners would never even know.

She watched to make sure the toilet tissue disappeared and then washed her hands in the middle sink. Why had she agreed to host the cook-out? She wanted to tell Justin she was leaving him after she put Chad to bed, not entertain a crowd, even if it was just Dee and Peg's families. Justin would most certainly drink. It was hard enough to have a conversation with him when he was sober. She might have to wait until tomorrow to talk to Justin. It wasn't that big a deal, she'd put off telling him a couple of hundred times over the past six years, what difference would another day make? It wasn't like anyone cared.

"Stupid jerk," she murmured when St. John's face filled her mind. What would he say if he found out she wasn't going through with her plan? She avoided the question and chose instead to think about what he'd asked her: why was she ready to do battle with him but with Justin she cowered?

Why indeed? Maybe it had to do with the fact that Justin had managed to oppress her for so many years she knew it was futile to argue. Her brief attempts at defiance were always trampled before the words ever finished leaving her mouth. But with St. John... What was it? What part of her said it was okay to challenge him?

Shit. Again with the throbbing groin.

She looked at her crotch and fumed, "Would you give it a rest and let me think?"

Jasper looked up at her, his ears flat against his head, the whites of his eyes giving him a sorrowful expression.

"Oh, baby, Mama's not mad at you. Come here."

She crouched and rubbed his ears, and it came to her. St. John threatened her. Not her exactly but her, the impostor her.

The woman who'd been raising Chad, calling herself Shannon, was a phony. A fraud. She wasn't a cowering wimp, even though that's the part she played as Justin's wife.

She was strong, capable... And she was ashamed about giving Justin full control over her soul.

And St. John knew it.

Ha, wait until she told him she'd figured it out. She gave herself a mental high five and started walking but stopped and frowned when she remembered they wouldn't be speaking.

Chapter 20

*"There are days when solitude is a heady wine that intoxicates
you with freedom, others when it is a bitter tonic, and still
others when it is a poison that makes you
beat your head against the wall."*
Colette

With the canoe strapped to its trailer and Sadie snoring on the back seat, St. John sped along Wexford Street. He glanced at the LCD numbers on the dashboard. Ten o'clock. It would only take him twenty minutes, tops, to swing by Shannon's development. Maybe she'd be outside, and they could talk. He'd be wise to stay away; if they did talk, they'd most likely end up battling again. She probably wasn't at home anyway, more likely out shopping for her upcoming barbecue.

What were the chances she would actually walk away from her marriage? It wasn't an easy thing to do. He'd watched his mother in a very similar situation, and all his pleading for her to leave his ass of a father had fallen on deaf ears. Not because she was weak. Far from it. Neither was Shannon. No, just like his mother, she'd stay with Justin because the familiar, even if it was crap, was a whole lot better than stepping into the unknown.

He took a sharp right onto Cardinal Street and tapped the brakes. He pulled alongside the road and turned off the engine. She was walking with her head down, Jasper at her side. If she'd look up as he passed, she'd just see a black truck, not an uncommon sight in New Hampshire. However, the white lettering on the doors and tailgate advertising ASJ Development might tip her off as to who owned the truck.

She raised her face and slowed to a stop. Just like at Canobie, she smiled, and just like at Canobie, her smile quickly faded.

He removed his cap and ran his hand through his sweat-slicked hair, his leg bouncing with nervous energy. Here he was, almost fifty, and he had butterflies in his stomach.

Sadie, who'd been sleeping on the back seat, raised her head. She stretched and yawned and, seeming to sense something was up, stood and looked out the window. And barked.

Shannon resumed walking, and when she arrived at the front of the truck, she stood by the bumper.

"Get in, Shannon," he muttered under his breath.

******

Sadie hung out the back window and barked at Jasper, and Shannon reached for the door handle. She couldn't resist the power of St. John's presence, and like a paper clip hurtling toward a magnet, she let Jasper in and then pulled herself onto the front seat of the truck.

A blend of scents filled the cab. They swirled around her, creating a dizzying effect. Or was being near him so soon after feeling his kisses causing her disorientation?

He offered the grin she'd come to know as his trademark. That and eyes the same color as the sky. Is that where the universe had found the color when it was forming him? The color of the sky, the scent of the forest, the strength of the mighty oak, and a passion forged in the eternal flames of Hades; they all combined to build the man watching her.

She held his gaze for a moment and then turned away. She didn't have a clue what kind of assumptions he'd made by her getting in the truck. Whatever they were, he was probably correct. If asked, she would willingly open her lips, arms, and legs for him. He might not even have to ask. So much for her resolve to stay away from him.

He didn't make any small talk but started the truck, pulled onto the road, and drove.

He cast a look sideways. "How about we get something cold to drink?"

She should just open her mouth and tell him to stop and let her out. That would be the wisest thing to do. "That would be great," she said. So much for being wise.

He chuckled that easy laugh of his, and she found herself relaxing, the smooth sound like a sip of warm ambrosia.

"What's up with women only wanting to talk to me today? I must have lost my charm."

Oh, don't be so sure, her brain replied. She had a list of things she wanted to do with him, and none of them involved speech.

They drove in silence, each lost in their own thoughts. St. John drove into the neighboring town and pulled into the parking lot for Honey Dew Donuts. Shannon asked for an iced tea, and he replied with, "Scoot on under the seat so nobody sees you," as he hopped from the truck.

She remained firmly in place. "Tell me you're kidding?"

He winked and closed the door.

Once they were on their way again, St. John took them back to Wexford. He skirted the center and drove toward the south end of the town.

Shannon looked at her surroundings and then at him. "Are you taking me home?"

"Relax, I'm not letting you go just yet."

They neared the development where she lived, and he passed the entrance and drove on for another mile before taking a left onto a dirt road that entered a thickly wooded area. The truck dipped and jostled as it passed over tree roots, dirt ruts, and rocks.

"Where on earth are you taking me?" She held the handle by her head to keep herself from bouncing off the seat. "I'm in no mood for a hike, St. John."

"You're no fun," he said and pulled up to an iron gate.

He hopped out of the cab and unlatched the gate's padlock. He drove through the opening, got back out, and locked the gate behind them. For another ten minutes, they passed over a road that made the first leg of the journey seem smooth.

Eventually, they emerged into a partially cleared area. Unlike the development she'd earlier spent her time in, only one house stood ready for occupancy. All the other lots were marked with bright orange flags and white placards with black numbers but contained nothing else, save for the trees.

"This is phase two of the development you live in," St. John said. He drove them to the house and tapped a remote attached to his visor.

To see the top of the four-story structure, she had to crane her neck completely. "Is this the sample, or has someone purchased this behemoth?"

"Yes, on both counts." He parked in the five-bay garage and grabbed their drinks. After handing them to her, he removed a stadium blanket from behind the back seat. "Come on. I'll show you around."

At the door he entered a code and stepped aside for her to enter the house.

They removed their shoes and walked through a kitchen that made the house she'd stopped at a short while ago look like a doll house. When they entered what could only be called a Great-Great-Great Room, she bent her head back to find the ceiling. "What is the owner going to do with this room: install a Ferris wheel?"

"You'd be surprised the ways people fill up the space. What do you fill yours with?"

"Ours is not this big."

"Almost. People like big houses."

She wrinkled her nose at his comment. "No offense, St. John, but I don't like our house."

He looked at her and feigned pain. "I'm crushed. I built that house."

"And you did a wonderful job, but your houses are too big. They lack charm."

He chose a sunny spot by one of the tall windows and spread the blanket on the hardwood floor. "No offense taken, but in my experience, I've learned warmth and charm have to come from the people living in the house, not the building itself. A bungalow can feel like a gymnasium if the people living in it don't like each other. Me," he continued, "I wouldn't be caught dead in a house this big."

Shannon walked inside the fireplace occupying a large portion of the outside wall. "Yet, you build them," she said, her voice echoing up the chimney.

"I give the people what they want. If it's not me—"

"Yeah, yeah, I've heard it already. If not you, then someone else will do it. Blah, blah, blah. That's a lazy excuse."

"And we're off." St. John settled on the floor and patted the area of the blanket next to him. "Do you think we could forgo the barbs for a while, maybe even be civil to each other? They seem to be managing." He indicated Sadie and Jasper lying in a patch of sunlight streaming through the French double doors that led onto the deck. Jasper lay on his side with Sadie's muzzle resting on his rump.

Shannon knelt by St. John's outstretched legs. "Then it's agreed," she said. "We'll behave is if we're dogs." An image of two dogs humping came instantly to mind followed by her and St. John doing it doggy-style. She grabbed her iced tea and sucked on the straw, avoiding his eyes.

"Agreed," he said and chuckled.

She watched him from under her lashes as he removed his baseball cap. He rested the back of his head against the window frame and closed his eyes, giving her a chance to study him in detail. Not his looks—the details of his face and body were fully embedded in her mind—but the man himself. The guy must be seriously damaged if all three of his wives had run to the arms of other men. Based on how he'd behaved before he left her last night she could see why. She should be fleeing instead of sitting in a stranger's house with him. Yet, here she was, not budging an inch, feeling safer than she'd experienced in her entire adult life.

Without prompting, St. John began to speak. "I grew up in a place that was under eight hundred square feet. It was a hip-roof style house, and my half-brother and I shared the second-floor bedroom. I could fit fifty of that house in the ones I build, but to me, it was the grandest home in Wexford, absolutely perfect in every way. If I could, I would build houses where families would be forced to be together instead of spending time in rooms crammed with stuff they don't need."

"But you said even small houses can feel empty."

"They can," he replied, opening his eyes. "But it's a lot harder to hide. Sometimes that's all it takes, to force people to look at each other." A sadness drew over his face. "Then again, it doesn't always work."

She didn't know what to say, so she said nothing. He was a complex man, and she wasn't sure she'd ever figure him out.

The clouds blew away, and his face brightened. "If you hired me to build a house for you, what would you want?"

The house from her vision came to mind, as did his truck in the driveway. They weren't on the porch any longer, though. They were inside, in front of a crackling fire. Her, Chad, and him. A puzzle lay in pieces on the floor, the two dogs snoring by the hearth.

He tapped on her leg. "Where'd you go?"

"I..." She removed her own hat and shook out her hair. "Sorry, I'm operating on very little sleep. Let's see, my house. Well, I want it small."

"Small's relative," he said. "I work in square footage."

"I don't know the square feet; now let me finish. The roof kind of bends where the second story begins. It's not a big second story. As I said, the house is small. Cozy. There's a porch along the length of the front." More of the house's characteristics came to her as she spoke. Details that weren't in her vision, but she knew just the same. Her cheeks warmed as she continued. "The living room has a brick fireplace, and a curved staircase leads up to the two rooms on the second floor. One room faces the front, and the other looks out over a pond in back. The house in on a hill, so the view is magnificent. Oh, and there's a copper beech tree in the front yard, and there's a flower garden. Surrounding the lot are trees, lots and lots of trees. Pines, hemlocks, oaks, birch. A whole forest of trees. And there's an old wooden swing hanging from this massive oak tree in the side yard, and down by the pond is a bench where'd I sit and feed the ducks." She finished with, "I guess I described more than the house," and looked at him.

He was sitting forward, staring at her.

"What's wrong?"

"You're teasing me, right?"

"I'm sorry, what?"

He removed a pen from his shirt pocket and began drawing on his palm. "You just described the house I grew up in."

Chapter 21

*"The best way to find out if you can trust
somebody is to trust them."*
Ernest Hemingway

The pen glided over the calloused skin of St. John's hand. An image took form, and soon Shannon was viewing a miniature ink drawing of her quaint house, complete with trees and smoke coiling from the chimney.

"That's my house," she said.

St. John tapped his hand with the pen. "No, this is my house, including every detail you mentioned, down to the copper beech in the front yard and the ducks in the pond. How do you know this house?"

She followed the blue ink lines with her fingertip. "It's a house that came to me the other night."

"Came to you?"

"In a vision. It's silly. Never mind. This is just a coincidence."

He took hold of her hand and joined their palms. The drawing of the house burned against her skin. Their fingers merged. "Being a witch, do you really believe that?" he said.

"At this point, St. John, it's hard to know what to believe." She pulled away because his touch was shutting down her brain and she wanted to tell him what she'd figured out. "I have something I want to tell you."

"Which I'll listen to after I've had my say."

"Why do you get to go first?"

"My house, my rules."

"This isn't your house. You said you sold it."

"If I built the house, my rules."

"Yeah, you and your rules." She lifted her iced tea. "I'm

making a list too, you know?"

"And I'll be willing to hear them as soon as you let me finish."

"Fine, go." She started sucking on the straw.

He took the cup from her hands and set it aside. "I behaved like a jerk last night, and I'm sorry."

"You're doing it again."

"I know, I'm apologizing when I haven't been given a reason to; got it. Let me finish, and I promise I'll listen to you. I don't know what came over me last night; I was an ass, and I'm sorry."

"For which time?" She leaned past him and reclaimed her cup.

"What?"

"You said a few nasty things, so I'm wondering which one you're sorry for."

"Everything. How's that?" He removed the cup and placed it behind his back. "My question is, do you hate me?"

"May I have my iced tea?"

He lifted her hand to his lips and placed a lingering kiss on the inside of her wrist. "Answer me first."

"I don't hate; it's a waste of energy. I do, however, loathe. Now may I have my tea?"

He kissed the middle of her palm. "Do you loathe me?"

She closed the remaining distance between them and straddled his lap. "Yes," she said as she lifted her T-shirt over her head. She reached behind her back and unhooked her bra. By leaning forward, she provided easy reach to her breasts. "I loathe you," she murmured. She loathed him so frigging much she couldn't stand to be away from him.

"Good." He slowly caressed her breasts, stopping to tease her nipples as his fingers passed by, and then he leaned forward, his breath a furnace against her skin. "Because I loathe myself too." He ran his tongue over each taut nipple.

She moved her hips, rubbing her crotch on the zipper of his jeans as he nipped and sucked. Arching her head back, she increased her speed.

"Oh, no, you don't." He swept her onto her back. "Close your eyes, please."

She listened as he removed an ice cube from one of the cups and shook when the frigid surface touched her. He trailed the cube over her skin: neck, collarbone, between her breasts, her nipples, her belly, and under the waistband of her shorts. When the ice had fully melted, she was as much a puddle as the trails of water cooling on her body.

He pulled on the waistband of her shorts. Next to go were her panties, and then his mouth was at her ear. "Touch yourself. Please."

Damn straight she'd touch herself. No man had ever asked her to do that, but she'd fantasized about it all the same. She widened her legs and gasped, her hand shaking.

He cupped her butt cheeks and lifted her hips. "Here, I'll help." His tongue moved past her finger and entered her. She squeezed her eyes, savoring the waves of pleasure she was riding on. He licked, and the floor tilted; he sucked, and the floor swayed; he bit, and the floor spun; he sucked again, and she cried out his name.

When her legs stopped shaking, he consumed her again, sending her spiraling through a second maelstrom of pleasure.

She lay spent with barely enough energy to lift her hand and twirl the strand of dirty blond hair hanging over her. "Hi," she said, smiling up into his blue eyes.

He grinned down at her. "Hi. Ready for more?"

"Yes, please."

"Good."

It amused her he had a condom ready. He'd done the same thing last night, like he was some mystic condom-dispensing machine.

She rose up on her elbows. "How do you do that?"

"Do what?" he asked, his attention on the matter at hand.

"Make condoms appear out of thin air."

"Ah, that." His pirate grin appeared. "It's a secret."

He lifted her legs and draped them over his arms. Then he bent her knees toward her shoulder. His steady movements were having an amazing effect on her, and she cried out "Don't—"

"What is it?" He stopped and pulled out, panic flooding his features. "Are you okay?"

All she could do was laugh, which she did, uncontrollably.

"What's so funny?"

"I was going to say 'Don't stop.'"

She laughed again, and he joined her.

"I think we've killed the mood," he said and lay next to her.

"Oh, don't be such a Debby Downer." She reached into a long, luxurious stretch and stroked him. When he was back to full power, she climbed on top of him. "See, it's like magic."

"You are a beautiful witch," he said, pulling her face down to kiss her.

St. John lay on his side, his hand supporting his head. "What did you want to tell me?"

"How come you're dressed, and I'm naked?" she asked.

"My house, my rules."

"Cute."

"I want you to take note that I didn't forget you wanted to talk to me. What's on your mind?"

She twisted and reached for her clothes, but he yanked them away. "What part of 'my house, my rules,' are you having trouble with?"

She squirmed and giggled. "Rules are meant to be broken." She jumped to her feet and walked to the opposite side of the room.

"Not mine."

He offered the grin she'd come to expect whenever he seemed to be thinking about being mischievous.

"Stop doing that," she said.

"Doing what?"

"Looking at me like that."

"And how am I looking at you?"

"Like you're a wolf and I'm dinner."

He rolled onto his back and released a groan. "Is this better? What do we need to talk about?" He sat up and reclaimed his earlier position of leaning against the window sill, then tossed ice cubes from his coffee to the dogs. "I'm listening," he said, glancing her way.

She refused to give in to the sexy way his brow was furrowed under that damn piece of hair. Really, what was she doing wanting to talk when he was willing to do so many other things?

"Seriously, it's unfair you're completely dressed. At least take off a sock or something."

"A sock? Okay, I have an idea." Standing, he offered a raised eyebrow and retrieved a thin packet from his jeans back pocket. Placing it between his teeth, he then removed his socks, shirt, and everything else, his erection ready for action, and sauntered her way. When he arrived at her end of the room, he scooped his hand behind her head, pressed his face in her hair, and inhaled slowly. "God, I love the smell of you."

"Stop." She moved away. "I have things I need to say, and I can't say them with your tongue in my ear."

"I could put something else in your mouth." He stepped her way, and she shifted to the right, but he managed to catch her.

"St. John, this is important, and you're not listening." She wiggled to get free, but the more she fought, the more restrictive his hold became. She gave up fighting, which truthfully hadn't been much of an effort, and allowed him to run his hands over the front of her body. His fingers pressed into her crotch. "I do want to hear what you have to say, but how do we know if we'll ever get this chance again? Why waste being alone by talking?"

"Fine," she exhaled. "Let's skip the talking."

He laughed and released her. "And here I thought what you had to say was important."

"You're a bastard." She bent and grabbed her clothes.

"So I've been told. Here, look..." He swiped her shirt from her hands and carried it with him as he repositioned himself on the opposite side of the room. "How's this?" he shouted, resting against the wall. "You'll have to speak up, though."

She hid her snicker under her breath at the ridiculous way she was acting. She should just screw him again and go home; talking was for wimps.

"I can't hear you," he called out. "Did you say something?"

"You're a cocky bastard, you know that?" she replied, not even trying to hide her amusement.

"So you've told me."

"Would you come here?"

"Gladly."

"But don't touch me."

"That's no fun."

"There." She held up her hand. "Stop right there."

"Not going to happen." He walked over to her and kissed her, his tongue surrounding hers and slowly sliding along it. His kiss became insistent, and he lowered her to the blanket and licked the length of her neck. "Talk."

She chewed on her bottom lip. Was it even worth saying what she'd figured out? They weren't together to talk.

He pushed himself up on his hands. "Shannon, if you're going to chew your lip like that, then talking is off the table. So, unless you're just trying to tease me and you have nothing to say, let's have you kneel this time."

"Absolutely not." She shoved him away and scrambled to her feet. "We need to set some ground rules."

"Is this what you wanted to talk about? Ground rules?" He stood behind her and looped his arms around her waist. "Okay, what rules?"

"Rule number one, no butt fucking. No licking my anus. No anus plugs. No ice cream in my anus or any place else, except my mouth. Leave my anus alone."

"First off, they're called butt plugs, not anus plugs, and where did you get the idea I wanted to do those things? However, I am intrigued about the ice cream. Would chocolate work? I'm assuming without nuts, right?"

"I'm serious."

"I am too, but I get it now. You thought when I told you to kneel that I was heading in the back door. No, I'm perfectly happy with the openings you have in the front. However, I do want to try a different position. Haven't you ever fucked doggy style?"

"Yes, and why didn't you say that to begin with?"

"I thought I had. Moving on... Will you please kneel?"

She managed to turn and face him, his excitement pressing against her lower abdomen. The guy was a frigging machine. "Rule number two."

"Go, rule number two, and I'm giving you ten seconds to finish your rules. Then I'm fucking you."

"Deal. Rule number two, no painful equipment."

He narrowed his brows and looked down at his erect penis. "You're not talking about my—"

"No, that piece of equipment is perfectly fine."

"Just fine?"

He raised his eyebrows, creasing the furrows across his forehead even more, and her legs went weak. She pushed his hair from his eyes and said, "Absolutely perfect."

He laughed and scooped her in the air. "I promise the only equipment I'll use on you will be what God gave me."

Again she found herself on her back with his body against hers. He positioned his hands on the sides of her head and, holding her face steady, forced his tongue into her mouth. She had no problem with his desire to consume her. In fact, she helped him by immersing her hands in his hair and twisting the blond strands into knots around her fingers and pulling. A chuckle vibrated through his chest, and he exhaled his breath into her mouth. Her toes curled, and warmth streamed from her crotch, dampening the blanket under her butt.

He reached between their bodies and inserted his hand into her, after which he raised his glistening fingers to his mouth. She'd never tasted herself and licked along with him, her actions making him growl, "You're incredible."

Next, she was on her stomach with her ass lifted toward the ceiling.

It didn't take him long, and almost as soon as the packet tore, he was in. His fingers pressed into her hips as he ground into her. She pushed back against each of his thrusts, but when he reached under her, she lost her rhythm and focused on the pressure building in her core.

He increased his pace, banging against her ass and rubbing her clit.

"Oh... St. John, no... I mean, OH!" Her arms gave out and she dropped forward as a seismic quake ripped her apart.

He lay on her, and she smiled as the pounding of his heart vibrated through her to match her own pace. Then he rolled onto his back. "Good talk," he said and pulled her close.

Chapter 22

"Thou art to me a delicious torment."
Ralph Waldo Emerson

Shannon and St. John lay on the floor in each other's arms, him staring up at the ceiling and her resting her cheek on his chest.

"This isn't the end, Shannon," St. John said. "I want to see you again."

"But you said—" She raised her face to see his expression. Was another rule biting the dust?

"I don't care what I said." He bent his head and looked at her. "I need to see you again."

"What about your rules?"

"Screw my rules."

"What about the rumor?"

"You're divorcing Justin, so what does that matter?"

He must have sensed her muscles tighten because he opened his arms and released her. "When did you change your mind?" he said, reaching for his jeans.

She sorted through her clothes and dressed with her back to him. She was adjusting her bra when she answered, "I haven't changed my mind. It's just that this might not be the best time. I have company coming tonight, and Chad's birthday is next weekend."

He walked in front of her. "Is this what you wanted to talk to me about? To tell me some bullshit excuse?"

She smoothed her T-shirt, adjusted her shorts, and then looked at him. "Last night this was just sex, right? Today it was just sex too. Correct me if I'm wrong, but you did say that. So where the fuck do you get off judging my life, my actions, or anything about me? And, no, this is not what I wanted to tell you. I thought through what you said last night, about me cowering to Justin and not you. I figured out the reason, but screw it. I don't even care at this point." The whole while she'd been talking, she waved her arms around like she was trying to signal a plane for take-off.

"Okay, tell me," he said, taking hold of her arms and settling them by her sides. "What did you figure out?"

"No."

"Tell me, please."

Without looking at him, she said, "While walking, I came to a conclusion. I get in your face because you threaten me."

"Excuse me? I what?"

"You threaten me."

He changed direction and stood away from her. "Are you kidding me? I've threatened you?"

"What?" She had to shake her head because she was certain she'd heard him wrong. "What are you talking about? No, I said—"

He paced the length of the room. "So, this has all been about money. I am so fucking sick of people thinking I'm their ATM. I have to say, though, you had me fooled." He stopped and released a dry chuckle. "I would have never expected it from you. Well, cry all you want. You'll never get a dime."

Each one glared at the other, their breaths coming fast and hard. Shannon spoke first. "I swear you'd be the perfect man if you would keep your stinking mouth shut. Will you let me explain?"

St. John crossed his arms. "Go, but make it snappy because I'm losing my patience."

Here they were again, like two rattlesnakes ready to strike. The one who drew first blood would be crowned the winner. Well, she wasn't interested in playing any longer. "Losing, I would say; you've already lost your patience."

"You're not helping my mood, Shannon."

"Fine, I said you—"

"Yeah, I heard you. I threaten you. So, you getting into my truck today was me threatening you? You opening the door for me last night was me threatening you? Now what? You tell Justin I forced myself on you, and we go to court? Great, let's do it. Marty will eat the two of you alive."

He ended his speech, and she held her silence, refusing to be baited. Let him jump to his conclusions. She already had a raging lunatic at home; she didn't need another one. She whistled for Jasper, clipped his leash to his collar, and pulled on the sliding door. Of course *this one* would be locked. She ran from the room.

"Shannon, wait." He caught up with her in the kitchen when she stopped to grab her sneakers.

"I'm sick of your apologies," she said. "You're just like Justin, saying whatever you want, lashing out, hurting me, and then apologizing." The harshness in her voice seemed to shock him, but it startled her even more. She was doing exactly as he'd said, coming at him with hackles raised. The poor guy didn't know she was giving him years of pent-up anger. "Do you honestly think saying your 'sorry' fixes everything? You both make me sick."

"Fine, go. But tell me this before you leave. If Justin's so bad, why are you going to stay with him?"

She didn't bother answering or putting on her sneakers but walked to the front door in her stocking feet.

"You have no idea what I've been through," he called out.

She twisted and stormed back into the kitchen. "What you've been through? Let me tell you something: *you* have no idea what *I've* been through, so save your sob stories for someone who cares. This is what you do though, isn't it—you make everything about you?"

He raised his hands as in defeat. "Yup, that's me. Selfish to the core. Go ahead and leave. At least you're willing to leave someone."

She doubled Jasper's leash around her wrist. "Goodbye, St. John. What was it you said last night? Oh, right, thanks for the fuck." She ran for the front door. He arrived at the same time she did and held his hand on the wood. "Get out of my way," she fumed.

"Don't leave like this," he said. "I'm sorry. Please, let's try this again." He reached for her, and she pushed him away.

"Leave me alone." She didn't want his apology; she didn't want anything from him or anything to do with him. She'd meant what she said. She wanted to be left alone. Why couldn't she just take Chad and be rid of everyone who felt they could kick at her whenever they liked?

"I'm sorry," he said again. "Come back, and let's talk. I'll listen, I promise. Just don't leave. Please."

She remained looking at the door. He'd been right, and she'd just proven it. She could behave any way,, even like a raving lunatic, and he still accepted her. If she'd said the things she'd just shouted at St. John to Justin, he would have ripped her apart. But not St. John. No belittling. No insults. Just good, old-fashioned fighting. She'd been able to rage and had still remained safe.

"Shannon, please." He surrounded her with his body and held her. "I'm begging you, don't leave."

Shannon's cell phone woke both her and St. John. Long shadows, cast by the late afternoon sun, stretched across the floor of the Great Room.

St. John held out her phone. "It's Justin. Do you want me to leave while you talk to him?"

"No, it's okay." She swiped the phone's screen but hesitated, choosing to wait and hopefully gage Justin's mood.

His voice blared from the speaker. "Shannon, where the fuck are you?"

She pressed the phone to her ear with a shaking hand. "I'm here, Justin. Where are you?"

"Where am I? Where do you think I am? I'm home in a house without any food or beer. Where the hell are you?"

"I went for a walk. I'm heading home now."

"Well, get here quick."

"Justin, where's Chad? Did he have fun at the water park?"

"Do I sound like I want to have a conversation?"

"Okay, I'm on my way. You can get the grill ready for—"

"I'm not going to cook my own food, Shannon. That's what I have you for, so get your fat ass here now."

The call ended, and she stared at the phone, eventually looking up to find St. John watching her. She had nothing to say and settled on a nervous smile. "I have to go."

"No, you're not."

"Don't do this, St. John. You're not my protector." She bent and gathered her shorts and slipped them on.

St. John kept his voice steady. "You have to be smart, Shannon. He could hurt you."

She didn't have the energy to argue; she just wanted to get home and make sure Chad was okay. "Please don't do this. Chad's there; I have to go."

"Shannon."

"Drop it, St. John, okay? My son is there, and I'm not leaving him alone." She soon realized her raised voice hadn't been necessary; he was just trying to help. "I'm sorry." She stood on her toes and kissed him. "Thank you," she said and left, half of her hoping he'd follow her and the other half hoping he'd stay and let her go.

"This turmoil in my life be gone; this turmoil in my life be gone..." She repeated the mantra over and over as she sprinted through the construction site. At the green porta-potty, she stalled and grumbled and looped Jasper's leash around the door handle. "Mama will be right out." Sucking in her breath, she entered the dark interior. If she passed out and fell into the hole, it would serve her right. She was such an idiot, dumping on St. John as she had. If she were him, she'd run as fast as she could, which is what she should be doing instead of sitting in a dank, airless closet. What was Justin doing home so frigging early anyway? She checked the time on her phone, something she should have done long ago. Holy shit, she'd spent almost six hours with St. John. Six glorious hours.

When she emerged, the bright daylight temporarily blinded her, and it took a moment for her eyes to adjust to what she was seeing—St. John's truck and the heads of two Labrador retrievers, pink tongues and all, hanging out the rear window.

"Get in. Please," St. John said. "I'll drive you to the beginning of your development."

"Thank you, but I'm tired of listening to how I'm making mistakes with my marriage. I can walk."

He opened the driver's door and was in front of her before she could blink. "I'm well aware that your feet and legs work, but I'm not asking. However, if you're concerned, I won't say anything about your marriage."

"Promise?"

"Promise."

He followed her to the passenger side of the truck and helped her up. "Before we leave, I have something to say about your marriage."

"You promised."

"I lied."

"I thought you were the one with the rule about lying. Quite the double standard, don't you think?"

"My house, my rules."

"Actually, we're outside, but please, finish and make it snappy. I have someplace I need to be."

He raised his index finger and rested it on her lips. "Stop talking and listen carefully. You're right. Your relationship with Justin is none of my business, but if you think I'm going to stand by and watch that living pile of shit hurt you or Chad, think again. I grew up under the thumb of a douche bag like Justin, and I watched him kill my mother with his fist and mouth, and let me tell you from firsthand experience, if Justin is willing to physically hurt you, he'll hurt Chad. Stop making this about you, Shannon, and start making it about Chad, and get him the hell away from that maniac." He kissed her softly. "Now buckle your seatbelt; accidents happen less than a mile from the home."

Chapter 23

"Knowing yourself is the beginning of all wisdom"
Aristotle

Running along her driveway, Shannon passed Jeff Boyle's Explorer, Howard O'Neil's pickup truck, and Justin's BMW. She flew through the side door, through the garage and into the kitchen, where she snatched a bottle of water from the fridge and raced into the Great Room. Five kids, draped over the furniture, had their faces focused on the television. From the dropping of F-bombs and rapid-fire shots, the show certainly wasn't PG.

"What are you guys watching?" She gasped as a man's brains splattered against a brick wall. "No, no, no, okay, enough of this." She located the remote, and the screen went black. "Go outside and play." Realizing Chad wasn't among them, she said, "Where's Chad?"

Kevin Doyle, one of Dee's twelve-year-old twins, stood and stretched. "He's upstairs."

His brother, Jeffrey, yawned and said, "We're kind of sick of being outside. Can we go downstairs and play pool?"

"Yeah, sure. Kevin, will you go upstairs and get Chad?"

"Um, Shannon..." Kevin gave her a sheepish look, "He's grounded."

"What?" She glanced through the open slider at the three men out on the deck. One of them had his back to the screen, his legs opened in a wide stance. She'd always hated the way he stood, almost as much as she hated him. Oh, right, she'd told St. John she didn't hate; she loathed. Well, then, she absolutely, with every cell in her body and every fiber of her hair, loathed the misogynistic, pretentious asshole who had his back against the screen.

The kids bunched together around her, and she said, "Sorry, brain fog. Kevin, run upstairs for me, please, and tell Chad he's not grounded and can come down, and then take the kids and play in the game room. Play pool, ping-pong, whatever, but no more television. Got it?"

They took off in the direction of the basement door, Kevin cutting to the right while she mentally prepared herself for what was to come. "Hey, guys," she said through the screen door. "What are you all doing back so early?"

Howard and Jeff cast their eyes to Justin before saying hello. Justin finished the beer bottle in his hand, placed it on the deck table, and opened the door to step inside. He took her by the arm and pulled her into the kitchen. "Where've you been?"

Footsteps clomped down the staircase, and Chad ran into the room. "Mama, you're home." He flung his arms around Shannon's legs. "May I go play in the basement?"

"Of course, sweetie. Go have fun."

"Don't you dare move," Justin said. "He's grounded."

Shannon stepped around Justin and scooted Chad along. "Go ahead, sweetie." To Justin, she said, "Can't you, for one day, stop being a bully?"

Justin folded his arms and jutted his chin forward. "I asked you where you were."

She'd never noticed it before but with his chin positioned the way it was, he resembled a bulldog. Not a ferocious one but one of those little designer breeds that were all bark and no bite.

"Let's try this again and see if your simple brain can keep up. Where. Have. You. Been?"

Shannon withheld speaking. He'd gone from resembling a dog to pretending to be a bouncer at some seedy nightclub with his folded arms and wide stance. "I don't have time for this. I have company coming. If you want to show off for your friends, do it with someone else." She moved but not fast enough, and he grabbed her by the arm.

"Answer me," he demanded, giving her a violent shake.

It was over. She was done being pushed around by him. "Take your fucking hands off of me," she snarled, surprising herself and him alike. It was about time her backbone got here.

"I said—"

"And I said let...go...of...me."

His touch nauseated her, and she shoved his hand away and began laughing. Her laughter grew until tears formed in her eyes.

"You think this is funny?" He glared at her. "You wait until we're alone. Then we'll see if you feel like laughing."

Between gasps for air, she said, "Thank you."

"For what?" he spat.

"For giving me the courage to finally say this." She waited for her breath to catch up and then settled her sights on his dead, doll's eyes. "You're a pathetic man, and I loathe you. Oh, and by the way, I'm divorcing your fat ass. Now get the fuck away from me."

The sounds of splashing water and a tune about little fishies swimming over a dam filtered out from the first-floor bathroom and kept Shannon company while she wiped the kitchen counters. She peeked in and saw Chad hold a sponge shaped like a fish, bright red and dripping, in the air. The sodden fish swooped and flipped through the air as it tried to clear the massive height of the make-believe dam, which was, in fact, Chad's knees.

"Swim, little fishy," the invisible mother fish called out in Chad's voice. "Swim as fast as you can."

Shannon returned to her cleaning and hummed along. Wiping, washing, rubbing—working to restore order to a kitchen she would soon be leaving. Her face hovered stark white in the window pane. Beyond her own reflection lay her future, buried in the inky blackness of the night. She blew at the strand of hair that had freed itself from the pile on her head. It felt unreal that she'd actually done what she'd been pissing and moaning about for six years. The big question was: now what?

Justin hadn't reacted at all as she'd expected. What *had* she expected? Screaming? Yelling? Throwing punches? Threats? He'd done none of those things. If he had given some reaction other than simply snickering and walking away, she might not have felt so jittery. After everyone left, he'd taken his car keys and driven off. She knew him well enough that he wasn't going to make a divorce easy, but she had no clue what his next move would be.

"Mama, I'm wrinkly," Chad called out.

"Oh, no," she replied. "It won't do to have a wrinkly child."

With her worries tucked securely in their place, she entered the bathroom and stood in the doorway. Her son's glistening body resembled a pink rose after a summer's rain. She wouldn't let him down. No matter what hardships lay in store for them, she'd protect him and keep him safe.

She wrapped him in his bath towel and carried him upstairs. "My bed or yours." Most child experts frowned upon children sleeping in their parent's bed but screw them; they didn't live with Justin.

After Chad fell asleep, she prepared herself for bed, but before climbing in next to Chad, she took Jasper out for one last sniff.

A pin of light shot across the starry sky. She'd often fantasized about fireworks going off when she finally stood up to Justin, but a shooting star would do just fine. "I am strong, fear me," she whispered. "Bane to all who try to harm me."

She allowed herself to think about her parting words to St. John before she'd left the truck. He'd asked if he could see her again. She had wanted to tell him yes. Every cell in her body had screamed the word, except for those comprising her brain.

'If I ask you to stay away from me, will you?' she'd asked.

His nod had been slow in coming. 'If you ask me, I will. Are you asking me?'

'Yes,' she'd replied.

Over time she'd accept she'd made the right decision. She touched near her lips where his passionate kisses had left the skin raw. He'd brought her to life again, and she didn't want him to stay away. But being with him, no matter how exciting, was unwise. They wanted different things, and even though she didn't have a clue what she wanted, she understood it was more than he was willing, and capable, of giving.

"Sometimes what we want isn't meant to be."

She heard her quiet words and nodded. So mote it be.

******

"Are you listening, Shannon? You should tell Justin you were angry and didn't mean it," Dee said. "Jeff and I talked about you guys; you're not great together, but Justin's your husband, and you should make it work."

Shannon, who'd been toying with the condensation on the side of her glass, frowned. She didn't want to talk, but Dee and Peg had come over to see her because they'd been concerned. She owed them an explanation. "Fine. I'll tell you what happened this morning but you..." She cast a stern expression at Dee. "Shall remain silent until I'm done. Deal?"

"Deal, but make it snappy. I have to be in Manchester by eleven."

"What's in Manchester?" Peg asked.

"I'm meeting St. John for an early lunch."

Taking an interest, Shannon raised her eyes. No way would St. John tell Dee about yesterday or the night before. Right? "What's going on?"

"It's nothing. I have a favor to ask him, that's all," Dee said. "And you have to be in Concord by eleven?"

"What's in Concord?" Peg wanted to know.

Shannon gave an unenthusiastic reply. "Justin asked me to pick up some papers he needs for a client."

"You're divorcing him, but you're running errands for him?"

"He asked very politely. Of course, that was after he threatened to take Chad and disappear."

"Okay, Shan, hop to it," Dee said.

Shannon began her story by telling what had happened yesterday when she'd returned home and ended with Justin walking out after everyone had left last night.

"He didn't say a word? Just left?" Dee asked.

"Yup."

Peg scowled and asked, "What if he had come back? What would you have done?"

"I kept Jasper outside my bedroom and barricaded Chad and me inside. Plus, I had the panic button for the alarm with me."

Dee half snorted and half chuckled. "What'd you do, drag your bed in front of the door?"

"Dee, stop with the questions." Peg's impatient scolding earned her a glare.

Undeterred, Dee said, "Didn't Chad think that was weird?"

"He was asleep."

"Okay, that's it." Peg smacked the table. "Dee, no more questions."

"I'll ask all the questions I want."

Shannon took a sip of coffee and glanced around her yard. Tonight was the Summer Solstice and she had plans to celebrate by lighting a fire. The biscotti were already made, and she had a new bottle of bourbon waiting to be cracked open. She smiled at Dee and Peg, who were still going at it.

"Enough," Dee announced. "Shannon, continue."

"Justin arrived this morning when Chad and I were having breakfast. He poured himself a coffee and sat at the table with us. Chad was kicking the chair leg, and Justin barked at him to stop. Then he looked at me and, without caring that Chad was there, said, 'I'm not divorcing you, in case you wanted to know.'"

"What did you say?"

Peg snapped, "Dee, quiet. Go ahead, Shan, what did you say?"

"Since Chad was finished with his cereal, I told him to go upstairs and brush his teeth. Then I said to my darling, soon-to-be-ex-husband, 'I didn't ask your permission, and there's nothing you can do to stop me.'

"'Save it,' he said. 'I already told you, you're not going anywhere.' I got up and carried the dishes into the kitchen. He followed me and said, 'If you want to leave, fine. I knew you never loved me and were using me for my money.' He's a pro at guilting people, but I stood my ground and told him he was right about the love part. Then I said, 'As for your money, I don't need it. You'll buy out my portion of ownership in the house.'"

"How much money?"

"Peg, shush," Dee said. "How much money, Shan?"

"Four hundred thousand. It's half my inheritance from my grandmother. She may have been a bitter old coot, but she was a loaded bitter, old coot, and I was her only living descendant. The other half I put into decorating this place, buying the SUV, and I put some aside for Chad."

Dee waved her hand. "Who cares? Finish."

"Right. So I said, 'Face it, Justin, you don't have a say in this. By the end of the summer, you'll be a free man to do whatever you want with Shelby, and Chad and I won't have to endure your abuse any longer.'"

"You mentioned taking Chad?" Peg asked. "He must have flipped."

Shannon took a sip of her coffee. Justin's response concerning Chad had been frightening.

"Shan, hello. Finish," Dee said.

"Justin said it'll be a cold day in hell before he lets a witch raise his kid and that if he has to, he'll take Chad and disappear."

"Oh, my God." Peg held her hand to her mouth.

"He's just blustering, Peg. Don't worry. He called me a few choice names and said he knew I wasn't right for him." She forced her voice down so she sounded like a guy. "'This is the thanks I get for marrying you when you were pregnant. What were you going to do? Raise the brat on your own?'"

Dee leaned on the table. "What did you say?"

"I told him to expect to hear from my lawyer. Then I went upstairs to get Chad. We left, I brought him to school, dropped off the scones Jimbo ordered, talked to him a bit, and came back here." Shannon pushed away from the table and stood. "And now I have to drive to Concord." She kept the other errand she had to make a secret. Jimbo's advice about visiting the bank was worth heeding.

Chapter 24

"If we don't disappoint people,
maybe they won't disappoint us."
Unknown

The expression on St. John's face displayed disbelief as he witnessed the waiter getting skewered because of an under-cooked cheeseburger.

"I could have gotten food poisoning," Dee said.

The young man stammered out a second apology and included, "I've already offered to prepare a new meal for you, so I'm not sure what else you want from me?"

Dee's cheeks blazed a violent shade of ruby. "What I want is to speak to your manager—that's what I want. How dare you talk to me in that tone?"

"Okay, I've had enough." St. John dropped the now cold fry onto his plate. He reached for Dee's dish and handed it to the waiter. "Ben, I apologize for Mrs. Boyle's behavior. Please bring her a chef's salad, no ham, house dressing on the side."

"I don't want a salad," Dee complained.

St. John ignored her and finished with the order. "You can take my dish too and bring me a bourbon. Make it a double, and a glass of ice."

"Sure thing, Mr. St. John."

Ben almost sprinted from the table with the two plates in his hands.

"How can you even eat here?" Dee said. "That burger was not made from cow meat, I can tell you that."

St. John drained his iced coffee while she vented about her lunch. When she stopped to take a breath, he said, "I happen to like it here. The food is good as is the service. Maybe you should have a beer to calm your nerves; you look like you're going to have a coronary."

"I'm not upset," Dee disagreed. "It's just that I heard something that's upsetting me."

"Well, I am sorry. How about we move this lunch along, and you can go deal with whatever it is that's bothering you?"

"Don't you want to know what's upsetting me?"

"Not particularly."

"Has Hancock's daughter gotten back to you about the farm?"

"Is this what we're here to discuss?" St. John set his glass down. "No, they haven't, but I'm sure they'll accept the offer. Do something for me, will you? The next time you talk to Shannon, mention how hard I work to keep as many trees as possible when I'm building. I'm not MacMillan; he's the..." He shifted his eyes toward the nearby table. A child was listening to him, and he'd almost added a new, colorful word to the kid's vocabulary. "Just tell her, okay."

Ben returned with the chef salad, which earned him a sour look from Dee, and St. John's drink. St. John thanked him and poured half the bourbon over the fresh ice and tossed the other half into his mouth.

Dee inspected the ingredients of her salad, stabbed her fork into the lettuce, and bit into the crisp leaves. "Mm, not bad." She swallowed and narrowed her eyes. "Why do you care what Shannon thinks?"

"Just tell her, okay?"

Dee responded, her mouth full of lettuce. "Anything I say to her about your sterling business practices will go out the window once she learns that you're planning on developing twenty-eight thousand acres."

St. John spun the whiskey around the ice cubes and took a sip. "I never said I'm going to develop it."

"Then why do you want it so bad? Let MacMillan have it and move on."

"Let's move on. Why are we here?"

Dee chewed a piece of ham and said, "She did it."

St. John set his glass on the table. 'She' had to mean Shannon and 'it' had to mean—

"Shannon told Justin she's divorcing him," Dee blurted out. "I didn't think she'd do it; actually, I was sure she wouldn't. She's not a confrontational kind of person. I told her she's made a mistake, and I can only hope she'll come to her senses. I'm really upset about this. She's going to get hurt. Chad too. And they only gave me one hardboiled egg," she said, tossing her salad ingredients around the plate.

Leaning forward, St. John spoke quietly. "Stop complaining and eat the damn thing." He rested against the back of his chair, lifted his whiskey, and took a long sip. He was thrilled Shannon had actually followed through, but where did this leave the two of them? She'd told him to stay away, and he'd honor her request, unless Baldos did something to hurt her. Then all bets were off.

He set his elbows on the table and bided his time until Dee's mouth was empty. "How did Justin react when Shannon told him?"

"He called her some names, I guess, and said he'd never give her a divorce."

"Did she back down?"

"Nope, she told him he didn't have any say in the matter and to expect to hear from her lawyer. I'm sure she was bluffing about the lawyer unless she plans on calling your guy." Dee went back to putting vegetables into her mouth.

"Marty's very good at what he does. Does she have a timeline, such as when she'll move out? Where is she planning on living?"

Dee bit off a piece of turkey and nodded. "Mm, not bad." She swallowed and narrowed her eyes. "Don't go getting any ideas, St. John. I appreciate you doing me the favor the other day, and she did say you were a perfect gentleman, which I question, but she's still off-limits to you."

"You have nothing to worry about. I have rules against that sort of thing." St. John drained his drink and signaled for Ben.

"Yeah, well, we all know rules can be bent." Dee pierced a slice of cucumber and nibbled on the edge before dropping it back to the plate and choosing a narrow slice of cheese. "I still think she's going to regret this. She has no idea how hard life as a divorced, single mother can be."

When Ben returned St. John asked Dee, "Do you want dessert?"

Dee crumpled her napkin and dropped it on her salad. "Is the pie here good?"

"You won't like it, but let's give it a try." He ordered two slices then responded to her previous comment about Shannon. "I'm intrigued. How do you have such a wealth of knowledge in the area of being a divorced, single mother?"

"Don't forget I've placed loads of Wexford divorcees in condos around town; they can't be happy."

"Why? What's stopping them?"

"Their guilt. They know in their hearts walking out of a marriage is wrong, and despite being pagan, Shannon knows it too. There are rules against divorce, and breaking them is frowned upon by the church and God. I'm really afraid He'll take revenge on Chad to punish her."

St. John cocked an eyebrow and stared at Dee. "Excuse me? Did I just hear you correctly? Punish her? Are we living in the fourteenth century?" He accepted Denise's zealousness for her religion. A lot of people were passionate about their faith, but she was supposed to be Shannon's friend.

"Is this what you wanted to discuss, Shannon burning in the eternal flames of hell?"

"Nope, I have other news. Ready? Meredith's house is going live. Malcolm called me Friday and asked me to handle the sale.

He also said to tell you, and I'm paraphrasing, that he won't sell it to you and to rot in hell."

St. John stared at the slice of pie Ben had placed on the table and scowled, his appetite suddenly gone. "My brother always did have a flair for words. Why am I hearing this now and not last Friday?"

"I tried to tell you yesterday. Besides, what difference does it make? You can't do anything until it's listed."

"This is unbelievable." St. John mumbled a few more expletives under his breath. He was fully aware the kid next to them was more interested in their conversation than the chicken fingers on the plate in front of him.

"Relax," Dee said. "I'll keep you posted. He wants to have some work done to the place to get it ready. Do you want the job?"

"I most certainly do."

"I don't get it. You've never really explained why you hate each other so much. You two were thick as thieves when you were young. What happened?"

Denise's question was a fair one, but not something he planned on answering. "Thanks for telling me. I owe you."

"I was hoping you'd say that because I need a big favor. Jeff's fortieth birthday is coming up, and I want to do something special for him."

"And what does that have to do with me?"

"Well, I want to have a really big shindig: invite all the members of the lodge and half the town."

"I still don't see what... No." St. John shook his head. "Not going to happen. Find someplace else."

"But your property is a thousand times the size of mine. And you have that great beach."

St. John signaled for the check and asked for a container. Tonight, after practice, he'd build a fire, have a little bourbon, or maybe a lot, and enjoy the pie. "Are you going to eat your dessert?"

Dee made a nasty expression with her face. "No."

"Fine." He claimed her plate and set it next to his.

"Come on, St. John. Say yes. There's no place else in town."

"You mean no place else that's free. Have it at the lodge."

"Do you have any idea how much they charge?"

"I tell you what." He removed his wallet from his pocket. "Book the damn thing at the lodge, and I'll cover all the costs. Order a champagne fountain for all I care. Happy?"

"Actually, yes, I am."

"Oh, I get it," he said. "You were hoping I'd say that."

"I played you like a violin."

They both stood, and Dee walked around the table and hugged him. "I don't care what people say about you—you're a great guy. I gotta go. Thanks for lunch. Send me an estimate for the repairs for Meredith's, and I'll have Malcolm approve them."

"Will do," St. John said. "Say hi to Jeff for me." He waited as the pie was packaged and when given the container he handed Ben a fifty and two ten. "Thanks for everything, Ben," He then sighed and walked out into the midday heat. The only good thing that had come out of the lunch was learning what Shannon had done, but he couldn't even talk to her about it because she'd asked him to leave her alone, and he'd agreed.

He should have stuck to his rules and stayed away from her, but there was no going back.

Even if he could go back he wouldn't change a thing. He'd do it all over again.

He'd break every goddamn one of his rules to be with her.

Chapter 25

"No one saves us but ourselves."
Buddha

Each morning, rain or shine, sleet or snow, Mr. Ron, the principal of Wexford Academy, greeted his charges as they disembarked busses or the endless line of mini-vans and SUVs. He knew each student's name, their teacher's names, along with the student's academic standing and any extra-curricular activities the boy or girl enjoyed. At the close of the school day, Mr. Ron would return to his post by the flagpole and bid each child farewell along with tidbits of advice for staying out of trouble.

This day was no different. Moments before the first dismissal bell, Mr. Ron strolled to his post, his partially bald head bobbing up and down as he greeted the waiting parents. A petite woman with long hair the color of corn silk followed, the pointed tip of her nose held high as she strutted past the other mothers. When Mr. Ron positioned himself under the flag, Leeann, two e's-two n's, claimed her spot to his left.

Shannon parked where she always did, in the lower lot, and walked the incline to the school. She was heading for the stone bench off to the side, her and Chad's meeting place when Mr. Ron called out to her and met her halfway.

"How are you holding up, Shannon?" Mr. Ron's narrow face held a worn expression, his kind eyes showing a measure of concern.

"Hi Ron, I'm fine. How are you?"

"I am well, a few personal things are happening, but I am more concerned about you." Mr. Ron lowered his voice and bent her way. "I heard about your situation, and I am sad that you will be leaving Wexford. Rest assured Chad will be in good hands. I will make sure of it."

Shannon knitted her brows and asked, "I'm sorry, but what are you talking about?"

The principal blinked rapidly and stammered, "Oh, I... Leeann told me—"

A shrill ringing pierced the air, announcing the first round of dismissals. Mr. Ron smiled and returned to his post as the K through one classes began filing from the building.

The question as to how the town's height-challenged minion had learned about the divorce wasn't hard to figure out. Justin must have stayed at the lodge. Shannon spied the smug smile heading her way and, not for the first time, she wished for some super cool power, as the witches had used in the old television show *Charmed*. Then the blond elf might not be so uppity when she realized she was a wart on a toad's ass.

"Mama."

A happy squeal came from the boy running her way. She bent and scooped him into her arms and kissed his face. "How was your day, munchkin?"

"Can we get donuts?" Chad asked after quickly kissing her face. "I'm hungry." He ran on. "Let's go."

Shannon followed him and another boy with whom he'd joined hands. She'd hoped to speak to him about divorce in general before she and Justin broke the news. She'd even purchased a book at Barnes and Noble: *The Three Bears Get a Divorce*. Obviously, sharing their porridge with Goldilocks had been a sticking point, and Mama and Papa bear couldn't get past it and ended up parting ways. Baby Bear spent weekends with his father. Even children's stories weren't safe from the harsh realities of the world.

With a mouth full of chocolate donut, Chad sang as Shannon pulled into their driveway.

She wiped powdered sugar off her fingers and pressed the garage door opener. And pressed the button again.

And again.

And again.

She stared at the bay door still in its down position.

And she pressed the button again.

"What the...?"

Chad unbuckled himself and stood behind her seat. "Mama, what's wrong?"

"The door won't open."

"Can I try?"

"Sure, here." She handed him the remote. "Maybe you'll have better luck than me."

Chad pushed his thumb against the yellow button. He kept pushing. "Mama. It's broke."

"Actually, sweet pea, the correct word would be broken, and yes, I agree, it does seem to be broken. Maybe the battery is dead. Okay, let's go use the keypad."

"Can I do it?"

Chad ran ahead and stretched his arms. "Lift me, please."

Holding Chad under his bum, Shannon raised him high enough to reach the buttons. "Push six, two, and nine, and then hit enter."

Sticking his tongue out of the corner of his mouth, Chad pressed the buttons with careful precision.

The triple bay door remained firmly in place.

"It's broke—I mean broken, Mama."

"I can see that." Shannon returned him to the ground and re-pressed the numbers. "What the f...?" She swallowed the curse and settled for, "...heck is going on?"

"What the heck?" Chad shouted, directing his frustration toward the door with a solid kick. Jasper barked, and Chad jumped up and pointed at the window. "Hurry, Mama. Jasper has to pee. And I do too."

"I'm coming," Shannon called up to Jasper, whose response of increased barking got Chad hopping faster. "Relax, Chad," she said and walked over to the door tucked under the breeze-way. She inserted her key and twisted.

And again.

And again.

"Okay, now I'm getting pissed."

"I'm getting pissed." Chad stomped on the driveway.

She stepped back and stared up at Jasper, refusing to give credence to her new thought. Justin was a despicable man, but this would be a new low, even for him. "Chad, you go pee, and I'll try the front door."

"But, Mama, there's no toilet."

"Use a tree."

He willingly obliged and sang at the top of his lungs while he sprayed the tree bark with his urine. "You come pee too, Mama."

"I'm good."

Chad ran up the front steps as she was jiggling the key. "Is that key broken too, Mama?"

"It seems so. Let's try the Great Room door."

With Jasper following their movements by jumping from window to window, they circled around to the back.

Chad ran ahead, raced up the deck stairs, and pulled on the sliding door, grunting with his effort. "It's stuck."

"Let me try, honey." She already knew it would be locked, but insanity *was* doing the same thing over and over and expecting different results, and she did feel like she was going insane, so... "Give me a frigging break." She slapped the door handle.

"Give me a friggin' break." Chad slapped the handle as well.

"Chad, you don't have to repeat everything I say."

"Are you mad, Mama?"

He stared at her with wide eyes, and she opened her arms.

"No, baby, but I am frustrated. May I have a hug?"

"Okay, but no kisses."

"Fine."

They sat on the deck floor, her with her head down and Chad with his arms around her shoulders.

"It's okay, Mama. Maybe the key will work now."

"No, Chad, the key won't work now. Let's check the windows."

All were closed and locked; even the bulkhead was sealed tight.

She stood on the grass and studied the house, her hands on her hips while chewing on her bottom lip.

"Try the key again, Mama."

"No, honey, it won't work. It's time for Plan B."

That piqued Chad's curiosity, and he perked up. "I'm a big boy. Can I help?" The faintest of lines formed between his brows, a common occurrence when the answer to a question eluded him. "Am I a big boy, Mama?"

Shannon kissed the creased skin and smiled. "Yes, Chad, you are, and I'm proud to be your mama." She hugged him tightly, taking the time to store the memory. Very soon she would need it. She didn't know how or why, but she felt it as clearly as she was feeling him in her arms. "I love you, my child."

Chad freed himself and kissed her cheek. "I love you too, Mama. Can we do the B plan now?"

"Sure thing, but first we need to go to the shed." She took long strides over to the shed. Instead of the original keyed padlock, a new, super-sized combination lock hung from the door.

"Fuck."

"Mama, you swore."

"Yes, sweetie, but I don't want to hear you swear, got it?"

"Can I swear when I'm old like you?"

"Yes, you may. Plan B is a bust. Let's move on to Plan C."

"Yay, I love plan C."

Jasper had grown silent, but at seeing them moving, his barking resumed.

"Keep your panties on, Jasper. I'm doing the best I can." She thought her voice had been too low for Chad to hear. No such luck.

"Keep your panties on, keep your panties on," Chad repeated as he raced ahead of her in the direction of the garage.

She selected a large rock from her lily garden and stared at the multi-paned window of the side door that also led into the garage. The problem? Her aim sucked.

"Stand back, Chad." She threw the rock at the glass panel closest to the deadbolt and watched it bounce off the door frame. "Shit."

"Shit." Chad ran and collected the rock. "I want to try, Mama."

"Go ahead, but stop repeating everything I say, okay?" She tapped the pane she wanted broken. "Aim for this one, right here. Can you do that? Stand back, so the glass doesn't get on you."

Chad wound up like a pro pitcher for the Red Sox and sent the rock spiraling toward the door and through the glass.

"I did it." He jumped, waving his arms over his head. "Wait till I tell Coach John. I bet I get a trophy."

Shannon high-fived his hands and said, "Definitely. If he doesn't give you one, I will." She reached in and unbolted the door. To her relief, Justin hadn't change the inside lock to the house or the alarm code.

"Shouldn't have gotten lazy, Justin," she muttered. "Snooze, you lose."

She took Jasper out and, after returning him to the house, opened the bay door and parked her car. She went back into the kitchen. "Chad, go upstairs and change into pants and your baseball T-shirt. You have practice tonight."

"But, Mama, *Aquanauts* are on TV."

"Chandler Baldos, now."

He came barreling out of the Great Room and danced up the stairs to a bouncy tune about baseball.

Proudly serving Wexford for over twenty years. That was the slogan printed in blue across the top of the Jay's Lock and Load receipt sitting on the counter under a set of new keys. Justin had paid a pretty penny for the prompt replacement of all the door locks, the garage door opener, and the lock on the shed.

Two could play this game. She used her phone, did a quick Internet search, and called a company in Hampstead. She next phoned Dee.

"Hi, can you take Chad to practice? I'm in the middle of something."

"Sure thing. You sound stressed. What's going on?"

Shannon offered a shortened version and ended with, "I have to wait for the locksmith."

"Do you need anything?"

"Courage."

"Don't have any. See ya soon."

"Thanks."

She placed a third call and soon had a newly coded alarm system. While she waited for the locksmith, she entered the garage, a broom and dustpan in hand, and cleaned up the broken glass. She found a piece of plywood in the basement and was in the process of a attaching it over the broken window when a yellow van entered the driveway. Her bill would surpass what Justin had paid, but no bother. When she'd dropped off the scones that morning, she'd told Jimbo about the divorce, and he'd offered some advice, which she'd taken.

It was a shame Justin hadn't gotten to the bank first.

Chapter 26

"When one door closes another one opens."
Helen Keller

Nineteen-thousand, fifty-five dollars, and twelve cents remained of the initial twenty-two-thousand she'd removed from the joint checking account. The money lay safely in a new private account in a Manchester bank, solely under her name. She hadn't planned on spending a small fortune on the new locks, but if they kept Justin out, they'd be worth every stinking penny.

She told herself she hadn't stolen the money and that she'd deduct it from the amount Justin would pay to buy out her ownership in the house.

She checked the time. Six-fifty-nine. If Justin *was* coming home, he would arrive soon. Racing up the stairs, she entered the guest room and dug two suitcases out of the closet. To one she added Justin's socks, underwear, shorts, T-shirts, a sweatshirt, and a pair of jeans. Into the other suitcase, she tossed a couple of suits, hangers included, button-down shirts, dress slacks, and a stack of polo tops. Crumpling up several ties, she shoved those against the inside edge and topped off the pile with a pair of dirty sneakers.

In the nightstand drawer, she found a box of extra-large condoms. "Yeah, in your dreams." She contemplated poking holes in the foil packs but changed her mind. Even *she* wouldn't stoop that low. However, she could put a curse all of them, something that involved a latex allergy.

"Too much work," she sighed and inserted the box.

When she opened the bottom drawer, her heart stopped. She'd never held a high opinion of Justin, but this brought him to a whole new level of stupidity. She knew next to nothing about guns but was damn sure they needed to be kept away from curious six-year-olds. What was he doing with a gun, anyway? She reached in and took hold of the handle. Pointing the gun toward the floor, she carried it to the master bedroom and placed it in a shoe box before hiding it in the linen closet. Tomorrow she'd ask someone for help. St. John would know how to use a gun. He'd been raised in the wilds of New Hampshire; he'd probably killed his first moose before he'd finished teething. Or Jimbo. Bikers owned guns. Nearly everyone in the State owned a gun; they were easier to get than toilet paper. But for right now, it was safely out of Chad's reach, and that was the important part of the equation.

She ran back to the guest room, opened the window overlooking the driveway, and removed the screen. The first suitcase traveled without incident but split upon hitting the pavement. The second suitcase opened mid-flight. Oh, well. She must have forgotten to zipper it all the way around.

The glint of sunlight on chrome caught her eye, and she glanced at the street. She raced down the steps to the kitchen and snatched her keys and cell phone and placed a call to the Wexford police. She repeated what the lawyer in the YouTube video had instructed. After ending the call, she clipped on Jasper's leash, ran through the garage, and opened the side door, closing and locking it behind them.

Justin stood by his car, staring at his clothes, and then he looked at her. "What the fuck is all this?"

What she was doing stretched the fibers of her already thin courage, but she'd taken the plunge; it was time to see if she remembered how to swim. She folded her arms and indicated the suitcases. "Take your shit and leave."

"The fuck I will."

He walked calmly to the door and tried his key in the lock. Then he faced her again. "I have to say, Shannon, you're more resourceful than I gave you credit for. Normally you would have crawled in to a ball and waited for someone to figure things out for you. Now that you've made your point, open the fucking door."

She paid no attention to the shaking in her legs and in a surprisingly steady voice said, "I told you to leave. I'm not going to say it again."

"This is my fucking house, and I'm not going anywhere. Now let me in." He moved but stopped short when Jasper growled.

"You're a bastard," she said, her anger blossoming. "What were you thinking? You not only locked me out, but you locked Chad out too. What did you expect, that he'd sleep in the car with me? And a gun? In a drawer where he could find it?"

Justin laughed. "I don't care where you and the brat sleep. As for the gun, I kept it in case I had to put a mad dog down... Or an insane wife." He bent to pick up his underwear and threw them in his car. "I don't need the gun. Maybe some night when you're sleeping, I'll just blow the whole fucking house up. *Kaplo-oey.*" He raised his arms and wiggled his fingers. "Little pieces of Shannon floating down over the town."

She slapped him across the cheek, the snap of skin on skin silencing the robin. His face, where she'd hit, turned a rosy shade of pink. "You're sick. First, you lock your son out of his house, and now you're threatening to kill him. Or have you forgotten he sleeps in this house too?"

Justin formed a fist and raised it, lowering his hand when a police cruiser entered the driveway. Moving away quickly, Justin went and stood by his car and smoothed his hair. He wore a wide grin and waved at the cop getting out of the police car. "Hey, J.C. What are you doing here?"

"We got a call."

Shannon spoke up. She knew that if she didn't cut off the good-ol'-boy chatter, she'd never get help. Trying her best to remember what the lawyer in the video had said, she started slowly. "Officer, I... I fear for my life and that of my son, and my lawyer...attorney, Martin Decker, has advised me to request the removal of my husband, but he's refusing to leave."

"Let me get this straight..." J.C. scratched his multiple chins. "You want me to remove Justin from his own house because you're skittish? That seems a bit harsh, even for you, Shannon." He sucked in as much of his obtrusive gut as humanly possible and hitched his utility belt up to what should have been his waist. "Why don't you conjure up a spell or something?"

From his spot by his car, Justin chuckled. "Good one, J.C."

"Okay, I see where this is going." Shannon tapped her phone and raised it to her ear. "Hello, this is Shannon Baldos. May I speak with Attorney Becker? Yes, thank you, I'll hold."

She met J. C.'s glare and listened to Peg's phone recording. "Yes, hello Attorney Becker. What? No, things are not going well." She paused for effect and then repeated what J.C. had said. "You'll call the sergeant? Great, thank you, and I'd like to file a formal complaint against the officer. His badge number?"

J. C. said, "Hold up there, Shannon. I never said I wasn't gonna do nothin'."

"I'm sorry, Attorney Decker, hold on." Shannon held the phone close to her chest. "What, J.C.? I didn't hear you."

"There's no need for that. Tell your lawyer I got things under control."

J. C. walked over to where Justin stood, and they talked privately, shared a quick laugh, and shook hands. "I'll keep Justin away for forty-eight hours," J.C. said to her. "That's about it. You'll have to get a restraining order after that. Come on, Justin, get your stuff and move on."

Shannon thanked her fictitious attorney and ended the call. The two men picked up the clothes and dumped the load into the trunk of Justin's car. J.C. waddled back to his cruiser, oozed his gut behind the steering wheel, and backed out of the driveway.

Justin remained. "Your life is about to become a living hell. Don't say I didn't warn you."

He blew her a kiss and climbed into his car.

Shannon scratched behind Jasper's ear and released a stream of breath as Justin followed the cruiser. She'd be foolish to take his threat lightly but short of barricading herself and Chad in the house, she didn't have many options.

As for Justin's threat that her life was about to become a living hell... Well, there wasn't much else he could do that was worse than what he'd already been doing.

******

Periodic breezes offered brief respites from the remnants of the day's heat. Parents sat on the bleachers in the waning sunlight and fanned themselves while their young children made valiant efforts to play baseball. Only two teams were partaking in the practice session: St. John's and Arnie Chambers'. Neither team surpassed the other when it came time to catch, throw, field, or hit the ball, but they were neck and neck in their excitement about being on the baseball field. Unlike St. John's coaching of even temperament and steady guidance, Chambers preferred the method called throwing his hat to the ground and yelling and screaming at the top of his lungs. During one such flare-up, St. John decided he'd had enough. He liked Arnie; he was a decent guy, but he needed to leave his frustrations at home.

He walked over to the opposite side of the field.

"What's up, St. John?"

Chambers didn't look angry, but if body posture was a clue, the locked arms meant things might go badly.

"Come on, Arnie, the kids should be having fun and all the yelling is upsetting them," St. John said. From Chambers' expression, St. John's plea had fallen on cement ears. He would give him another minute and then drop the subject and find another coach for Arnie's team. "Okay, I get it. No harm in trying."

"Hey, St. John, wait."

"Yeah."

"You're right. I get so caught up in wanting them to win I forget they're kids. I'm becoming my father, and I hate it."

St. John removed his cap and scratched his scalp. There were too many things to unpack in what he'd just heard, and he wasn't a shrink. Both of their fathers had been pricks, but that's just how the cards had been dealt. There was no use in crying about things they couldn't change. Right now he had two goals: get through practice and find out why Shannon hadn't arrived with Chad. Chambers would have to deal with his own crap.

"Good, let's give the kids some fun and have a mock game."

On the way back to his team, St. John scanned the bleachers. Shannon still hadn't arrived. He'd tried to extract information from Chad, but after learning about a rock and a trophy, more kids arrived at the field, and Chad had become distracted. Denise and Peg's heads were still locked together like a couple of lovers whispering sweet nothings to each other. Something was up, and he'd be a real asshole if Shannon had gotten hurt and he looked the other way. He was just being neighborly; he'd do the same for Denise or Peg.

"Save it, St. John," Dee told him. "Shannon's business has nothing to do with you."

Practice was over. The kids had received their pep talk and were now standing in line at the ice cream truck. He had decided he needed to find out what was happening.

He raised his hands in mock surrender. "Okay, I get it."

"Tell the truth, St. John. Why do you care about Shannon so much? It's like you're obsessed with her."

"I'm not obsessed with her. I'm just concerned, that's all.

For Christ sake, you make me sound like a stalker."

"Why the concern, then?"

"Are you kidding me? I ask about your friend, someone you supposedly care about, may I remind you, and you turn it into an episode of *America's Most Wanted*. You know what my father did to my mother? Do you want that to happen to Shannon? I can help."

He'd have to wait and see how it played out, but from the look on Denise's face, she didn't believe him. "You know what? Just forget about it," he said.

"Alright, I'll tell you, but you can't tell Shannon I did."

"I won't," he said, keeping his grin to himself. Thank God Denise loved to gossip.

"All the locks..."

As Dee relayed Shannon's saga, the spot between St. John's brows creased, the folds of skin deepening the more Dee spoke.

"So, now you know. If you tell Shannon I—"

"I said I wouldn't," he snapped. "Sorry. Does anybody know where Justin is?"

"I have no idea, but I'm surprised he didn't show up here and try and take Chad. I tell you, St. John, this divorce is going to get ugly if Shannon doesn't stop it now. She's not capable of standing on her own, and she's going to get hurt. Chad too."

"I don't think you know Shannon very well. She impresses me as a remarkably self-reliant woman."

Dee scoffed by issuing a loud chuckle. "There you go, thinking with your dick. Anyway, I told you everything. Now leave it alone. Peg and I will help her. You'll only confuse her more."

Her comment puzzled him. "Why would you say that?"

"Because you're a handsome man, and Shannon's lonely. She might confuse sexual attraction with love, and you and I know how that will end."

"I think you're inflating the effect I have on women. Anyway, I have no intention of confusing her; I just want to help."

Dee looked past him and called out to a group of boys. "I'm coming." She finished with St. John by saying, "Shannon doesn't need your help, and whatever happens to her is none of your business, so do me a favor and stay away from her, okay? I gotta go. I have to bring Chad home."

St. John placed one hand in the air and the other over his heart. "I swear on my Boy Scout's honor, I'll stay away from Shannon."

He pecked Dee's cheek and sauntered away, his hands in his pockets.

Too bad he'd never been a Boy Scout.

Chapter 27

"You cannot find peace by avoiding life."
Virginia Woolf

Concentric layers of brick formed a paved patio located at the rear of the Baldos' yard. Four cushioned wicker chairs hugged the centrally located fire pit. It was in one such chair that Shannon sat and studied the blaze before her.

Flames licked along the oak logs, reaching swirling coils of blood-orange into the night sky. At her feet, on a red scarf, lay six white cloth pouches, each tied closed by a red ribbon; a porcelain cup; an apple; and her athame. At the side of her chair, she'd placed a bottle of bourbon, a hand towel, and the baby monitor she still used when Chad was asleep in the house while she was outside conducting magic. She'd already consecrated the sacred fire, called the four elements, and welcomed the goddess to her Litha celebration. All that remained of her midsummer's ritual was to voice her intentions. Goddess willing, the Universe was paying attention.

Holding the first pouch containing three leaves from the St. John's Wort bush in her herb garden, she tossed the pouch into the flames and spoke clearly, directing the protection spell toward the fire. "By the power burning within this midsummer's pyre, I call to thee; form a protection from those who wish to harm my son and me. So mote it be."

The next pouch contained lavender.

"By the power burning within this midsummer's pyre, I release thee; calmness and peace within my soul, I beckon you to bring me."

The pungent herb pierced the air.

Mint followed with a spell for luck, then sage for the cleansing of her soul. The second to last pouch held petals from a starflower. Roman soldiers consumed the plant in preparation for battle, believing in its power to instill bravery in a person. Fingers crossed the legend of the flower's powers was true.

"By the power burning within this midsummer's pyre, I call to thee, Jupiter; battles await me, and I ask that you arm me with the strength to be victorious. So mote it be."

The pouch hit the fire, and a rapid burst of energy shot upward in a shower of glowing sparks.

With the last pouch opened on her lap, she used her athame and sliced into the apple, the juice running over her fingers. She scooped out five seeds and added them to the meadowsweet flower heads on the cloth and retied the ribbon, but she kept hold of the packet. At present, her life held no room for a third person. By opening the door with the love spell, she would make herself and Chad vulnerable all over again.

She pressed the soft fabric. What was the harm in welcoming all possibilities? In the end, that's what magic was all about—a willingness to allow all that could be to be.

"By the power burning within this midsummer's pyre, I release thee; return with the one who shall love Chad and me." She quickly added, "But please make him kind...and safe...and gentle...and...and... Oh, screw it; bring me the one who will care for us and us him."

She tossed the bag, hoping to see more sparks. What she saw was the pouch on the log, the flames refusing to touch the sack. No smoke. No nothing.

This type of thing had never happened before. Should she leave the pouch? Remove it? Throw bourbon on it? Maybe she needed to do some visualization to get it to catch. She closed her eyes and focused, finding herself once again on the porch of the quaint house, watching Chad playing in the yard with Jasper.

The truck rolled to a stop.

She accepted the truth of what she was seeing. Perhaps St. John *was* meant to be part of her and Chad's journey. The aroma of pine and musk filtered into her brain, her name on his lips.

"Shannon."

She opened her eyes in time to watch the enchanted pouch ignite into blue-and-green flames.

"Shannon."

She turned her gaze to the right, got to her feet, and fell into his arms.

Her savage hunger returned, and she opened her lips to grant his tongue entry. A different fire ignited and tore through her body, burning with the intensity of a thousand flames.

St. John spoke, keeping their lips touching. "God, I've missed you."

She pushed him away and sat down. What difference did it make that she wanted him in her life? He didn't want the same. "Why are you here?"

"I wanted to see you." He dragged over a nearby chair and settled himself before handing her a packet of sunflower seeds. "Happy *Litha*." He bent and looked at the collection of items on the red cloth. "Is that your athame? Can you use any knife, or do you have to buy a special type?"

She stared at him. "How do you know about Athames?"

He returned to a relaxed position. "I figured if I'm going to be involved with a witch, I should learn about her ways and holidays. Oh, sorry, *sabbats*."

"I don't understand." Seriously, her thoughts were a tangled heap.

"What's not to understand?" He looked at her. "You're Wiccan, and I wanted to know more." He tenderly touched the skin above her lip. "This is from me, isn't it?"

She swatted his hand away. "What does that even mean? Involved?"

A shrug served as his explanation. "What's the bourbon for?"

"You're the one who did 'research.' You tell me." Ouch. The sharp tone in her voice had been bad enough, but she hadn't needed to add the air quotes.

"Good thing I studied for this test. Okay." He cleared his throat. "Fruited drinks are the more traditional offerings, but you'll serve the goddess a cup of bourbon as refreshment. By the way—" He looked at the items spread on the scarf. "I don't see any honey cakes. Did you forget to make them?"

"I made honey-lavender biscotti." She pursed her lips and studied the photograph on the seed packet. His gesture was so frigging sweet, and extremely confusing. For a man who ran from relationships, he seemed to be running in the wrong direction. "You should leave," she said.

"Not a very hospitable witch, are you? I was under the impression all were welcome at *Litha* celebrations."

She met his eyes, always a mistake because her will wasn't her own. "I... Did you shave?"

The grin of a rogue appeared, and he ran his fingers over his chin. "I noticed your skin looked raw yesterday and didn't want to hurt you when we kissed."

"You are the cockiest bastard I've ever known."

He leaned her way and traced the line of her mouth, refueling the furnace under her skin.

"An honor I'm proud to hold," he said.

He held her chin and retraced her lips with his tongue, and drew her into his arms. The kiss was slow and deep and long, and her toes curled and her insides melted.

When he finished, he said, "I'd like to hear what happened today, but, before you start, will your goddess mind if I have some bourbon? And may I have a biscotti? I haven't eaten since lunch."

******

St. John chewed a cookie and sipped his bourbon while Shannon tended to Chad. He set his glass on the bricks and raised the baby monitor to his ear.

"I want to have a fire, Mama," Chad said.

"Go back to sleep, sweetie. It's late. Tomorrow night we'll have a fire, and I'll even get marshmallows for you to toast."

"But, Mama."

"No buts. Close those eyes and dream."

"Of running and playing?"

"Yes, my love, of running and playing."

St. John returned the monitor to the concrete wall and rested his head against the chair cushion. He allowed the lullaby Shannon hummed to open his thoughts. Life presented chances, and if not taken, they passed by. Some were offered again, others were lost forever. Was he being given another chance? Was meeting Shannon an opportunity to finally get it right?

He cared for her—that went without saying—and he enjoyed her. But love... He wasn't capable of loving anyone, and would she even want him? He was damaged goods, beyond fixing. Even if she opened her life to him, he wouldn't know how to begin. He'd be wise to say goodnight and return to his life and his rules.

When she returned and sat down, he said, "I'm going to leave. Thank you for the food."

Shannon held onto his arm. "What's going on, St. John? Why did you come over?"

He found all he could do was chuckle.

"I'm serious," she insisted, her voice taking on a serious tone. "I deserve to know."

"I was concerned," he answered.

"About?"

"You. Who else would I be concerned about if I'm sitting here, in your yard, with you?"

"Why are you angry all of a sudden?"

She removed his plate and stood.

He stayed sitting and gave her what he'd hoped was a 'what the fuck' look. "Why am I...? Why do you keep pushing me away?" He left the chair, walked a few feet away, and then turned to her. "It wasn't me who kissed you."

"Don't be so immature. I just asked a simple question. You agreed we wouldn't see each other anymore, and yet, here you are."

He didn't have a response because she was dead right. He'd only wanted to be sure she and Chad were safe, but just as Denise had said, whatever happened was none of his business. He turned and walked away.

"St. John." Shannon ran to him. "I'm sorry. Stay."

He feigned a frown. He had every intention of staying, but it wouldn't hurt for her to beg a tiny bit. Hell, he'd begged enough, now it was her turn.

"Please," she said. "I want you to stay."

Making love to her hadn't been part of his reason for stopping by, but the thin dress she wore hid none of her curves, especially with the firelight behind her. Before she could stop him, he had her in his arms. The way she trembled under his touch drove his passion, and he couldn't stop himself from lifting the skirt of her gown. Her body yielded to the pressure of his hands.

"I can't," she said and stepped away. "Chad."

"I'm sorry. I didn't come over to do this."

"Now who's lying?"

It wasn't so much the question but her grin that caught him off guard. He quickly regained his mental footing and responded with a dry, "I don't lie."

"Really? You said you shaved so *when* we kissed you wouldn't hurt me—not *if* we kissed. Face it, St. John, you're human, just like the rest of us."

Her stance, with her arms folded and her right hip thrust out to the side, increased the pressure behind his pants zipper. A night spent with his right hand and the memory of her loomed in his future. "Guilty as charged. Am I about to be banished again?"

"Oh, I have a more severe punishment in mind," she said.

"Such as?"

"Bring those lips over here and kiss me."

He didn't need her to ask him twice.

Chapter 28

"The loneliest moment in someone's life is when they are watching their whole world fall apart, and all they can do is stare blankly."
F. Scott Fitzgerald

Even though it was hot in the SUV, Shannon remained. The walk up the incline didn't appeal to her. She repositioned herself and leaned against the door and closed her eyes. Remaining outside with St. John until the wee hours of the morning had seemed like a good idea at the time.

St. John had asked why she'd started the blog and one thing had led to another, and she'd found herself explaining about life under Justin's thumb and her post-partum depression. She should have kept her mouth shut instead of sharing information better left buried. Her blabbing obviously hadn't added to her sex appeal. At the end of her story, all St. John had said was he needed to get a few hours' sleep. A quick hug and kiss, and presto change-o, he'd disappeared into the shadows as he crossed the lawn.

The shrill bell disturbed her thoughts, and she left the car and hurried up the incline. She reached the bench and looked for Chad. Kindergarten and first-grade students dispersed, and a second bell released the next two grades but no Chad.

She refused to give in to the panic creeping her way. Chad was most likely still in his classroom under the watchful eyes of Miss Brewster...who happened to be walking by.

"Miss Brewster," she called, hurrying to intercept the teacher. "Do you know where Chad is? I don't see him."

"He was dismissed," Miss Brewster said and continued her path to the flagpole.

Shannon followed. "What do you mean he was dismissed?

Who dismissed him?"

The woman's loud huff preceded, "Perhaps you should see Mrs. Hogan."

Finding herself in the school's main office, Shannon stood facing the high counter and Rhonda Hogan, the pleasant voice behind all school announcements. "What would you like to know?"

The dismissal bell for the upper grades startled Shannon, and she hugged her bag to her stomach. The unimaginable was happening, and she was powerless to stop it. "Can you tell me who dismissed Chad?" It was a stupid question; she already knew the answer. "I mean, what time did Justin dismiss Chad?"

She wanted to also ask why Chad had been dismissed when she'd signed paperwork that very morning barring his removal by anyone other than herself.

Mrs. Hogan flipped open a black binder. "Chad's father collected him at seven-thirty-five."

"Seven thirty-five?" Justin must have been in the parking lot when she and Chad had arrived at the school, but that still didn't answer why the fuck they'd let Justin take him.

It didn't matter; Chad was gone. Justin had exacted his revenge with the marksmanship of a sniper.

"May I ask, Mrs. Hudson, if my husband mentioned where he was taking Chad?"

The elderly woman studied her with a quizzical look. "Your husband didn't tell me his plans."

Shannon offered a nervous laugh as she added an incoherent reason for not knowing the location of her own family. She left the office and, keeping her head down, sped along the walkway, praying no one would speak to her. After she sealed herself in the hot interior of her car, she pulled out her phone. A boy with two missing front teeth grinned back at her. She touched the screen as if the cool, hard glass was a conduit to his actual skin. "Oh, baby, where are you?" Her throat burned, and she swallowed the desire to cry. Tears weren't going to bring Chad back; she had to keep calm.

She swiped the phone and spoke to Justin's voicemail. "Justin, please... I need to know where..." Sobs wracked her chest, making speech difficult. "Please... I'm begging you. Please call m...me."

So much for staying in control. She'd provided exactly what he'd wanted—the crying, her tortured pleas; he loved stuff like that. He'd probably jerk off while listening to her message.

"Hello, Shannon."

She glared at the person standing outside the car and lowered the window. "What do you want?" she snapped.

Leeann stepped back, a startled look on her face. "I saw you crying and—"

"Wait, don't tell me. You saw me crying and thought, hmm, what else can I do that will make Shannon's life suck?"

"No, I want to help."

"Save it. You've never done anything for anyone in your whole life."

"I admit I haven't been the nicest to you, so I deserve that, but you've been a bitch to me too."

"Really? Is this why you stopped by for a visit, so we could have a pissing contest? Well, how about this? Piss off." Shannon raised the window, sealing Leeann's voice outside the car.

Leeann knocked again, and her voice pierced the glass. "I may know where Justin took Chad."

"Attorney Decker's office."

Shannon took an unsteady breath. "Um, hi, this is Shannon Baldos. I spoke with Attorney Decker yesterday and have an appointment with him tomorrow, but may I talk to him, please? It's important."

The line switched over to a preprogrammed music link, and she sat in the car and watched the remainder of the school population file by as she listened to a piano rendition of the theme to *Phantom of the Opera*. By the time the third cycling of the song ended, she'd soiled the remaining tissues in her bag and had started on the napkins in the glove box.

Martin Decker came on the line, his voice as pleasant as it had been the day before. "Sorry to keep you waiting, Shannon. What can I do for you?"

"Attorney Decker, my husband..." She tried to conceal the hysteria taking control of her but was failing miserably. "Justin... Chad... Please..." Her voice cracked and silence followed.

"Slow down and start at the beginning. Has Justin done something to your son?"

Too bad the lawyer couldn't see through the phone; he'd see her nodding, and she wouldn't have to speak.

"Shannon? Do you want to come in to the office?"

Another assault of tears buried her voice. No, she indicated with her head. She wanted to find her son.

"I'm going to need you to stop crying and tell me what's going on. Can you do that?"

Maybe. She squeezed out, "Justin took... Chad's gone."

"Justin took Chad?"

Yes, her brain screeched. He took Chad. Chad is gone. "He's gone. I don't know... Please, help me."

"I can't do anything if you don't pull yourself together and tell me what happened."

"I pretended to call you," she said. Sniffing back more tears, she explained about the locks and calling the police and finished with Justin dismissing Chad from the school. "Another mother seems to think he's taken Chad to California."

"Why would she think that?"

"Justin asked her husband about Disney."

"That can also mean Florida. Has Justin ever expressed an interest in going to Disney?"

"No."

"Well, just to make sure, I'll have one of my staff call the airports and inquire about a man traveling with a six-year-old."

"His mistress... She might be with them."

"Okay, three people, then. Have you tried calling him?"

"Yes, I left a m...message."

"Good. Maybe he'll call you back. Are you home?"

"No." A sudden idea unfolded, and she said, "The police... Should I go to the police?"

"No need to involve the police more than you have. As for what happened yesterday, I'll file for a Temporary Protective Order asking for a Stay Away Provision. I'll try and have it cover the next five days, but I may not be able to do more than three, after which Justin will be allowed back into the house unless we can prove he's a danger to you or Chad. I do wish you had called me earlier. Does Chad have a passport?"

"No."

"That's good. That means wherever they are, they're still in the country. The best thing you can do is go home."

What on earth did he expect her to do at home? Bake a pie? "I don't want to go home. I have to do something to find Chad."

"There's nothing you can do except to wait and let me handle the paperwork."

"Shouldn't I go to Justin's girlfriend's apartment? See if he's there? Or the lodge... He could be at the lodge."

"Shannon, I want you to pull yourself together. I've dealt with this type of situation more than I care to count. By no means are you to go looking for Justin. Go home and try and relax. He's just trying to scare you."

"It's working," she whispered.

"Go home, Shannon. For all we know, your husband might be there waiting for you. If he is, and you feel threatened, call the police again and then call me. I know it's not much, but that's all you can do for the time being. We'll find your son. Don't worry."

She was afraid if she said the words out loud they might come true, but she had to know. "What if he never brings Chad back?" A knife cut into her chest. She doubled over and let her tears drip onto the steering wheel. She'd only wanted to give Chad and her a chance at a better life, and now she might have lost him forever. "I have to do something."

"There's nothing you can do except wait. If Justin calls, ask to speak with Chad and try and find out exactly where they are. Ask Chad questions that would relate to Disney, such as has he met Mickey or what type of decorations the hotel has. Disney hotels are themed, and we might be able to pinpoint where they're staying. Can you do that?"

"Yes, but—"

"Do you happen to know Justin's attorney's name?"

"I don't know... He's used Eugene Draper in the past."

"I know Gene. I'll place a call to him and find out what's what. Would you like to come in earlier than eleven tomorrow? I have a meeting at six and could see you around seven-thirty?"

"Thank you, I can't, I have to drop Chad at scho... Never mind. I'll be there. Thank you."

"Why don't you call someone to stay with you tonight? I wouldn't suggest you be alone. I'll see you tomorrow. And, Shannon, call me if anything changes. I'll text you my cell phone number. You have *carte blanche* to call any time."

"Thank you."

She took the lawyer's advice and left messages for Dee and Peg. Neither answered, so she started the car and faced the rear to back out of the parking spot. She bit into her lower lip when she saw Chad's empty car seat.

✳✳✳✳✳✳

"Stop asking. You know I can't discuss my clients with you."

St. John frowned at his long-time friend and lawyer. He'd listened to Marty's side of the conversation and had the gist of what had happened. Justin had taken Chad, and their whereabouts were unknown. He hadn't heard what Shannon had said, but he had a pretty good idea of her state of mind.

"Screw the attorney crap," he spat back. "I was sitting right here the entire time and heard everything you said, so you might as well fill me in. Who said Justin might be at Disney?"

"I can't tell you."

"Whether you tell me or not, I'm going to make him pay dearly for what he's doing to Shannon and Chad."

Decker's chair squeaked as he leaned forward and wrote on a yellow legal pad. "Watch what you're saying, St. John. Do you happen to know the name of Justin's mistress?"

"Dooley. Shelby Dooley. Should I call Tony?"

"No. I need to pinpoint a location first, and you need to stay out of this. I know Shannon's an acquaintance, but I'm her lawyer."

St. John rubbed his jaw. By remaining silent, he'd just given away the truth.

"If this wasn't such a mess, I'd break out the champagne," Decker said. "I never thought I'd see the day."

"You haven't seen anything," St. John grumbled. "Don't go making assumptions."

"If you say so. You do realize you could be named in the divorce? Do you honestly want the good name of St. John dragged through what's likely going to be a dirty fight?"

"What good name?" St. John scoffed. "Anyway, I didn't say I was involved. Shannon made the decision to leave Justin without any influence from me. She's been thinking of doing this for a while."

"That doesn't matter. You're involved now. Take my legal advice and step away."

"No can do."

"It's your funeral."

Decker buzzed one of his paralegals and instructed her to check the flight manifestos.

On his own, St. John placed a text to Tony Santos, his favorite, and only, private investigator.

Chapter 29

*"We are healed from suffering only by
experiencing it to the full."*
Marcel Proust

"You've reached Justin Baldos. Leave a message."

Shannon cradled the phone against her shoulder and removed the wax seal from around the bourbon's cap. "Hey, asshole," she said. "It's me again. I want to talk to Chad, you fucking idiot. Call me back, you fucking jerk."

Decker had told her to call, so she was calling. Granted, he hadn't said to insult Justin, but since this had been her thirteenth message, why not? Being nice had gotten her zilch.

She fingered the soft terry fabric of the stuffed clown in her lap. Every night since Chad's birth, he and Clowny had slept together. What would Chad do when he discovered his constant companion was out of reach?

She took a long draw from the bottle.

It had been foolish to go looking for Justin, but after taking her shower, she couldn't just sit around and do nothing. At least she'd learned he and Shelby had left Shelby's apartment early in the morning, each carrying a suitcase. Praise the gods for nosy tenants.

A stop at the lodge and the police station had each yielded zilch. The only saving grace had been the young cop on duty. He took down a description of what Chad had been wearing and said he would send out an unofficial bulletin.

She arched her head and swallowed more of the woodsy liquid and brought forth the words to a spell.

"Through the piercing black I will find you; sing, my son, like the call of a bird; sing and let your voice be heard; sing my child, my all, my love; sing that I may hear, sing that I might see, and I promise, once again safe with me you will be."

She lifted the bottle of bourbon and emptied the remainder into her body and lowered herself to the rug. A lonesome wail erupted from her throat, and she buried her face into the sweet-scented body of the doll. And then she heard the plea. Faint and distant. She shook as the image of Chad materialized in her mind.

'Where are you, Mama?' he said, his face drenched with tears.

"No. Please, dear goddess, no."

She clawed at his bed, pulling herself to standing, but her legs crumbled under the weight of the alcohol, and she collapsed back to the floor.

'Mama, where are you?'

"Please, no," she shouted. "Chad, goddess, help him. He needs me."

'Mama.'

"NO." Her shouts drowned out Chad's voice, and she no longer heard him calling. "Chad, come back."

A man shouted her name. Justin. She had to keep him from finding Chad.

"JUSTIN, NO, STAY AWAY FROM HIM. CHAD, HIDE. RUN."

******

Jasper stood barking on the inside of the sliding door, and St. John stared at the second story window from which Shannon's cries were coming. Justin must have come home. Why else would she be yelling for him to stay away and for Chad to hide?

St. John ran to the garage door and smashed the glass by the lock. He leaned in, reaching for the latch. Of course there wasn't one.

"Fuck this."

He stepped back and slammed his foot against the door. A snapping of wood rewarded him for his effort, and he pushed into the garage. At the door that led to the house, he caught his breath. "Please be unlocked." The doorknob turned freely. Mumbling thanks, he ran to the staircase, Jasper leading the way. Strange, he still only heard Shannon. By now, he should be hearing Justin's voice, even Chad crying. Something wasn't right.

He took the steps two at a time and raced to what had to be Chad's bedroom. The setting sun gave the room an eerie feel. The shadows on the faces of the stuffed animals made them look more like zombies than innocent toys. But no Justin. And no Chad.

An empty bourbon bottle lay next to Shannon.

He bent and lifted her. "I'm here, Shannon. It's okay, I'm here." She was a dead weight in his arms. A dead weight that reeked of whiskey.

By now it was clear Justin and Chad weren't in the house. From the circle of candles on the bookcase, it looked like she'd performed a spell of some kind and might have gotten lost in some sort of trance. A drunken trance.

He carried her into Chad's bathroom, leaned her over the toilet bowl and braced her from behind. What he did next was going to take their relationship to a whole new level. Nothing said 'I'm into you' like forcing your partner to vomit.

With a strength he hadn't expected, she bucked with her legs and sent them both to the tile floor. She pulled away from him and stood and swayed. He knew that look.

A deluge of hot, partially digested, alcohol-laced food splashed the back of his head, neck, and shoulders even as he scrambled to his knees. He reached out for her. She staggered, and her head wavered. From her expression, the front of him was next. Not if he could help it. He spun her to face the toilet but she missed the bowl entirely.

"Stop," she groaned.

He held her in place. "Who am I?"

"Let me go."

"Not until you tell me who I am."

"St. John, let—"

A third wave topped off her first, making sure this time to include his pants and shoes.

"Feel better?" he asked.

She nodded.

"Good. Time for a shower."

He brought her into the tub with him, shoes and all, and blasted them both with cold water.

St. John placed a mug in front of Shannon. He was wearing a pair of Justin's sweatpants and one of his T-shirts. While she'd gotten herself dressed, he'd cleaned Chad's bathroom and brewed some coffee.

"How did you get in?" she asked him, an ice pack held to her forehead.

He didn't answer, choosing instead to focus on her eyes. Her story, the way she'd been treated—it had been like witnessing his mother's suffering all over again. Justin Baldos. Charles St. John. They'd both been carved from the same pile of crap.

"St. John, I asked—"

"I was worried about you," he said and filled a mug for himself. "When I heard you screaming... I'll send someone over to fix the door."

"The door?"

"Yeah, the side door."

"That's okay." Shannon snickered. "You're not the first person to break one of the glass panes."

"It's a bit more than glass. I kicked in the door."

"You kicked... You're unbelievable."

"A thank-you might be nice."

"I'm supposed to thank you for destroying my door?"

"It would be the polite thing to do."

The rapid scowl on her face seemed to imply she didn't like his answer.

"Why, exactly, are you here?" she said.

He returned the pot to the coffee maker. "I'm here because I was concerned."

"You can't keep coming over here to check on me every time you get worried."

He rested his hip against the counter. "Why not?"

"Because."

"That's not an answer."

"It is when I have a headache."

"You'd feel a whole lot worse if I hadn't been here. A bourbon hangover is nothing to toy with."

"I've been drunk before, and I'll still have a hangover."

"I'll bet not with bourbon."

"Actually—" She met his eyes with a look of defiance. "I have. It more than sucks; it's akin to a slow, painful death. But you see, daddy-dear, tonight I didn't fucking care. I wanted the suffering. I still do. At least I'd have a physical reason for wanting to die."

"Making yourself physically ill won't do a damn thing to help the situation," he said, the mug held to his mouth.

Shannon face contorted into a mask of anger. "Of course, I should have known the great and wise St. John would have an opinion."

"I'm not the enemy, but if it makes you feel better, go ahead and treat me like I am. I can help if you'll let me."

"I don't need help. I need my son."

He didn't outwardly react when she slammed her mug against the island, but inside he was flailing, completely helpless to comprehend the depth of her anguish.

"Say something," she demanded.

"I get what you're going through," he stated in a calm, reassuring tone.

"You can't even begin to *get* what I'm going through," she said.

He rushed to her side when she stood and faltered. Holding her by the shoulders, he said, "You're right, I can't. But believe me when I say Chad *will* come home. Until then, tell me what you need me to do to get you through this."

She clawed at the T-shirt he wore. "I need you to make it go away, please. I'm begging you."

He steadied her hands. "That won't fix anything."

"I'm not stupid." She struggled away. "You asked, and that's what I need." With a nasty look, she finished by saying, "Are you man enough to help me or not?"

He could laugh—if sex was the answer he'd have gotten rid of his own pain a long, long time ago. "I guess I'm not," he said.

"Then get the fuck out of my house."

"No." He held her face between his hands and kissed the tears winding down her cheeks. He'd drink an ocean of her tears if that's what it would take to help her. "Come on, let's go upstairs."

She clutched to him, and he helped her up the steps. After getting her settled in her bed, he leaned over and whispered, "I'll find Chad. I promise. Get some sleep."

"Please stay."

He lay behind her and pulled her close. "Don't worry. I'm not going anywhere."

******

St. John bolted from the room and down to the kitchen. He met Shannon in the stairwell and handed her the phone. "It's Justin."

She dropped to one of the steps, and St. John settled behind her, placing her in a safe cocoon of his arms and legs.

"Justin, bring Chad home," she demanded.

"Still haven't learned anything, have you, Shannon?"

Her eyes stung. No more tears, she pleaded with herself. Be strong for Chad. She would do whatever Justin asked at this point, anything to get Chad back. "I'm sorry. Please bring him home. I'm begging you."

Justin switched to a slippery-sounding voice. "That's what I like to hear. Are you on your knees?"

St. John reached for the phone, but she shook her head. "Why are you doing this? You're hurting Chad."

"Oh, I'm not the one hurting Chad. You are. This is all your fault. You were stupid for removing the money from the house account."

"You can have the money," she told him. "I'll even let you keep my inheritance."

"Oh, don't worry. I plan on it. But right now, I have a few things for you to do. Ready? Pay attention. Bring the money back to the bank and deposit it in the new account I've opened. Then pack your stinking potions and cooking shit and that rabid dog and get the fuck out of my house. I don't care where you go, but I don't want you or that hound there when I get back."

"You have to give me time to find a place for Chad and me to live."

"You're not paying attention, Shannon. Chad is staying with me."

"No, please, no." Her determination not to cry crumbled, and she folded into herself, tucking her face against her knees. "Please, no," she sobbed.

Again, St. John tried to take the phone, but she twisted away. Justin was issuing orders like she was some kind of spy. Her mission, should she choose to accept it, was to roll over and admit she'd failed.

"I'm not finished. Tell your lawyer you changed your mind about the divorce."

"I can't."

"Then you'll never see Chad again. Goodbye."

"Justin, wait."

"What?"

"I... Okay, I'll tell him. I want to talk to Chad."

"You're in no position to be making demands, sweetheart."

"*Please*, may I talk to Chad?"

"He's not here."

Had she heard him correctly? Chad wasn't with him? It was two in the morning. "I don't understand. Where is—?"

"Back at the hotel. Shelby and I are out getting something to eat."

"He's *alone*?"

"He's fine. I gave him something to keep him asleep. He won't be waking up till noon if the stuff works as good as Shelby says. I'll call you in a few days, and Shannon, remember one thing: you have no leverage, not as long as Chad is around. Sleep tight."

In a daze, she let the phone slip from her hand. Chad was alone and drugged. And it was all her fault.

The strong arm that encircled her shoulder did little to ease her guilt. She'd decided to leave Justin, thinking she'd be able to create a better life for herself and Chad, but the reality was she'd messed everything up. Now Chad was paying the price for her stupidity.

"Come on," St. John said. "I'm putting you back in bed."

She allowed him to do what he said, but only after she'd claimed Chad's clown. She settled her head against the pillow and hugged Clowny to her chest and whispered, "I will find you, my love, I promise."

Please, goddess, make it so.

Chapter 30

"In all things it is better to hope than to despair."
Johann Wolfgang von Goethe

A woman dressed in a navy blue, tailored suit stopped at the receptionist's desk of Attorney Martin Decker's office and then faced Shannon. Closely cropped black hair accented smooth, ebony skin, and lips, tinted with red lipstick, opened into a smile.

"Give me one minute," the woman said and hurried down a hallway.

Shannon nodded in return. Screw the ability to fly on her broom. Right now she'd take being able to change her appearance with the snap of her fingers. She wouldn't be surprised to find the people at the firm thinking the newest client partied like a rock star, what with the puffy face and bloodshot eyes.

She'd have looked a lot worse if it hadn't been for St. John. She owed him a world of gratitude. He'd stayed by her side and had kept her from jumping off the emotional ledge she'd been on. He'd been there when she closed her eyes, and his arms had still been wrapped around her come morning.

She'd learned a lot about the man behind the self-confident armor. He'd started with an apology for his behavior the night before, just walking out of the yard. Her interpretation that he thought she was weak couldn't have been farther from reality.

'My father manipulated my mother, and it still sickens me how easy he made it look,' St. John had offered. 'I was too young to get what was going on, and I used to think my mother was crazy when she accused him of trying to confuse her. Hearing what you've been going through stirred up some stuff I couldn't handle, and I'm sorry I ran. I promise I won't run anymore. I'll be with you until Chad comes home.'

She couldn't decipher what that last part meant. Would St. John bolt when they found Chad, eager to repair his broken rules and move on to someone else?

How would she feel if he did?

The woman from earlier approached and extended her hand. "Hi, Shannon, I'm Jayla, Attorney Decker's assistant. We're almost ready for you. Let me get you situated in the conference room, and I'll bring some fresh coffee. This way."

Jayla opened the double doors of a lengthy room. The floor-to-ceiling windows offered a panoramic view of Manchester's skyline and, in the distance, the tips of the Presidential Range, with Mount Washington's snow-covered crest rising above them all.

"I hope you don't get dizzy," Jayla said.

Shannon stood near the glass. "I'm good, but I can see how this would get to a person."

Jayla laughed. "There's been some late nights when Martin brings out the Scotch, and let me tell you, the room sways. Have a seat. How do you take your coffee?"

"Black, please."

"I'll be right back."

Jayla left, and Shannon turned to stare out the window, but all she could see was Chad's face. "Hold on, munchkin. Mama's going to find you."

"Shannon."

She turned at the mention of her name and found herself on the receiving end of St. John's grin. He strolled into the room, looking handsome in a white, short-sleeved shirt and

black cargo shorts, his hair combed away from his freshly shaved face.

"What are you doing here?" she wanted to know.

He strode her way. "I'm here for you. Do you mind if I stay?"

"Not at all, but you didn't say—"

"I wanted to surprise you," he said and leaned close.

Shannon jerked away when someone new cleared his throat.

St. John said, "This ugly son-of-a-bitch is Martin Decker, Attorney at Law." He motioned toward Jayla as she walked into the room. "And this lovely lady is—"

"We already met, St. John." Jayla set a cup of coffee in front of Shannon and then sat and opened a laptop.

Attorney Decker dropped a folder onto the table and shook Shannon's hand with an aggressive pump. "Don't listen to him. He's still jealous over me getting more bids than he did. It's good to meet you. How are you holding up?"

"I'm as good as can be expected, thank you." She flexed her fingers and gave St. John a quizzical look. "Bids for what?"

"Ten years ago, the New Hampshire chapter of the Sons of Italy held a fundraiser and auctioned dates with local business owners. Marty hasn't stopped boasting about his win, which is in poor taste if you ask me. Nobody likes a poor winner."

Marty said, "Nobody likes a poor loser, either, St. John. I won fair and square."

"By fifty cents," St. John grumbled.

Shannon found herself smiling at the friendly teasing the two men were engaged in.

"A win's a win," Decker said. "Have a seat, Shannon. Before we get started, do you mind if St. John sits in on the meeting?"

"Not at all." She gave St. John a quick smile and then returned her attention to the lawyer.

St. John claimed the seat next to her and took hold of her hand. "We have something to tell you, but I'm going to let Marty do the honors. I'm just a bystander."

"More like an active participant," Marty mumbled and

grinned at Shannon. "We've located Chad."

"What?" Shannon was on her feet. She looked at all three people seated at the table, ending with St. John. "Why didn't you tell me?" She directed her next question toward the attorney. "Where is he?"

"Sit," said St. John. "Marty will explain."

She allowed St. John to guide her back into her chair.

"Your woman friend was correct," Marty said. "Justin and his companion are at Disney World. They're staying in the Animal Kingdom Lodge and have booked the room until the seventh of July."

Questions flew from her mouth. "Is Chad safe? Has this associate of yours seen him? Has he talked to Justin? Is Justin bringing Chad home now that we've found him?"

Decker pressed his lips in a tight line and gave St. John a nod.

St. John said, "Our guy *has* seen Chad."

"Then what's wrong? You're both hiding something." She was up and out of her seat again. "Is Chad hurt?" That had to be what they were keeping from her. Justin must have harmed Chad. "What did Justin do to him?"

St. John joined her and lowered them both into their respective chairs. "Chad's fine, Shannon. Actually, our guy has eyes on him right now."

She swept her attention toward Marty. "Then tell your guy to grab him and run."

"We can't remove Chad because it would be kidnapping," Decker said. He wore a frown and opened the folder. "Justin has every right to bring his son on a vacation."

"Can I at least see Chad?" Shannon clutched St. John's hand. "Tell your guy to take a picture, please."

"He already did, but I want you to relax and remember Chad is fine." St. John swiped at his phone and held it out.

"No, no, no," she cried out, her brain refusing to accept what she was seeing—Chad, sitting on a bench wearing the same shirt he'd chosen yesterday morning. He looked as if he was crying.

Marty offered, "Shannon, don't worry. I'm in the process of making arrangements to bring Chad back, but it will take time. Before I can make it happen, we have a lot to discuss."

"I told you, Marty," St. John said, his voice gruff. "We don't *have* time. Baldos gets wind that we've found him, and he'll take off again. This is a game to him."

The attorney shook his head, his disagreement evident. "Your way is illegal, St. John. You could go to prison for kidnapping."

"Excuse me, Attorney Decker. This came for Mr. St. John." A youthful-looking man stood in the doorway, a white envelope in his hand.

St. John got up, walked around the table, and claimed the envelope. "It won't be kidnapping if Shannon comes with me." He removed two airline tickets from the envelope and waved them in the air. "Our flight leaves in two hours."

St. John's feet extended into the extra leg room provided to all first-class passengers, and having lowered his seat into a reclining position, he seemed to have fallen asleep. Meanwhile, Shannon impatiently flipped through the pages of the magazine she'd been looking at since takeoff.

"Can you turn the pages a little louder?" St. John kept his eyelids closed and his hands folded on his stomach. "I don't think they can hear you in the back of the plane."

Shannon huffed and closed the magazine, then opened it and began smacking through the pages again.

"You need a drink." St. John straightened the back of his seat and signaled for the flight attendant.

"I don't need a drink," Shannon responded, giving a page an especially aggressive slap. "I'm fine."

After St. John ordered their drinks, he grabbed the magazine and shoved it into the storage pocket. "Being antsy isn't going to get the plane to Orlando any faster. Try to relax."

"I don't want to relax." She reached for the magazine, but he swiped it away. It was easy for him to relax; it wasn't his son sitting in a strange place surrounded by thousands of strangers.

When their drinks arrived, St. John asked for a snack try, minus the pretzel sticks. He added an ice cube to Shannon's whiskey and swirled the glass before handing it to her. "Here, it will make you feel better."

"I don't want it," she said, taking hold of the drink. She sipped the cold, fiery liquid. "Will you check your phone and see if Tony sent an update? Please?"

"The FCC hasn't changed their rules about no cell use since we've been on board, so if you don't want to relax, at least finish your drink."

She gulped her drink and cast a greedy glance at his.

"Don't even try it," he said.

"Fine. What will we do if Justin sees Tony?"

"Don't worry about Tony. He's very good at what he does. I've used him enough to know."

She twirled her glass, making the ice cube spin. "When? I mean, why would you need a private investigator? Also, how are you here and not at work?"

"I'm the boss. Taking days off is one of the perks. Plus, I've hired people I can count on. To answer your first question, Marty and I used Tony during my last divorce."

Now she was intrigued. "You had your wife followed?"

"Let's talk about something else."

"Is there anything else I can do for you two?" The attendant asked when she delivered the snacks.

"Yes, may we have two blankets?" St. John asked.

Shannon took the package of Lorna Doone cookies he

offered. "Thank you for getting the blanket, but I'm not cold."

St. John ripped open a package of smoked almonds. "You might be."

She unbuckled her seat belt and shifted to face him. "Okay, now that you have your treats, it's time for you to share."

"I shared this morning. Isn't that enough for one day?"

"Too bad. Was your wife cheating on you?"

"No comment."

"Come on, St. John. We're stuck here for another three hours, and talking is about the only thing we can do."

He grinned and leaned her way. "We could join the mile-high club."

As much as she would have enjoyed the new membership, she stopped his hand before it got any further up her leg. "There are kids on board. Face it: talking is our only form of entertainment."

"Remember my fourth rule?"

"Is that the one about no second nights?"

"Nope, that's rule number three. Number four is the one about never allowing someone close enough to hurt me, which, if memory serves me, is your number-one rule."

"I thought that was number six. Wasn't number four about love? Anyway, I think it's too late for the close thing."

St. John raised an eyebrow and asked in his typical, pragmatic way, "What are you saying?"

"Look around. We're on a plane, flying to get my son. You've infiltrated my life. I have to accept that I broke my number-one rule. I've let you in, and at this point, you could do some serious damage." She opened the pack of cookies. It was the truth, only she'd left out the part about the rule having been broken back when they'd first met. Now she was wondering if she'd said too much. His expression, and silence, indicated the answer was yes. "I'm not saying I want you in my life," she included before indecision stopped her from speaking. "As you said last night, when Chad gets home, you and I are done."

"That's not what I said."

"Yes, it is."

He leaned her way and touched her lips, causing a thrill to ripple through her. Wanting to be with him was only sexual. She had to believe that because if she was wrong, that would mean...

"You weren't paying attention," St. John said. "My exact words were that I'll be with you until you get settled."

"That's a lie, and you know it. You said until Chad gets home."

His grin materialized and lingered. "Well, I meant until you get settled."

"What does that even mean?"

"It means I'll help you find a place to live, move you, and make sure Justin knows to stay away."

"And then?"

He slid his hand over the side of her face. "Then I need to step away."

It hadn't been what she wanted to hear, but she couldn't fault him for being honest—although his eyes didn't seem to agree. There was almost a plea for her to contradict him. Or was it wishful thinking on her part? Did it matter? He'd made his point.

"Thank you, but I don't need nor want your help. When we get home, feel free to pursue other avenues of entertainment."

She faced the window. It would be better if she focused on Chad and let go of idiotic, romantic ideas.

Chapter 31

*"It's better to lose your ego to the One you Love than to lose the
One you Love to your ego."*
John Keats

St. John removed the magazine Shannon had previously been beating up and started his own assault.

Shannon glanced at him. "You okay?"

"Yeah, why?" St. John said as he flipped a page too hard, tearing off a piece.

"Maybe because you're beating up a magazine. And don't say that I did it first. You're supposed to be the adult."

He shoved the magazine under his seat. "And why is that?"

"Because you're older. How old are you?"

"Old enough to know better."

"St. John, what's the matter? And don't say nothing's the matter. Are you angry with me for saying I don't want your help?"

"Let it drop, Shannon. I'm not mad." He signaled the flight attendant and ordered another drink. "Do you want something?"

"Water, please. I'm expecting you to hold Justin down while I gut him."

St. John's brow creased. "I thought you wanted to rip his throat out."

"The throat ripping is still on the table. The gutting comes after and before the disemboweling."

"I would never have guessed at this violent side to your personality. Does this have anything to do with Wicca?"

"Nope, the Wiccan creed states do no harm. This violent side comes from my maternal ancestors. The Müllers were known for their gangster moves."

He accepted his drink. "You could have warned me. I might have stayed away from you."

She faced him. "Would that have stopped you?"

"Not in the least," he replied and took a gulp of bourbon. Her fire excited him, made him feel alive.

"We still have to discuss the tickets," she said.

"I already told you I'm not taking your money."

"But you can't—"

"Yes," he said, meeting her eyes. "I can." He hadn't argued with all three of his wives as much as he'd done with her. And hadn't enjoyed himself half as much.

She knotted her fingers around his. "I never truly thanked you for what you're doing for Chad and me. I'm blessed to have you in my life."

The determination to walk away with his dignity flew out of the window, and he almost blurted out, 'Not blessed enough to want to keep me.' But then he remembered it had been he who'd started the beginning of their end, and so he kept his mouth shut.

"Are you sure you're okay?" she asked.

"I'm fine."

"Okay."

Shannon covered herself with the blanket and closed her eyes, and St. John finished his drink.

******

"It's Mickey." Shannon pointed out the taxi's window at a person standing in the street dressed like Mickey Mouse. "That was so cool. I am definitely bringing Chad down here for a vacation. Maybe around Christmas time. Or for my fortieth birthday."

"When is your birthday?"

"February."

"And?"

"And?"

"The date?"

"The twenty-ninth."

"You're a leapling?"

"Yeah, how did you know what we're called?"

"Someone very dear to me was a leapling. She was born in 1932. I knew there was a reason I was drawn to you."

"Save the sweet talk, St. John. You're only drawn to me because I have a vagina, and you know it." Drawn to her, ha. If he was so frigging drawn, then why didn't he want to be with her?

"I'm crushed you think so little of me." He answered the call coming into his cell phone.

She listened and quickly realized the person on the other end of the call was the private investigator. From St. John's side of the conversation, she gleaned that Justin, Shelby, and Chad were at the Mount Kilimanjaro roller coaster in the Animal Kingdom Park.

"Okay, we're nearing the main entrance now. Keep an eye on them, and we'll be there shortly, I hope. I have no idea how long it'll take us to get to you." St. John ended the call and repeated to her what he'd learned. A text came through, and he opened it, anger spreading across his face.

Shannon reached for the phone. "What's wrong? Is that a picture of Chad?"

St. John held the phone out of her reach. "I don't want you to flip out."

"Give me the fucking phone, St. John, or so help me—"

"That's exactly what I told you not to do."

She snatched the phone and studied the picture on the screen. Sure enough, Chad was alone on another bench, his knees drawn up to his chin. "That fucking moron. When I see him, I'm going to rip his balls off and feed them to him, and then I'm serving him his dick for dessert."

"Ouch, I'm glad you're not mad at me."

"Look at my son." She held the phone in front of St. John's face. She was back on the ledge and ready to take a swan dive. "Can you see what they're doing to my son?" she shouted. "Look."

St. John held the phone and her hand. "Pull it together," he said in a soft, calm voice.

"I am together. Watch me when I'm in front of Justin if you want to see what I look like when I'm not together."

"And that is why you will not be seeing him."

She yanked her hand away. "What do you mean I won't be seeing him? I damn well better see him."

"Not going to happen. I want you to take Chad to one of the other parks. Take him on a few rides. Tony and I will deal with Justin."

"No."

St. John placed his finger on her mouth. "I'm not giving you a choice. We don't need the Mickey Mouse brigade hauling our asses off to Loony Tune jail."

"Wrong company."

"Excuse me?"

"Loony Tunes is Warner Brothers, and if I want to confront my husband, you have nothing to say about it. You don't own me."

"I don't think I own you, but I am much calmer than you right now. My dime, my rules."

"You and your stinking rules." She scowled at him. "I'd like to smash every single one of them."

'You're off to a good start' he was about to say when the taxi driver said, "*Mèt, nou isit la.*"

The driver pointed at a sign welcoming them to Disney World, and a line of cars.

Shannon opened her mouth, but St. John patted her hand and, leaned his face through the divider where he spoke in a hushed voice.

The driver gave a rapid reply in Creole, flipped on his flashers, and zipped around the line of traffic waiting to pass under the blue-and-yellow arch welcoming everyone to *The Happiest Place on Earth*.

"You speak Creole?" Shannon whispered.

"I've picked up bits and pieces of different languages; the construction business attracts a variety of non-English-speaking individuals."

The taxi driver drove along the road's shoulder, stopped and had a heated exchange with a security guard, and then zipped the cab onto an access road where he finally delivered Shannon and St. John to the Animal Kingdom main entrance.

St. John handed the driver four hundreds, and said, "*Mesi zanmi'm*."

"Now what did you say?" Shannon asked while St. John presented their passes at the ticket window.

"I said 'thank you.' Let's go."

They asked for directions and raced to the Expedition Everest entrance.

"He's over this way." St. John took Shannon by the hand and pulled her toward a gift shop.

She spotted a short, intimidating-looking man standing next to a bench on which sat an elderly couple, and one sad child.

"Chad."

She ran to him.

Chad looked up, and his face brightened. He climbed onto the bench and waved his arms. "Mama, I'm here." He leapt straight for Shannon and wrapped his arms and legs around her. "Mama, you came."

"Yes, baby, I came."

Chad pressed his lips to her ear. "I'm sorry, I had an accident."

"It's okay, sweetie." She let joyful tears flow from her eyes and kissed his filthy cheeks. He was in her arms, and she was never letting ago. Except to clean him. "We'll find a bathroom."

Chad leaned away and held her cheeks with his sticky hands. "I tried to hold it. Daddy yelled at me. I tried, honest."

Her heart broke as she studied round eyes much too serious for a six-year-old. "Oh, sweetie, it's okay. Accidents happen. That's why they're called accidents." She drew him into another strong embrace.

"Look, Mama, Coach John is here." He pointed over her shoulder and shimmied from her arms. "Coach John, hi. It's me, Chad."

St. John crouched to Chad's level. "Hey, Chad, you okay?"

Chad looked up at Shannon. "Am I okay, Mama?"

"Yes, darling, you're okay," she replied.

Chad stood between Shannon and St. John and pointed at a nearby ice cream vendor. "Mama, can I have a Mickey head?"

"A what?" Shannon looked where Chad was pointing and nodded. "Of course. In fact, I think we all should have ice cream Mickey heads."

St. John held out his hand and said, "Come on, Chad, let's go buy some while your mom talks to my friend."

Shannon turned her attention to the Tony, the private investigator, and offered a sincere, "Thank you. I'll never be able to repay you for what you've done for me."

"Don't thank me thank St. John, he's the one who put me here. I'm just glad I could help. So, how long you two been together?"

Shifting her gaze back to the ice cream vendor and the man holding her son's hand, Shannon half whispered, "We're not together."

"Hey, sorry, I didn't mean to imply... I know you're married and all, it's just that... Aw, shit, just drop it; my wife is always telling me to keep my yapper shut."

Shannon grinned at Tony and laughed. "Don't be silly,

you're his friend and you're just curious. However..." She let a shrug end her thought and took a step in the direction of her son who was running her way, a chocolate-smeared grin on his face

"Mama, Coach John said he's gonna take me to see the world."

"The world?"

St. John handed her a Mickey head while he licked at the remnants of vanilla ice cream on his own stick.

"You made short work of that," Shannon said. "You can have mine, but I want one of his ears. And what's this about showing my son the world?"

"The ride. Chad said he wants to go on the big world ride, and I said I'd take him." St. John added his cocky grin and held the edge of Mickey's ear to Shannon's lips. "You can come too, little girl."

"You mean the Small World ride?" She gratefully accepted his offering and sighed as the smooth, chocolate coating melted along her tongue. Mickey ears ruled.

"Small, bit, what's the difference?" St. John added a shrug and devoured the remainder of Mickey's head.

She couldn't hold back her laughter. "You're a brave man, St. John. You have no idea what you're getting yourself into."

"I'm sure you'll tell me. However, right now, I want you to take Chad out of the park. Go to the world ride and wait for me, please."

Tony tapped his watch at St. John, and she instinctively pulled Chad against her legs, half burying him in the folds of her skirt. "What's wrong?"

"Relax. Nothing's wrong," St. John said.

"Please stop telling me to relax."

"When you relax, I'll stop." St. John spoke to Chad. "Hey, pal, will you stay with my friend while I talk to your mom?"

Chad scanned Tony and slowly faced Shannon. "Do I have to?"

"It will only be for a few minutes, munchkin." She wiped at his face and opened her wallet. "This is forty dollars. Hold on to it and go into the store with Mr. Tony and buy yourself a toy. I'll be right outside here with Coach John, okay?"

Tony leaned over and held out his hand. "Hey, Chad. My name's Tony, and I have a little bud just like you. His name's Oscar."

"Is he a grouch too?"

Their conversation about Sesame Street filtered away as they walked into the gift shop, leaving Shannon to continue wondering what had suddenly gone wrong.

Chapter 32

*"When you feel like giving up, remember why you held on for
so long in the first place."*
Unknown

Touching Shannon's elbow, St. John nodded to a shady area. "There's nothing to worry about. I don't want you here when Justin comes back, that's all."

"No," she responded with a hearty level of conviction. "I already told you I want to see him." Her refusal bordered on a tantrum, with foot stamping and arm crossing. "I have things I want to say."

"That's why I don't want you here. Wait until he's back in Wexford, and then you can rip his dick off."

"No."

St. John ran both of his hands through his hair as he released a low groan. "For once, would you do something I ask without arguing? *Please*."

Shannon folded her arms. She tried to come up with a reason she should remain, but every scenario involved Chad getting upset. "Fine. I'll take Chad over to Magic Kingdom. That's where the world is."

"Thank you. I'll text you when I'm heading there. Don't go on the big world ride without me."

"Small World ride."

"Right, got it. Just don't go on it without me."

"Okay, we'll see you at *It's a Small World*, but don't say I didn't warn you."

He held her waist and placed an easy kiss on her lips.

"Mama. You're kissing Coach John."

Turning her attention to Chad, she scrambled for an explanation and, coming up empty, said, "Hey, let's go over to Magic Kingdom."

Chad held up a plastic bag. "But I want to show you what I got."

"You can show me on the bus."

She offered a second thank-you to Tony and a nod to St. John, and turned to walk with Chad in the direction of the main gate. They struggled to maneuver through the congested walkways. She wanted to stop in a bathroom and clean him, but when a passerby stepped on Chad's foot, he wailed like one of the monkeys in the park, so she carried him the remainder of the way to the bus stop. He would have to remain dirty a little longer. When they were safely on the bus heading to Magic Kingdom, she let him show her what he'd gotten with her forty dollars.

"That's it? Forty bucks, and all you got was a bathing suit?"

"It has Mickey on it."

"I see that but...okay...great. Did you try it on?"

"No, but Mr. Tony said it will fit. Can I wear it?"

"You can't very well undress here on the bus. When we get to the park, you can change in one of the bathrooms." She frowned at the wide stain in the crotch. "Those shorts have seen better days, anyway."

"I sorry I had an accident."

"Sweetie, it's okay, really. When people are scared, they sometimes have accidents. It's perfectly normal. Here, sit on Mama's lap and take a nap."

A thin worry line creased Chad's forehead. "Am I a bad boy?"

"Absolutely not. Why would you ask that?"

"Daddy said I was a bad boy when he spanked me."

"Your dad spanked you?"

"Ah-uh. When I had my accident. I tried to hold it, but I was scared."

She kissed his forehead and rocked him. "You're not a bad boy. When we get to Magic Kingdom, I'll buy you clean undies and socks and shorts and get you cleaned up."

"I want to wear my bathing shorts."

"Okay, I won't buy shorts. Now take a nap."

It didn't take long before Chad was asleep. Despite the vents blasting cold air into the bus, sweat seeped through her blouse from his wet hair. She wiped his damp forehead with her hand and tried to figure out what St. John planned on saying to Justin. Calculating Justin's response was easy—he'd flip out and start pointing his frigging finger. If he swung a fist, would St. John respond? Seeing Justin face down would be worth the price of admission. And if he was knocked out cold, she'd have an easier time of gutting him. Too bad the Wiccan creed was such a killjoy; just thinking about disemboweling Justin was probably costing massive amounts of karma chips.

What *would* she do when she did come face to face with him? She could see herself slapping him. Maybe adding a knee to the groin. How badly did a head butt hurt the person delivering it?

Sick of thinking about doing things to Justin she wouldn't actually do, she rearranged Chad and reached in her bag for her phone to place a call to Martin.

"Hi, Shannon," Jayla said. "Marty's in a meeting. Are you in Florida?"

"Yes. I have Chad with me."

"Great. Marty is going to be pleased. I have good news too. Your paperwork is with the court, and copies were given to Justin's lawyer. You have officially filed for divorce. And I also filed the TPO, which will protect you through Saturday."

"Wow. That was fast, but seriously, you and I both know restraining orders don't work. I'd rather move and get it over with. Do you know if I can buy a house before the divorce is finalized?"

"Sure you can. However, by New Hampshire law, Justin will own half of it. I'll have Marty call you. When everything calms down, let's go out for some fun. My treat. Unless St. John would mind me taking you barhopping."

Shannon stammered. St. John kissing her in the conference room must have had the law office buzzing. "He doesn't... We're not... It's complicated."

"When it comes to St. John, things usually are. Call if you need anything."

"I will, thank you." She tucked her phone away and stared out the window. The happiest place on earth was like a small sovereign nation inside of Orlando, which posed the question as to which Disney characters comprised the ruling party. Maybe Simba kept things orderly by threatening to eat anyone who didn't follow his rules. If so, it would be an easy way to dispose of Justin. Chomp, chomp, goodbye.

"Mama, why are you forcing Daddy?"

Chad knelt on a chair outside Main Street Bakery, a sweet roll in one hand and a Donald Duck cup in the other. Shannon sat opposite him, her plastic cup of iced tea dripping with condensation from the scalding heat. She'd like to revisit Disney, but, note to self, not in June. Or July. Or August. Maybe it was the humidity that made the air so oppressive, but damn, she was finding it hard to breathe. Sitting in the shade didn't help either. She'd wanted to stay in the cafe, but Chad had insisted on sitting outside, so he could watch for Mickey. It was in this fugue state that she tried to figure out what he was talking about.

"I'm sorry, sweetie. Forcing Daddy to do what?"

"I don't know." Chad set his pastry on a napkin and licked at his fingers. "He said you were forcing him."

"Forcing him, forcing him..." She repeated the phrase two more times in her head before light dawned. "Divorcing him?"

"Ah-huh. Why are you forcing Daddy?"

She nibbled her bottom lip as she figured out what to say. She could start by telling him his father was a jerk for even mentioning the divorce. How did Justin expect a six-year-old to grasp something as complex as divorce? More likely, he hadn't cared.

"Honey, what did Daddy say, exactly?"

Chad set his cup on the table. "Am I in trouble?"

"No, sweetie, no. What gives you that idea? Mama is just asking what Daddy said. Did he tell you not to say anything?"

Chad folded himself into a neat ball, his feet tucked under his bum. "Ah-huh."

She dragged his chair close to hers and lifted him onto her lap. "You know we have no secrets, and I promise you're not in trouble. You can tell me."

"But Daddy will be mad at me, and he'll punish me."

"Sweetie, I don't want you to keep secrets from me, okay? Even if Daddy tells you to. You and me, we're a team. Please tell me what he said."

"'Kay. He said you won't let him live with us anymore." Chad wiggled around and straddled her lap, where he played with the damp hair clinging to her neck. "Is that true?"

There was no easy way to clearly explain divorce to a child, no matter the age, but for a five-soon-to-be-six-year-old, it was especially challenging. Chad was old enough to reason through things he found confusing—maybe not to where he understood all the ins and outs but surely to the point where one plus one equaled two. But understanding why she was leaving his father wasn't black and white. He might end up thinking she was an evil monster who'd cast his father aside.

She licked her napkin and wiped around his mouth. "Honey, you see... It's hard to explain, but... Well..." What was she trying to say? 'You're dad's a fucking loser, and he's been gaslighting me for years, and I hope that sticky bun was the balls because it cost as much as a week's groceries.'

Her cell phone vibrated against the table top, and she snatched it up.

I'm in the park. Where to?

She texted back their location. "Sweetie, Coach John is here. Keep an eye out for him. He should be walking by any minute now."

The discussion about the divorce could wait. It was time for some fun, Disney style.

Chapter 33

"Tis better to have loved and lost than
to never have loved at all."
Alfred Lord Tennyson

Chad dozed in the seat next to the airplane window, and Shannon held her hands to her face while St. John hummed "It's a Small World" and rattled the ice cubes in his glass.

Not able to take it any longer, Shannon said, "If you hum that song one more time, I'm going to feed your vocal cords to you."

St. John raised an eyebrow her way. "Wow, that's a lot of hostility for a woman who just spent time in the happiest place on earth. You should be filled with glee."

"I am filled with glee, so button it."

His response was a quiet chuckle.

"When are you going to tell me what you said to Justin?"

"When you ask nice." He lifted his drink and drained the alcohol.

She gritted her teeth. "Please tell me what happened. Is he coming home tomorrow?"

"That I don't know."

"Well, what did you say?"

"Before or after I punched him?"

She sensed the look of shock spreading on her face. "You didn't. Please tell me you didn't."

"I didn't, but I wanted to. I've run into men like him throughout my entire adult life, and even before that. Oh, I would have loved to deck him, but I didn't."

"I'm sorry." She didn't know what she was apologizing for; it had just seemed like the best thing to say.

"I'm a big boy. I can take it. He did have a few choice threats you might want to hear about, but you have to stay calm."

"I'm always calm," she said.

"Yeah, like a hurricane."

"No, thanks. You do know that anything Justin told you is a lie. He'll do the exact opposite."

"I hope so."

He set his glass down, reached for the last bag of almonds, and held them her way. She shook her head and he emptied the entire contents into his mouth and chewed. When he finished, he sighed and stretched out his legs.

His stalling worried her. "Please don't drag this out. Just tell me," she urged.

"He's going to fight you for custody of Chad."

"That's it?" She couldn't help but scoff. "Let him try. The courts always side with the mother." The longer St. John remained mute, the greater her confidence eroded to where she was almost begging him to agree with her. "It's true. I've done nothing wrong, and Justin's been unfaithful. They have to let me keep Chad. Right?"

"I don't know. You'd have to ask Marty. But don't worry. I think I set Justin straight."

"You don't get to do this, St. John."

"Do what?"

"Handle Justin. You're not in my life on a permanent basis."

"As you keep reminding me."

"As you've reminded me." She shrugged off his arm when he tried to slip it over her shoulders. "I am so done with Justin—and you."

"Meaning what?"

"You're smart. You figure it out." If she couldn't strike at Justin, she'd go after the closest target she had.

He leaned close. "For Christ sake, Shannon, have I deserted you? Are you alone right now? Please tell me because I seem to think I'm on a plane with you and Chad instead of at a job site."

"I didn't ask you to come to Disney. I could have done it myself."

"Yes, you could have. What you seem to be missing is I wanted to be here."

"You just said you'd rather be working."

"Don't twist my words. Save that little ploy for when you're talking to your husband."

She forced herself to meet his cold stare. "Then why *are* you here? Why care what happens to me or Chad?"

He crumpled the empty almond package and sent it skimming like a hockey puck across his tray. "You're smart. You figure it out."

"What are you saying, St. John? That you love me?"

There, she'd given him an opening. All he had to do was take the bait and run with it. She just needed to hear him say the words, or some facsimile of them. He touched her cheek, and she readied her response. 'I've fallen for you too. Let's fall together.' Enough of the is-she-isn't-she crap; she was in love with him. There, she'd admitted it to herself. And she was ready to tell him...after he told her.

"The last person you need in your life is me. You'll only get hurt."

Those were not the words she wanted to hear. Not betraying any sign of disappointment, she said, "Thank you for all that you've done for me, but I never said I needed you in my life, and I'm sorry to disappoint you—I don't care a fig about you."

She swung away and looked at Chad. She *was* sorry—sorry she'd given in to her desires and slept with him; sorry she'd allowed herself to fall for him; sorry she'd broken her rule about never letting someone close again to hurt her; sorry she hadn't run from Justin back when she had a chance; sorry for everything she'd done that put her where she was at that very moment. Sorry, sorry, sorry, sorry.

******

St. John asked the flight attendant for two drinks of water with lemon. He gave one to Shannon and other he nursed as he sorted through what he'd said to Justin.

'Let me tell you about a man I know. This guy is a weak fuck who wanted to punish his wife for what he saw as her betrayal at leaving him. So, what did the low-life do? He kidnapped his own son. He used an innocent child in his sickening game of revenge. But there's a problem the guy didn't foresee. There's another man who cares for the mother, and the child, and that man will do whatever it takes to protect them. Do I make myself clear?'

He would have added a more direct threat if Tony hadn't pulled him away.

When the waters arrived, St. John handed one of the glasses to Shannon. She remained with the back of her head facing him, so he set the water on her tray and settled against his seat to ride out the remainder of the flight.

He didn't have the words in his vocabulary that would get her to understand what he was feeling. He didn't want another failure. He'd given his last wives everything they'd wanted and then some. The sex had been fucking awesome. He'd taken them on trips, built them each a big-ass house, and they'd still left him for someone else. Granted, he'd never loved the last two, but still, with three marriages and three divorces under his belt, he had to know when it was time to take his bat and glove and go home.

St. John huffed and shifted in his seat.

Shannon cast a dirty look his way. "What's your problem?"

"My problem? What's yours?" He tried to make his question sound angry while keeping his voice low. Not an easy task.

"Me? I'm not the one squirming around like I have worms in my pants."

"It's ants in my pants, not worms, and I'm not squirming." As long as they were speaking again, he needed to know one thing. "Why did you stay with Justin?" He must have sprouted two heads because that was the look she was giving him, like he had two heads that she wanted to rip off.

"What?"

"I asked—"

"I heard you."

"Then why did you...? Just drop it." He raised his glass and emptied the water.

Shannon rearranged herself so her entire body faced his way. "What exactly do you want to know?"

"I asked a simple question. You've hung around despite the fact that he treats you like shit. You even moved to New Hampshire with him. My wives walked away from me for far less."

"Are you wondering why your wives left you even though you're this great guy, and I've stayed with a jerk like Justin?"

"Not exactly how I would phrase it but, yeah, something like that."

"I can't tell you why your wives left, St. John. Although, as I get to know you, I'm beginning to understand."

He rattled the cubes in his glass, and what could be a chuckle rumbled in his chest. "Cute. Thanks." As much as it sucked, she wasn't far from the truth. The only common denominator in all his marriages had been him. It didn't take a genius to do the math.

"That was a low blow," she said. "I'm sorry. I can't speak for your wives. I don't know why they left you. As for my staying with Justin, you have to remember I had Chad."

He started to say that having a child doesn't mean a woman has to stay with an abusive man but paused. If he was able to ask his mother, would she offer the same reason for having stayed with his father? He would never know the truth, and he didn't want to attack Shannon, but he had to clear something up. "You stayed with him because of his money, didn't you?"

The shock that registered on her face was like a slap to his. It had been a rotten thing to ask, but he'd needed to know.

"You think I'm that shallow?"

"I don't but... Then tell me the real reason you've stayed with Justin. You're not a fool. You had to know keeping Chad in that environment wasn't good for him."

She bit her bottom lip, which was a signal she was thinking. He'd give her the time she needed.

Instead of providing St. John with an answer, Shannon twisted away and looked out the window.

The sun was shining through the glass as the plane traveled over a bank of clouds.

"Do you think it's raining under all these clouds?" she asked.

"I don't care if the sky is falling." He reached around and cupped her chin, directing her to look at him. "You're leaving something out. Something important. Why, after six years, are you so courageous that you're willing to try living on your own with Chad?"

She glared at him, but it didn't daunt him from pressing.

"Why *now*? What happened to give you this newfound courage to stand up to Justin?" He was leading her. He knew it, and he hoped she understood what he wanted to hear.

The smile started out slowly, the corners of her mouth turning upward a fraction at a time until he found himself looking at a full grin, only it had nothing to do with joy.

"You want me to say that I left Justin because of you," she said.

"I never—"

"Cut the bull, St. John. I can see right through you. You want me to tell you the reason I've left Justin is because you came into my life."

"I..." Her narrowed brows shut him up. Yeah, he wanted to hear that, so sue him. He wasn't made of stone. He wanted her to need him as much as he needed her.

Chilling words fell his way.

"I'm sorry to disappoint you, but you have nothing to do with my reasons. You want to know why now and not one, two, three years ago? I stayed because I was a coward."

She turned away, leaving him in silence to do battle with the voices in his head.

Other women had come and gone—some wanting his heart, some wanting his cash, and some wanting both. None leaving a lasting impression.

Until he'd met her.

Something inside of him had snapped that first day he met her.

And here he was, in love with her but too fucking afraid to tell her.

She wasn't the coward.

He was.

Chapter 34

"The best thing we can do when it's raining is to let it rain."
Henry Wadsworth Longfellow

"Mama, Mama, wake up."

Lying under the covers of the master bed, Shannon opened her eyes. "Sweetie, we just got home. Let Mama sleep a little more, okay?"

"It's Daddy."

Daddy? Was he calling from Disney or had he decided to leave Florida and follow them home? Her heart seized as she stared at the phone Chad held out to her. She wasn't ready to do battle with Justin.

"Daddy wants to take me camping. I have to pee." He shoved the phone into her hand and ran into the bathroom.

Was she still sleeping, or had Chad said Justin was taking him camping? Chad hadn't seemed particularly happy about the news, nor had he seemed upset. Whether he was or he wasn't, the bowels of Hades would be icy cold the day she let Justin take Chad on an outing. He'd be lucky if she let him take Chad into another room of the house.

"PICK UP THE GODDAMN PHONE."

Justin's voice blasted through the speaker and looped around her neck, cutting off oxygen to her brain. She squinted at the screen. She wasn't ready to deal with him. She'd expected a call from him but not at four-thirty in the morning.

Hanging up was an option although he'd just call back. She could toss the phone out the window. Most likely, he'd still find a way to reach her. Her last option was to suck it up and talk to him. At least he wasn't standing in front of her.

"SHANNON."

"I'm here. No need to shout."

"Where the fuck have you been?"

"Justin, you woke us up. It's early."

"Who cares? I'm coming home tomorrow around two. Some of the guys are taking their kids up to Twin Oaks this weekend, and I'm taking Chad. I'll pick him up at—"

"No."

"What did you say?"

"I said no. Tomorrow is graduation and the end-of-the-school-year BBQ. So, no, you cannot take him camping. And besides, Saturday is his birthday, or have you forgotten?"

"My, my, aren't we brave when you don't have your boyfriend to hide behind? Now let me tell you what's going to happen: I'll be by to get Chad tomorrow afternoon at three. Have him ready and all his gear packed."

"No, I won't. You can't take him. You tried to steal him once, and I'm not giving you another shot at it."

"Funny you should say 'shot.' I also want my gun."

"I don't have it."

"Who does?"

"I turned it in at the station."

"That was stupid. You might have needed it for protection."

She'd be a fool to let him intimidate her. "Goodbye, Justin. Next time, call my lawyer."

"Whoa, whoa, whoa. Don't you dare hang up on me."

She disconnected the call and noticed Chad in the doorway.

"All set, munchkin? Come back to bed. I bought you a new book."

Chad's face lit up. "Where is it?"

"It's downstairs in my office. Let's go down, and I'll take Jasper to pee, and then we'll have hot chocolate and read." She double sighed at the rain coming down in nearly horizontal sheets. "After I dry off, we'll have some hot chocolate and read."

"Yay, hot chocolate and a new book. Let's go, Jasper."

She lowered the phone's volume and followed Chad, watching him jump from step to step. He wasn't singing. That was okay. At least he wasn't telling her he hated her like he had done last night.

She still wasn't clear what had set him off. He'd slept through the entire flight and the drive home, only to wake up when she'd begun dressing him in his PJs. Once he'd let loose, there had been nothing she could do to reverse the meltdown. She'd tried everything in her motherly arsenal short of promising she'd buy him a pony. If there'd been bourbon handy, she might have poured him a shot—and several for herself.

In the end, under the power of his own exhaustion, he'd quieted down, but that hadn't come soon enough.

'I hate you.'

Three words meant to transfer his suffering to her. She gladly accepted them, wishing she could have responded that, presently, she wasn't too fond of herself.

******

St. John propped his feet on his desk and watched the tall pines swaying in the wind. Not much happened in construction in weather like this so, basically, another day where he wouldn't be at a job site. He could go into the office, but spending the day inside four walls might likely drive him crazy. Physical labor, hard enough to break his back, was what he craved. Pain so intense the loss of control he felt wouldn't stand a chance.

The text sat ready: *How are you and Chad today?* Nothing Shannon could misinterpret for anything other than friendly concern.

He'd typed the damn thing over half an hour ago but still hadn't hit send.

This wasn't him, questioning his thoughts and actions. He was a decisive man, even when it came to women. He didn't pussyfoot around.

By the time he was seventeen he'd had more notches in his belt than all the other guys on the football team. He never second-guessed his decision to go steady with Coleen. And when they found out she was pregnant, he'd jumped at the chance to marry her. He wanted her to be his wife, and he'd wanted the baby.

The baby.

He carried his coffee cup over to the sidebar, where he added a shot of bourbon and stood looking out into the glooming rain. The baby's death had been tough on them both. He hadn't known what to say or do. He still wouldn't. What do you say to a woman who's lost her child? 'Sorry for the way things turned out. Better luck next time'? Coleen should have told him what to do, helped him understand. He would have gone through fire for her. But, as the story always goes, she found what she needed in his best buddy's arms.

Every Christmas the newsletter arrived, offering a glimpse into their lives: vacations to the Caribbean, a houseful of grand-kids—Yup, Coleen and Barry had hit pay dirt.

He saluted the air. "You're welcome."

The invitations still came—birthdays, christenings. She always included him in the celebration, and he always responded with a polite decline. One time he'd actually said he'd come. It had been two years ago, for their twenty-fifth wedding anniversary.

'Please come. If it hadn't been for you, Barry and I would never have found each other.'

Who could resist such a glowing invitation? Thanks for having the emotional range of a block of concrete, St. John, and forcing me into your buddy's arms. There'll be cake.

She'd been happy when he said he'd come, and he'd meant it, too. It would have been great to see them—a burying of the proverbial hatchet. He could have even brought a sexy plus-one to prove he was over getting trampled, but then he realized they'd see through the con, and he'd end up looking like a rich loser who had to buy affection. 'Poor St. John,' they'd whisper. 'Still doesn't have anyone who loves him.'

Yeah, well, to hell with them. He'd learned his lesson and had no desire to put himself through the meat grinder again. Besides, there wasn't a woman with a strong enough backbone to withstand his fucking truckload of baggage.

Except for Shannon.

Her features were etched across his brain: the green eyes that flashed when she was mad to the pattern of her freckles. And her smile. Damn, he could get used to seeing that smile every morning when he woke up and every night before he fell asleep. Plus, she could toss back a shot of bourbon like a pro, and she didn't let him get away with any shit. And the way she looked at him, as if she couldn't get enough of him, blew his mind.

And, true to his nature, he'd gone and fucked it all up.

He flopped into his chair. On the corner of the desk stood a silver frame containing the only picture he had of his adoptive mother. If he lost the photograph, it wouldn't matter. Over the years he'd memorized it down to the tiniest detail, to the number of rosebuds on the neckline of the yellow sundress she wore. He still felt the press of her hand on his shoulder as he smiled at the camera. He'd been nine in the photo and Malcolm twelve: him on one side, Malcolm on the other, and her caught in the middle.

He remembered the day being God-awful humid. He also remembered the sweetness of the lemonade she'd made as vividly as if he'd just taken a sip. That night, in the stifling heat of his and Malcolm's bedroom, they'd lain awake listening to the sounds the outside insects made as they beat against the window screen. In that stuffy heat, they made a pact to never let anything come between them.

They'd even carved their oath into the windowsill and had added two bloody thumbprints.

Blood brothers for life.

And now they weren't speaking.

How on God's green fucking earth could he hope to give Shannon and Chad his love when he withheld the emotion from the one person to whom he'd promised solidarity?

The short answer was he couldn't. He had to rectify his relationship with Malcolm or walk away from Shannon.

Too many people in the world were afraid to make the first move—he refused to be one of them for one second longer.

He pressed the number stored in his phone.

"Macy, Perry, and Sullivan. How may I direct your call?"

"Hi, this is Adam St. John. May I speak with Attorney Sullivan?"

"Hold on, please."

While he waited, he walked into the kitchen and poured a fresh mug of coffee. The receptionist came back on the line. "I'm sorry, Mr. St. John, but Attorney Sullivan stepped out of the office. May I take a message?"

Malcolm wasn't going to make this easy for him—which St. John had already known. "Look, I appreciate you're just doing your job, but I want you to tell Mal... Attorney Sullivan to pick up the phone."

"He's not—"

"I disagree. I'll wait. Thanks."

He hadn't had time to blink before his brother's angry voice got on the line. "Make this snappy, St. John. I'm busy."

"That's not a very nice way to greet the brother you haven't spoken to in ten years."

"You're not my brother."

"Oh, sorry, half-brother."

"What do you want?"

St. John scratched the new hairs growing on his chin. The urge to end the call was almost too strong to ignore, but he'd lose everything if he didn't at least try.

An aggressive "I'm waiting" cut through the phone.

"How's Bev and the kids?" St. John asked.

"Bev passed the bar, and both the boys are new fathers. Is this why you called? To catch up on my family?"

"Tell Bev I said congratulations. Is she going to join your firm? You two would make a cool power couple."

"Not likely. She's going to do pro bono work for the down-trodden. No money in that kind of law, but it'll keep her busy. Thanks for calling. Have a nice life."

"Stop being a dick, Malcolm. I called because I'd like us to bury the hatchet."

"If we're burying it in your skull, I'm all for it."

"Funny guy. I'm serious. We've been through too much in our lives to let some petty bullshit come between us. What you heard wasn't—"

"Is this how you eat crow, St. John, by dredging up the past and pointing your finger at me?"

"Would you let me finish? Meredith loved us both equally. I didn't—"

"I'm her biological son, not you."

"I know that. I didn't steal her away from you."

"You tried."

"Oh, cut the crap, Malcolm. You know what I was going through at the time. My father had died, then my mother, and next I found out Merry and my father were... If it hadn't been for her taking me in, who knows where I'd be now? She saved me; you both saved me. You and I, we made a pact."

St. John stood by his patio door and watched the rain. Why did relationships have to be so goddamn impossible for him? He could negotiate multi-million dollar projects but was inca-pable of retaining a connection with another human being.

"Tell me, St. John, does this call have anything to do with my putting Mom's house on the market?"

"This has nothing to do with the house."

"Sure, and I piss wine."

"That's a neat trick. Must come in handy at parties." His brother's quiet snicker heartened him to continue. "We're not getting any younger, and the truth is I miss you, man. You're my brother. We're family, and we're all we've got." He was intrigued to hear Malcolm's response.

"You're alone, not me."

Yup, his half-brother was still a prick. "I didn't say you were alone. I meant you and I are the only ones left of Merry's family. Tell me, do you think she'd be happy with us fighting?"

The call ended.

"I'll never make that mistake again." He was carrying his mug to the office when his phone rang. "Now what?" he said into the device.

"I'm having a party this weekend to celebrate Bev passing the bar. Come tomorrow, and we'll talk. I'll text you the address to our place in the Hampton's."

"Great, what can I bring?" he asked the severed call. "Prick," he added to no one except himself.

Chapter 35

*"Truth can be stated in a thousand different ways, yet each
one can be true."*
Swami Vivekananda

"You two didn't have to come over. Chad and I are fine."
Shannon set a tray of three mugs and a plate of cookies on the
coffee table.

"We'd be piss-poor friends if we didn't," Dee said, accepting
the mug Shannon offered. "I'm really sorry for doubting you,
Shan. Justin is a fucking jerk. If Jeff took the kids, I'd castrate
him." Pointing a biscotti at Shannon, she added, "I hope your
lawyer cleans him out."

Peg bit into a cookie and moaned. "I love these. What are
they called again?"

"Honey-lavender."

"Yum. Anyway, Dee's right: Justin sucks. I wish I had gotten your message Tuesday. I would have come over. How did
you get through the night?"

Dee agreed with Peg. "I'm sorry too. My phone died, and I
hadn't realized it."

"It's okay," Shannon said. "I got drunk and passed out."
She thought it best to leave out the part about St. John taking
care of her. The less said, the better. Besides, no sense getting
Dee going. Chad was home, and St. John was history. She'd
hoped he would have texted or something, just to check on
Chad if nothing else but not a peep. Maybe... "Hang on, I'm
going to check my phone." She ran up the steps and into her
bedroom. She hadn't heard the text come through because
she'd turned down the phone's volume.

How are you and Chad today?

His text had arrived two hours ago. The guy must have

though she was a bitch for not responding. As she walked down the staircase, she texted, *Sorry, I had the ringer off on my phone. We're fine, thank you for asking.* Then she quickly typed, *How are you?* and hit send.

Dee zeroed in on Shannon's actions. "Who are you texting?"

"Leeann," Shannon lied. Damn, she'd forgotten to text Leeann back.

"Yeah, what's up with that?" Peg said. "She's done a complete one-eighty. Justin's little stunt rattled her enough that she's now human. And..." Peg waved a biscotti at Shannon. "She's now your biggest fan. Does this mean we can't make fun of her name anymore?"

"Whatever we call her," Shannon said as she sat down, "I'm just glad she's not out for my blood anymore. Do you know she's even taken it upon herself to organize Chad's birthday party?"

Peg groaned. "Yes. All day yesterday with the texts: Have I heard from you? Where should we have the party? What kind of cake does Chad like? My God, she was a royal pain in my ass."

"Be grateful you got texts," Dee said. "She *called* me. We'd hang up and boom, another call. I liked it better when she hated you, Shan."

"Hold on. I forgot to text her back."

Shannon typed a quick message and hit send. She realized her mistake from the hardened set of Dee's mouth.

"You just texted her," Dee said.

"I, um, meant to say I needed to add something to my text of before." Shannon quickly turned to Peg. "Thanks again for taking care of Jasper."

"Aw, it was fine. When I came over to get him, St. John's guys were here fixing the door. Did Justin break it in?"

"No, I... That was from when I couldn't get in the house."

"Wow, what'd you use, a battering ram?"

Dee turned the topic to Chad. "Shan, have you told Chad about the divorce?"

"Yeah, I read him a book this morning. *The Three Bears Get A Divorce.*"

"Get out." Peg nearly chocked on her coffee. "Even the Three Bears have a lousy marriage?"

"Apparently," Shannon offered. "They realized they'd grown apart and decided it would be best for all of them if Mama and Papa Bear lived separately."

Peg leaned forward. "Do you think Chad understood?"

"There's no way to really know." Shannon gathered her hair and tied it back with a bungee she had around her wrist. Chad hadn't asked any questions except where Goldilocks was. "He just wanted to know what happened to Goldilocks." She puffed out her cheeks and exhaled as she pushed her bangs off her forehead. "Before he fell asleep, I heard him explaining about divorce to his toys, so something got through. I'm sure the other shoe will drop, especially when we move."

"Speaking of which…" Dee ran into the kitchen and returned with a folded piece of paper. "Do you guys realize it's still pouring outside? I hope they take the kids into the gym for recess. Otherwise, they'll be bouncing off the walls when they get home." She handed the sheet to Shannon. "I found you a temporary place to live if you're interested."

"A condo?" Shannon said. "I don't want to buy a condo. Plus, I can't right now."

"I said *temporary*. Every month this place doesn't sell, the owner gets all over me. I keep telling him to lower his asking price but, noooo, I'm just the realtor. He doesn't want to sign a year rental agreement, and because I'm showing it, whoever lives there needs to stay super clean and clutter free. You'd have to live like a mouse and not disturb anything. Oh, and disappear for a few hours when I get a showing appointment.

Interested?"

Peg snatched the paper. "Shan, this is perfect."

"Maybe, but what do I do with my stuff?"

"I have a moving company I recommend to sellers," Dee said. "They do storage too. I've already called them, and they can come by here, pack, and move you in one day."

"But..." Shannon's lower lip received a steady assault from her teeth. As she chewed on the already tender skin, she worried. How would Chad react to moving? And what about all the stuff she and Justin owned together? What about her freezer?

"Shan." Peg came and knelt by the recliner. "You have no other choice. You said the restraining order expires Saturday, and when Justin returns, you can't stay here. This way, you'll have a place to live until something permanent comes along."

"But..." Shannon looked over the paper again. Everything was happening too frigging fast.

"Stop with the buts," Dee snapped. "Peg's right. When Justin gets home, if you're still living here, all holy hell is going to let loose."

"What about my herb garden? And Jasper? Can I bring him to the condo?"

"Shan, would you stop?" Dee's patience appeared to be thinning. "I thought you wanted to do this? What did you think—you could tell Justin you're divorcing him but still want live with him? You yourself said he told you to get out, and yes, you can bring Jasper, but you have to keep the place spotless."

Shannon took Dee's s scolding in stride. "You're right, but... Sorry, it's just that... How much does storage cost?"

Dee proudly added, "Thanks to my wicked good negotiating skills, I got the moving company to give you thirty days' credit. St. John would be proud of me." Dee grinned and settled into her corner of the loveseat. "Speaking of the devil, have you slept with him?"

Peg was quick with a swat to Dee's arm. "We agreed you would ask nice."

"I did ask nice."

Shannon picked at some cookie crumbs on her lap. "It's complicated," was all she could offer.

"What's so complicated? Either you have or you haven't."

Peg grinned at Shannon. "Is he as good as the rumors say?"

"Peg, stop." Dee leaned forward and zeroed in on Shannon. "Come on, spit it out. Yes or no?"

"Yes," Shannon responded. "I've slept with him, on more than one occasion too, and I'd do it again if he asked." She returned Peg's grin. "I don't know what the rumors say, but he's like a frigging machine."

Dee wrinkled her nose and covered her ears with her hands. "No details, please."

"This is so exciting." Peg clapped and then shoved her hands under her legs. "Sorry, I hope that didn't wake Chad."

Shannon cocked her head. She listened for Chad's voice. Satisfied he was still asleep, she said, "All good. As for St. John and me, we won't be seeing anymore of each other. He ended it on the return flight." She returned to her crumb collection. Last night, the thought had come to her that St. John didn't want to see her because of how messy things with Justin would most likely get. He didn't want to get dragged through the mud. Maybe when everything settled down...

"Shan, have you fallen for St. John?"

Any judgment Dee might have harbored seemed to be gone, and her question came across with empathy and caring.

"Yes."

"Have you told him?"

"No." Shannon transferred the crumbs to her hand. "I'd be an idiot to jump from a marriage into a rebound relationship.

Nothing ever comes of that."

"This isn't rebound, Shan."

Peg stared at Dee. "Who are you, and what have you done with Dee?"

"Yeah, seriously," Shannon said. "Why aren't you telling me 'I told you so'?"

Dee reached for the last cookie and broke it in half, offering one side to Peg and Shannon. "It's complicated, like you said."

Peg snatched the biscotti and popped the entire section into her mouth.

Meanwhile, Shannon remained staring at Dee. "I don't get it, Dee. What's happened that you've now changed your mind about me hooking up with St. John?"

"Oh, don't get me wrong. I'm not thrilled he slept with you, but this thing you've got going with him *is not rebound*."

Peg swallowed her mouthful of cookie. "I'm really confused."

"Think about it." Dee nodded to Shannon. "According to you, you left Justin, mentally and emotionally, a long time ago, right? Your mind has had plenty of time to get used to the idea of living without him. I would say you've been ready to meet someone for a while, and now you have. It's not rebound, Shan. It's real. Unfortunately, it's St. John, and despite him being a great guy, he's still the same man who's torpedoed every relationship he's ever had. He doesn't even talk to his brother."

Peg chimed in with, "That's not true. He's friends with you and me and his lawyer. Plus, Howard and Jeff like him. Anyway, Malcolm started the whole not-talking thing, not St. John."

Dee said, "Great, he has friends, but he still can't maintain a romantic relationship."

"Don't listen to her, Shan. Adam loved Coleen, and his other wives were bitches who were after his money. All he needs is someone who isn't going to trash his heart and who'll yank him back in line when he behaves like a child." Peg dropped to the floor and lay on her back. She tucked her heels close to her butt and pushed up on her feet and hands, contorting herself into a full wheel pose.

Shannon stood and added the mugs to the tray. "It's hard to take you seriously in, Peg, when you look like a human spider, but St. John made his decision, and there's nothing I can do about it."

"I'll have a talk with him and tell him—"

"Dee, just let it drop, okay?" Shannon said. "I'm fine, and besides, I have bigger problems to focus on."

She carried the tray into the kitchen and set it on the counter. Despite her protest, she wasn't going to lie to herself. She wasn't fine. She hated St. John being gone, but she'd been honest when she said she had a bigger problem, and soon it would be returning from Florida.

Chapter 36

"Sometimes your mind needs more time to accept what your heart already knows."
Anonymous

Thursday ended without incident, and bright, sparkling sunshine announced the start of Friday. Shannon lay in her bed, the birds outside the bedroom windows doing their best to keep her from dozing back to sleep. The incessant chittering didn't seem to bother Chad, who was still asleep. She toyed with the idea of keeping him home from school but knew it wouldn't be fair. According to Dee and Peg, the entire baseball field would be taken over for the end-of-year celebration. Chad had to be there.

"Munchkin, time to wake up." She stroked his hair, and his eyelids fluttered open. "Good morning, sleepyhead. Ready for your last day of kindergarten?"

"Morning, Mama. I want to stay with you."

"Why, sweetie?"

"Daddy might take me again."

"Daddy's not going to take you."

Chad snuggled close and shook his head. "I don't want to go. Please."

It was super easy to envision herself letting him stay home. Hiding for one day had been enough. Now they both had to face the world. How else would they learn to survive in it?

Jasper leaned his muzzle on the bed's edge, his tail wagging, and licked Chad's face.

"See," she pointed out. "Jasper wants you to go to school too. He knows you'll have fun at the party."

"Party?" Chad sat up. "What party?"

"The school party. Remember, for the end of school?"

"I didn't miss it?"

"No, silly, it's today. And tomorrow's your birthday."

"I didn't miss my birfday?"

"Nope. After your baseball game, we're going to have a huge party for you at the mini-golf place."

"Yay." He ran to his bedroom, Jasper keeping up, and created a song about not missing the parties.

His singing was music to her ears, even if he was off key. "Thank you, goddess," she offered as she shuffled into the bathroom. "And thank you for Leeann too." Words she never thought she'd utter, but if it hadn't been for the blond gnome, Chad's party would have been a bust. Yup, having Leeann as a friend was a whole lot better than having her as an enemy.

When Shannon emerged from the shower, she found Chad lying on her bed, the new book open in front of him, Jasper next to him. "Mama, I haf a question."

She stood in the bathroom doorway, her toothbrush poised to enter her mouth. "Sure, munchkin. What's up?"

"Does Baby Bear haf to live with Daddy Bear?"

"Um, hold on. Why are you asking that question?"

Chad turned the pages of the book as he spoke. "Because Baby Bear doesn't want to live with Daddy Bear."

"Wait a minute." She returned her toothbrush to the bathroom and rinsed her mouth. Just when she thought she was out of the woods regarding the divorce and Chad's understanding, he triggered a land mine.

"Sweetie, scoot over and let Mama sit. How do you know Baby Bear doesn't want to live with Papa Bear?"

Chad rolled on his side and snuggled against Jasper. "He told me."

"Sit up, Chad, please. Baby Bear told you? What did he say?"

Chad hung his legs off the side of the bed and arched his

back, allowing his body to slide to the floor. "He doesn't want to live with the new Baby Bear."

The phrase 'new Baby Bear' wasn't setting well in her gut. A new baby, bear or not, indicated that...

"Chad, stand up. Is Daddy having a baby?"

"Silly, Mama, daddies can't have babies, only mamas."

"Yes, I know that, but did Daddy tell you Shelby is having a baby?"

"Uh-uh." Chad shook his head and tugged on Shannon's hand. "I'm hungry."

"Okay, go and get dressed while I do too. But first, did Daddy tell you not to tell me?" His refusal to answer spoke volumes. "You can tell me anything. No secrets, remember?"

"But, Daddy said—"

She drew him between her legs and raised his face so he looked at her. "Chad, no secrets. You have to trust me, okay?" His nod pushed her to ask again, "Is Shelby going to have a baby?"

"Ah-ha."

"How do you know?"

"I heard Daddy and Shelby say it. They thought I was asleep, but I wasn't."

She held him and pressed her lips to the side of his head. "Thank you for telling me. I'm going to get dressed while you do and then..." She nudged her voice to a cheerful level and said, "We'll have waffles for breakfast."

Chad raised his arms and cheered. Then he ran to his bedroom while she remained sitting.

Justin had knocked up Shelby.

Holy shit.

******

The house, with its faded wallpaper, held onto its secrets. St. John walked through the empty rooms, listening for a trace of Meredith's laughter, but the walls refused to release its ghosts.

"Where are you, old girl?"

Sadie came trotting into the room and looked at him, her head tilted. "Sorry, I was just talking to my... Never mind."

He climbed the stairs, remembering the times he'd run up and down them, his sneakers smacking against the worn wood. Malcolm had been the better runner, taking the steps two, and sometimes three, at a time. Some days their antics had driven Merry crazy enough that she'd told them to 'take their shenanigans outside.'

In the small bedroom, he stood by the window where his narrow bed had been. Outside in the front yard, the beech tree remained a sturdy reminder of the times they'd climbed to the top, each trying to beat the other's speed. That was how living as Malcolm's newly adopted brother had gone from the moment he'd stepped foot into the snug, hip-roof house. Who was faster? Who was stronger? Who could make the loudest farts or burp the longest? Who had more of Merry's love?

As Malcolm got older, he'd convinced himself she loved him less than his half-brother. All because he didn't understand what he'd overheard.

Merry's words had been innocent enough, 'You're my son, Adam. Never forget that.' That had been it. Not 'You're my favorite' or 'I love you more than Malcolm.' Just a simple proclamation of affection for the child of her deceased lover.

St. John strolled into the second room, the one they'd used as an attic. All that remained of the Christmas decorations were a few strands of tinsel, cracked by time and temperature. Malcolm had hired a disposal company to come in and remove every last piece of Meredith. Nothing was left except for the overgrown garden in the back and the bench by the pond where she'd sat each morning and sipped her tea.

He opened the short door leading to the eaves. A mouse

ran by his feet. Shannon being Wiccan might not mind having them around, but with mice came sharp teeth that liked to chew wires. He'd have an electrician come over and check over the place, along with an exterminator.

"Consider this your eviction notice," he said and shut and locked the door.

Back on the first floor, he decided it was time to summon Denise. She owed him for Jeff's birthday party.

"I was going to call you," was the hello he received.

"Yeah, about what?"

"I saw Shannon yesterday. Hold on."

He was treated to her shouting for Jeff to wake the kids and laughed to himself. If her raised voice hadn't done the trick, nothing would get the kids up.

"I'm back. I think you and I should discuss the Shannon thing."

Calling her had been a mistake. He should have texted her about his idea. He had to get on the road soon if he was going to reach the Hamptons by one. "I don't need a lecture, Denise."

"No, you don't. What you need is a smack to the head, but that's not why I want to talk to you. I want to hear your side of the story."

"About?"

"I don't want to do this on the phone. Why did you call me?"

"No, finish. What did Shannon say?"

"St. John, for a smart guy, you're not too bright. She's in love with you, you moron. What I want to know is how do you feel about her? And don't give me some bullshit about you helping her because you're a nice guy and you'd fly to Disney for anyone. I want to hear the words. Do you love her?"

"Yes, but get back to the part about her loving me. How do you know?"

"She told me. Actually, she told me and Peg."

"I don't get it. Why would she tell you, of all people?"

"What's that supposed to mean? Why wouldn't she tell me? I'm her friend."

"Yeah, a friend who's been on her case to stay away from me. I bet you did the old 'I told you so' bit."

"I didn't, and you can ask Peg. I'll tell you the same thing I said to her: I'm not happy you two let this happen, but it did. What I want to know is what are you going to do about it?"

"*That* is why I called."

"Hold on."

More yelling on Denise's side of the call gave him a chance to revisit what he'd learned. Shannon loved him. All her bluster about not caring for him had been a ruse. So why hadn't she reached out? Maybe she was willing to ignore her feelings and get on with her life without him in it. He might have missed his shot.

"I'm back, but you have to talk fast. I have to get the kids to school."

"I called Malcolm, and I'm heading to the Hamptons to attend a party he's giving—"

"Hold the fuck up. You called Malcolm, and he invited you to the Hamptons?"

"Sure did. We're going to work things out and hopefully go forward. I'm going to ask him—"

"I'm impressed, St. John. This is huge. What did he say?"

"I thought you had to get going? Please stop asking questions and let me finish. I plan on asking Malcolm if he'll rent the house to Shannon with an option to buy. What I need you to do is show the house to Shannon." He ran his hand over a crack in the wall. Even though the house was in disrepair, there was no doubt in his mind Shannon would say yes. This was the house from her dream or vision or whatever she called it.

Merry's house *was* Shannon's house. "Can you get her here this weekend?"

"Here? Are you at the house? How did you get in?"

"Trade secret. Will you do this for me?"

"What about my commission? If Malcolm's not selling the house, I'll lose money."

"I'll cover your commission, and I'll throw in one of those fun-house bouncy things for the kids to play in at Jeff's party."

"I have one final question," Dee said. "If Malcolm says yes and Shannon says yes, what happens then? With you and her?"

"That's two questions, and since I happen to live across the road, I'm hoping she'll invite me over for a drink. I'm not kidding myself, Denise. She might not want a relationship with me. It's not like she's banging on my door to see me."

"She said you told her you don't want to see her."

"Yeah, well, I sort of, may have said that, but only because I thought she didn't want me in her life. Does she? Want me in her life?"

"You'll have to ask her. I'll get her over there and feel her out. When are you coming back?"

"Sunday night. I have to work at the bar."

"Okay. I gotta run. I'll text you. Drive safe."

With the phone call over, he walked outside and got in his car. If only he'd told Shannon the truth when they were on the plane. Hopefully, he hadn't missed his chance.

He shifted into drive and headed down the winding driveway, inwardly pleading with her to not give up on him.

Chapter 37

"You cannot swim for new horizons until you have the courage to lose sight of the shore."
William Faulkner

With Chad safely at the school party and under the watchful eyes of Dee, Peg, and Leeann, Shannon finished packing the last of her clothes. Chad's bedroom had been the first to get sorted. Clothes he'd grown out of and toys abandoned as he grew from a toddler to a six-year-old big boy were deposited in a carton marked for donation. She'd like to keep everything for his own children, but storage space would most likely be a rare commodity in her life. When he had kids, he'd be a rich tort lawyer and could buy new toys, which would probably have the ability to procreate by then.

While she was whittling down her wardrobe, her cell rang. She'd just spoken with Dee, so Chad was okay, and Jayla had called too. There was only one other person she wanted to talk to, and she leapt over a half-filled carton, catching her foot on the edge and tumbling to the floor. Jasper seemed to think she wanted to play and landed on top of her, his tail wagging.

"Jasper, off. You're crushing me."

She pushed herself free and scrambled up the side of her bed to reach for the silent phone. "Stupid box," she huffed. Now she'd have to sort through all the mental turmoil of whether to call him back or not, assuming the call had been from St. John.

The number *was* a New Hampshire area code, so it had to have been him, although she didn't recognize it. Maybe he'd used a different phone.

A pinging noise announced the voicemail, and she settled herself to hear what he had to say. Fantasies of him telling her he loved her and had made a terrible mistake in letting her go flitted through her coffee-stoked brain.

"Here goes nothing," she said to Jasper and pressed the numbers for her messages.

"Hi, Shannon, um, I need to talk to you."

She paused the message. The soft, meek tone was familiar, but she couldn't produce a face to match. Most likely the woman was from the Conservation Committee. Leeann had said someone would be in touch about membership.

The message resumed.

"Would you, um, please, call me back? Oh, it's Shelby."

"What the fuck?" She flung the phone at the floor. The call had to be some twisted ploy of Justin's. He was trying to...to what? Confuse her?

Well, it had worked.

And she wasn't calling back.

Shannon entered the *Beans*, and Jimbo greeted her with a wide grin like he'd just eaten the cat along with the canary. He walked around the side of the counter, wrapped her in a bear of a hug, and deposited a damp kiss on her cheek.

"Congratulations, sunshine. I'm proud of you." He clapped his beefy hands. "This calls for a celebration. Want a cappuccino?"

"A tall espresso with a triple shot would be nice, thanks, and how did you find out?"

"You just missed St. John. He was grabbing a coffee for the road. Took a dozen of your blueberry scones too."

Jimbo's little piece of news knocked the wind from her momentum. St. John hadn't said anything about... She really was dense at times. Why would he tell her anything?

She pretended she was studying the pastry case. "Where did he go?"

"New York. Gone to see his half-ass brother."

"Do you have any boxes I could take? Did he say when he'd be back?" She hoped by slipping in the last question Jimbo wouldn't notice. Not a chance.

Jimbo laced his hands together, tucking them under his beard. "He came in all smiles and whistling some irritating tune."

"'It's a Small World'?"

"Yeah, that one. I figured it out immediately. St. John's *finally* in love."

"Does she live in town?"

"Don't be coy. I heard about the trip to Disney and put two and two together."

"And from learning that we flew to get Chad, you deduced St. John's in love with me? Dee told me a very similar thing, but the two of you are missing a very important fact: St. John hasn't said anything to me except he was moving on."

The confusion she felt must have surfaced onto her face.

"Don't you worry; you'll be hearing from him." Jimbo said more seriously, "St. John's a true person, and he'll never let you down if he can help it."

She buried herself against the Santa Claus belly and hugged as best she could with her arms not even reaching midway around Jimbo's girth. "What about the times when he can't help it?"

"Well, those, sunshine, are the times when your love, and a bottle of whiskey, come in handy. Let me get you those boxes."

Jimbo and one of his staff loaded Shannon's SUV with stacks of flattened cartons, tied into neat bundles.

"Let me know if you need more or anything else."

Shannon scrunched her mouth. She was going to owe Jimbo big time. "Do you mind if I store the food in the freezer here? You can take anything you want for the café."

"Call it what it is, for crumb's sake. It's a coffee shop, not some damn café, and I already cleared a spot. You want me to send someone over with the van to get the stuff?"

"That's okay. I'll be coming back into town to pick up Chad, and I'll drop them off. Thank you. Oh, and I did what you suggested and withdrew some money, but Justin is fighting for it back."

"Tell Justin to suck his own dick," was Jimbo's quick response. "You keep that money until Marty tells you otherwise. By the way, where you gonna be staying until the house is ready?"

She cast him a surprised look. "What house?"

"Nothin', I was just thinking you'd be buying a house, that's all."

When he became interested in a spot on her car's bumper, she said, "Come on, Jimbo, give it up. What house?"

Before she received an answer, her cell phone rang. It was Shelby again. "You're off the hook for now. Love you. Bye."

"See you soon, sunshine."

Wearing a scowl, Shannon swiped to answer the call. "Hello."

"Hi, Shannon, this is Shelby, Justin's...ah...Shelby."

"Hold on, would you?" Shannon said. She started the car and pulled from the parking lot and, while driving, held the phone out the window. First she had to deal with Justin and now his mistress. Who was next? Shelby's mother?

She brought the phone back into the car. "Sorry about that. I had to... I was... Never mind. What can I do for you?"

"I called to see if maybe we could meet and talk."

"I don't think that's such a good idea, Shelby." Unless Justin had fallen off Magic Mountain, and Shelby wanted to celebrate together, there was nothing to talk about.

"This is important," Shelby said.

"I'm listening."

"I'd rather tell you in person."

"Sorry, I have too much going on to stop for a gab session. You may not know this, but I have to vacate my house in two days, or maybe you do know."

The back and forth continued until Shannon reached her driveway. "Hold on, please." She maneuvered the car with the hatch facing the bay door and contemplated whether to back into the garage or leave the SUV outside. Since Shelby wanted to meet, that meant Justin was most likely back in town. But he'd have to be a complete idiot to come by the house. She turned off the engine and retrieved the phone. "Shelby, I have to go."

Shelby's small voice rose a notch. "Can't we sit down like civil adults and talk?"

Shannon opened the back of the SUV and removed one of the carton bundles. She didn't feel like being a civil adult and chose to give a direct hit. "I already know about the baby."

"Oh, um, I..."

"I'm not trying to be mean, and I am happy for you. Going through a pregnancy is a wonderful experience, and I truly wish you and the baby well, but right now I don't have time to do this."

"The baby is the reason I want to talk to you," Shelby said.

Shannon carried the boxes into the house and tossed the stack onto the floor. Was this woman for real? Had she even listened to what had just been said? She took Jasper outside and removed the other stack.

"Shannon, are you there?"

"Yes, I'm here. Would you please get to the point?"

"Okay. Would you— ? I mean, could you find it in your heart to please let Justin go?"

"Go where?"

"What I meant to say is please, will you divorce him so he can marry me?"

Shannon placed the phone on the counter and walked out of the room. It was either that or smash the frigging thing, and she'd need it. Justin's deceit had dropped to a new low.

She returned to the kitchen. "Shelby?"

"Yes."

"What has Justin told you?"

"Um, he said that you're willing to move out of the house so we can live there together and raise the baby, but you won't let him go because you still love him."

"I'm sorry to burst your bubble about Justin, but he's lying to you. My lawyer filed the divorce papers yesterday, and we're waiting for Justin's signature, not mine."

"Oh, but I don't understand. He said—"

"Shelby, let me give you a piece of advice: think long and hard about whether Justin is the person with whom you want to raise your child. I wish you well, and please don't call me ever again unless it concerns Chad. Goodbye."

With the last of the freezer containers in her arms, Shannon walked to her car and screamed, releasing her hold. Half-Moon cookies littered the blacktop.

"Surprise," Justin said, stepping in front of her.

She considered bolting back into the house but knew she wouldn't make it. Her only option was to swallow her stomach and stand up to him.

"What are you doing here?" Hopefully she sounded threatening.

"What? No welcome back from Disney?"

"You're not allowed on the property, not until Sunday. The TPO states—"

"Fuck the TPO and fuck you." Justin shoved his finger at Shannon's face. "This is my house, and I'll come and go as I please. What are you still doing here?"

Shannon bent and gathered the chocolate-and-vanilla-frosted cookies, which she threw back into the plastic tub. "You gave me until Sunday to leave." Asshole, her brain added.

"Yeah, well I changed my mind."

Screw you, she wanted to say. Instead, she straightened and walked away to dump the cookies in the trash. When she returned, she said, "Are you still here? Fine, I'm calling the police." There was one problem with her little ploy—her phone was in the house. Not looking at him, she picked up the un-opened container and added it to the others already in the back of the SUV.

Justin spread his legs and crossed his arms over his puffed-out chest. "I'm sleeping here tonight, and you and the mutt are not. And don't have any delusions about Chad. He's staying with me."

A kink in her courage appeared. And then another one. More followed.

It would be so easy to return to the old ways and her usual pattern of cowering to him. There'd be no packing, no moving all her stuff...but also no safety for Chad.

Screw that.

"As long as we're on the topic of children," she said. "How does it feel?"

"What the fuck are you babbling about?"

"I'm just wondering if you're excited about being a daddy again." Surprise couldn't describe the look passing through his eyes and in her head she performed a happy dance. She hoped he'd enjoy her next announcement. "I talked with Shelby today. She's so happy she could barely get her words out, but she did. I assured her I would eagerly sign the divorce papers so you two can get married. Congratulations."

She wasn't going to wait for him to catch up, so she added, "I don't hate you, Justin. I just wasn't the right woman for you."

"Anyone would be better than you." He spat on the

driveway. "You're just like my mother, always complaining and then walking out. You're both whores."

She finally understood him, and all the loathing she felt for him seeped away. He'd been doomed as a man from the moment his infant lungs had taken their first gasp of air.

But, hey, he was Shelby's problem now.

"I'm not your mother, Justin," she said. "And I don't care that she didn't hold you enough. Grow up and start acting like a man. Sign the papers and give Shelby and your baby a chance to heal you. But whatever you decide to do, do it far away from Chad and me."

She slammed the hatch closed, returned to the garage, and lowered the bay door.

So this was what courage felt like.

Pretty frigging cool.

Chapter 38

*"It's your road and yours alone. Others may walk it with you,
but no one can walk it for you."*
Rumi

Victorian Park Entertainment Center offered miniature golf, an indoor arcade, and over forty different flavors of ice cream. By two o'clock the party was in full swing with Leeann acting as ringmaster. The part she'd played in locating Chad had risen her to superhero status with the other mothers, including Shannon. She was quick to point out to anyone willing to listen that without Leeann, Chad might still be missing.

"Shannon, do you want me to gather the children for the cake before or after Chad opens his gifts?"

Leeann stood with a clipboard in hand, awaiting Shannon's instructions.

"I don't know what I'd do without you." Shannon said. Truly, she didn't. She wanted to hug the energetic blonde, but she wasn't sure if that would be awkward. Leeann obviously didn't think so because the perky woman's surprisingly strong arms soon wrapped around Shannon.

Leeann gushed, "We're going to be the best of friends, you just wait. Gifts or cake?"

"Honestly, I can't decide. I'd love it if you would since I'm sure whatever decision you make, it will be the right one."

"That's true," Leeann said with a hop in her step as she bebopped away, ponytail swaying.

Dee raised a very bushy eyebrow and sipped on a Diet Pepsi. "So, Peg and I are dog meat now, huh?"

"Not at all," Shannon said. "We'll just have to make room for her in our gang. She's even going to sponsor me on the Conservation Committee and the PTA." She stared at the children running through the play area and chewed on the inside of her top lip. A friendship with Leeann might prove to be a mistake. "Do you think I should trust her?" she posed to Dee. "What if she turns on me like she did last time?"

"Shan, chill. She thinks you're the bravest woman alive. Did everything go okay with the movers?" Dee walked to a nearby recycling bin and tossed the can inside. "

"Like a charm," Shannon said as Dee walked back her way. "Thanks again for taking Chad to baseball. I'm a lousy mother for missing his first game, but the packing took precedence."

"Trust me, you didn't miss anything. The only way the kids are going to keep the ball in their gloves is if St. John glues it there. I took a video and sent it to him."

"I bet St. John hated missing the first game. He's coming home around noon tomorrow, right?" Slipping a similar question into her conversation with Jimbo hadn't worked, but hopefully Dee was too distracted by the chaos around them to catch on. The narrowed glance she received suggested otherwise.

Dee said, "If you want to know his plans, text him."

"I was only—"

"Yeah, right. Are we on for later?"

"Yes, if Peg is still taking the kids."

"Change of plans. Leeann is taking a bunch of kids for a sleepover and pool party."

Chad, wearing a golden crown and a sash that read *I'm Six*, raced their way and pulled on Shannon's skirt. "Mama, Stevie's mama says to come now for the schedule."

"Okay, birthday munchkin, I'm coming."

Shannon turned to follow Chad, but Dee stopped her. "For what it's worth, Shan, I happen to think you're brave too."

At that, Dee clapped her hands and yelled at the kids to gather in the ice cream parlor.

Shannon maneuvered her SUV along Farmview Road. She'd done some research on the property where she was meeting Dee. The satellite image had been too pixelated to see specific details except for a small house, pond, and trees galore. A little digging in Wexford's property archives revealed a surprising fact, though: the house had been built by Chester St. John, St. John's grandfather.

She drove to the end of the rutted dirt road and turned left, passing a mailbox with a number twelve painted on the side. Spruce and fir trees encased the long driveway, giving her the feeling she'd been transported to Canada and was driving in a boreal forest. Add about three feet of snow, and the image would be complete.

At the top of the steep driveway, the road bent to the left. Time stopped as her vision and reality merged. In her mind, she'd stood on the porch of the quaint house many times; it was the very same house St. John had sketched on his palm.

She turned off the car and ran the remaining length of the driveway. Jasper bolted past her and disappeared into the dense woods, but she continued to the center of the lawn. The magnificent tree beckoned her, and she moved slowly forward until she stood under the sprawling canopy of study limbs and burgundy-tinted leaves. To her, beeches were the most magical of all hardwoods, their strength and wisdom bestowed upon them by the goddess Freya. Having a beech tree on the property was yet another good omen.

She dipped her hand into the space where the trunk separated and pressed her lips against the smooth, gray bark. The tree's energy eased into her, and she whispered, "Thank you, Freya, for the bounty you have bestowed upon me and will bestow upon me. Blessed be."

At a sound akin to the snapping of a rubber band, she raised her face and found a pair of black eyes studying her.

"Hello, little chickadee. Are you the welcoming committee?"

Jasper bounded out from the trees, his coat dotted with mud.

"I guess someone is having a bath tonight," she said. "Let's try the front door and see if it's unlocked."

The weathered porch creaked under her sandals, and she turned the doorknob. The door swung in, and she sniffed. A subtle aroma matching her own perfume lived under the dust and age.

"I'm home," she called out.

She stepped inside, and with her index finger resting against the faded wallpaper, traced along the wall of the living room until she arrived at the fireplace. She rested her hand on the sturdy oak mantle. It opened itself and in a hushed whisper offered, 'Welcome home.' Having lain silent for too many years, the house was ready to live again.

Echoes of footsteps ran past and up the staircase located in the corner of the room. Jasper barked and followed the unseen feet to the second floor, and she followed Jasper.

At the top landing she heard laughter, and she found Jasper wagging his tail as he stood in the center of the room overlooking the backyard. Someone or something had wiped away the dust from the windowsill, revealing two brown smudges and the words *Blood brothers for life*.

A blanket of soothing energy enveloped her, and she gave a small nod. The two boys, now men, had mended their hearts. All was becoming as it should be; the house was finally at peace.

"Shan, you up there?"

Jasper returned to the first floor, and Shannon called, "Yes, coming."

Dee stood halfway up the steps, holding two take-out cups with the *Beans* logo. "How did you get in?"

"The house."

"The house?"

"The house let me in."

"Okaay... Can I have some of what you're smoking?"

Shannon took one of the cups and grinned. "It's not pot, it's magic."

Dee snorted. "Forget the voodoo stuff and concentrate on reality. What do you think of the place? It needs a load of work."

"I don't care," Shannon said, her tone emphatic. "Whatever the owner wants, I'll pay it, even if I have to work three jobs. I want this house."

"St. John said you'd say that."

Shannon shook her head. "Wait a sec. I thought Malcolm O'Brien was the owner?"

Dee responded, "Let's go sit by the pond. We have a lot to discuss. But first, you carry the coffees, and I'll be right back. I bought a box of muffins, and it's in the van, along with the paperwork."

Dee joined Shannon and handed her the pastry box. "I only got corn figuring you'd want to feed the ducks."

Jasper laid his muzzle on Shannon's lap and stared at the pastry box. "Be patient," she said. Pulling off a section of muffin, she tossed it on the water. Jasper leapt straight into the pond, sending the mallards and two swans quacking and honking in a variety of directions. "Aw, Jasper," she shouted.

"Don't worry about it; they're used to dogs. When St. John is over here, Sadie terrorizes them.

Shannon dusted crumbs off her fingers. "Okay, it's time to tell me what's going on. Who owns this house, really?"

Dee finished swallowing her bite of muffin. "First let me give you a brief history. St. John's grandfather built the place—"

"I already know that."

"Feed the ducks, Shan, and let me finish. He built the house in 1934 and sold it, along with twenty acres, to a young widow from Derry for the whopping price of fifteen dollars. The sale raised some eyebrows, and after the widow—her name was Sadie—moved in with her young son, tongues started wagging about infidelity and an illegitimate child."

"Who's Merry?" Shannon crumbled more muffin and tossed the pieces to the newly arrived ducks near her feet.

"Merry was married to David, Sadie's son."

"And now I'm officially confused."

"Give me a chance to get it all out before you start asking questions," Dee said. "David was Sadie's son, the one people believed to be Chester St. John's illegitimate kid. He, David, married Meredith Sullivan, and they lived in this house. David died in a logging accident, and his widow, Merry, who was pregnant at the time, gave birth to Malcolm. This is where history repeats itself. Merry became St. John's father's mistress. After his mom died, Merry adopted St. John. He was ten or eleven. He lived here with her and Malcolm until he married Coleen."

"This is incredible!" Shannon's exclamation sent the ducks flying back to the water and got Jasper running along the pond's edge. "This is better than Peyton Place." She took a moment and then said, "I still don't get who owns the house: St. John or Malcolm?"

"Malcolm.

"Then where does St. John fit in?"

"It's convoluted, Shan, but right now St. John is in New York trying to mend his relationship with Malcolm."

"Which they have already accomplished," Shannon added.

Dee looked surprised. "You've talked to him?"

"No, the house told me."

"Okay, never mind. I did talk to him, and he managed to convince Malcolm to rent the place to you with an option to buy. I can't believe he pulled it off; he's a better negotiator than I thought."

"Why did he and Malcolm stop speaking?"

"I don't know the details, and believe me, I've tried to get them. St. John doesn't like sharing. Good luck with that part of his personality."

Shannon left the bench and stood at the water's edge, alternately tossing muffin chunks to Jasper and the birds. As she faced the pond, she said over her shoulder, "St. John has a lot more baggage than I realized."

"I told you so," Dee replied along with a chuckle. "Sorry, I had to say it."

Shannon returned and sat again, responding with her own good-humored laugh. "It's about time. The suspense was killing me."

Dee poured the last portion of her coffee into the grass and picked up the manila envelope at her side. "I have a list of the repairs the house needs. St. John already said he'll take care of them. This preliminary contract spells out most of the details."

Shannon studied the papers. She reread the selling price three times. "I can't believe the house is so cheap. Why?"

"Talk to St. John."

"I need to know something." Shannon returned the papers to the envelope. "Why is St. John doing this for me?"

"You're kidding me, right?"

"No, I'm not. He's made it clear—"

"The two of you are driving me batshit." Dee stood and poured out the remaining coffee in Shannon's cup and dropped both cups and stomped them with her foot. "I feel like locking you guys in a room and not letting you out until you've both duked it out."

"What did I say that was so bad?"

"St. John loves you."

Shannon tossed the last pieces of muffins into the water. "No, no, no. He said—"

Dee's face reddened. "Screw what he said. You've done the impossible—you got Adam St. John to break his stinking rules and let someone into his life. I'll ask you the same thing I asked him: what are you going to do about it?"

Chapter 39

*"Being happy doesn't mean that everything is perfect, it means
that you've decided to look beyond the imperfections."*
Unknown

"I own a house in North Conway, one in Windham, and a
third on Cape Cod down in Mass. I also have......."

Shannon nodded every few seconds. She imagined her eyes
glazing over as Larry or Barry—she forgot his name—droned
on, but she wasn't being fair to him. She was at *Pappy*'s to see
only one man.

Giving the bourbon in her glass her attention, she once
again mused about why he hadn't called, or at the least texted,
when he got back to town. By now he had to know she'd spoken
to Dee and learned how he felt.

"Do you know that guy?"

Her companion nodded toward the far end of the bar, and
she thrilled at the pair of shockingly blue eyes directed her way.
She offered a smile.

He returned the favor with a wide grin of his own and, with
a quick jerk of his head, indicated the hallway. Then he blended
into the crowd of bodies.

"Excuse me," she said to Larry or Barry. "I have to..." She
grabbed her purse and followed St. John.

The hall led to the bathrooms and the kitchen. She tried
the door for the woman's room. "Wait your turn," blasted
through the wood. The men's room door wasn't locked, but
after she opened it, she blinked and yanked it closed.

"What's your hurry?" the guy called out.

"Sorry," she shouted and continued on her way. St. John
wouldn't have gone into the kitchen, and he hadn't evaporated
into thin air, so where...? At the end of the hallway, steps

entered a darkened stairwell. At the top, a slice of light escaped an open door.

This was it, the moment of truth. Since Jimbo and Dee might be wrong, she'd be smart to play it cool and see where St. John took things.

She climbed and entered an office consisting of a couch, two well-stuffed chairs, a file cabinet, and a desk, against which he was presently leaning. He looked relaxed, ankles crossed, hands tucked into a pair of faded jeans. He didn't speak or move.

She closed the door. "Are you going to stand there all night, or are you going to bring those lips over here?"

"We need to talk first," he replied without moving from his spot.

She reached over her shoulder and freed her hair from the rhinestone clip holding it in place. "Okay, so talk." She gave her head a shake, hoping her hair looked tousled in a sexy way and not like she'd just gotten out of bed.

He stepped away from the desk, and her pulse doubled, tripling as he moved close and quadrupling as he fingered the lace ruffle draping from the off-the-shoulder neckline of her dress.

"First," he said, "you look great."

His fingertips grazed the exposed skin of her chest, sending her pulse rate off the charts. "What's second?"

"Excuse me?" His right eyebrow arched.

"You said first, which indicates there's a second as in 'first, second, third.'" It was his closeness that was turning her brain to mush. First, second, third: what was she even talking about?

He nodded. "Got it," he said and walked behind her. The click of the lock told her the talking would eventually end, but not fast enough. Soon he'd have to make love to a puddle.

"Second, you smell incredible."

She wasn't sure if his breath near her ear had caused it or

if it was the way he'd inhaled along her skin, but a warm trickle slid down her inner thigh. "And third?"

Strong hands, roughened from physical labor, held her by the shoulders and guided her against his chest. He angled her head back and stroked the length of her neck. Each pass of his fingers bringing them closer to her breasts.

"Number three is I've missed the feel of you," he said and moved his hand under the dress's material and stroked her nipples.

There were two things she wanted: to hear that he loved her and to feel him inside of her. At the present time, she didn't care one bit about the words; she needed some action. She spun and faced him. "Are you going to fuck me or not?"

He gripped her by the waist and kissed her. Then he flashed his cocky grin, said, "No," and let her go.

******

"You're a tease, St. John," Shannon told him while straightening her dress.

"Don't get me wrong, Shannon," St. John said. "I plan on having you multiple times tonight but not here. Would you like something to drink?" He walked over to the file cabinet and removed a whiskey bottle and two paper cups. "On second thought, water for you." He bent under the desk and reappeared with a bottle of spring water. "I hope you don't mind room temperature. I could run downstairs and get you some ice if you want?"

"Why can't I have a drink?"

"Because you had three down in the bar."

She smirked at him, which did little to stem the blood flowing to his groin. "Were you spying on me?"

"It's my job to keep an eye on what's happening in my establishment. You didn't look as if you were enjoying your friend very much."

"I was enjoying him just fine." She grabbed the water bottle. "Why can't we fool around? I'm sure you've screwed lots of women in here. What's your favorite spot: the desk, the couch and the chairs, the door?"

He poured himself a shot and tapped his glass against her water bottle. "Mostly the door, never the desk or the couch. The chairs are too uncomfortable and only a few times on the floor."

"You are a cocky bastard."

"Yes, you've told me." He sent the bourbon into his throat. "And now I want you to tell me what you're doing here."

She sat on the desk and opened her legs. "I heard the chicken wings are pretty good, so I thought I'd come by and see."

"Stick to the wings back in Wexford, and sitting like that isn't going to change my mind." He'd promised himself that the next time he made love to her it would be in a bed, not against a door, not a counter, not the floor, but a proper bed that was comfortable and where he could take his time exploring her.

"I bet I can get you to change your mind.

She lifted the hem of her dress and fanned her open legs, giving him a clear view.

He ran his hand over his face. He could barely hear his own thoughts his heart was pounding so loud. The chances of him waiting to make love to her until they were someplace less seedy were lessening by the second. "Denise told me about Justin and how you stood up to him. You should be proud of yourself."

She bent her leg and placed her sandaled foot on the desk. "What about you, St. John. Are you proud of me?"

"Stay with me tonight."

"Tsk, tsk, tsk," she said. "That's not a very polite way to ask."

"Will you to stay with me tonight, please."

"I'd love to stay with you."

Then she touched herself, and his resolve crumbled.

******

Once their sexual appetites were satiated, St. John descended to the kitchen and brought back a plate of BBQ chicken wings, coleslaw, and a stack of moist towelettes. While they ate, Shannon detailed Shelby's phone call and Justin's visit. When St. John asked, she also described the condo where she was now living and added, "I came here tonight to thank you for what you did with the house."

"You're welcome. Merry would be happy to know you're living there." He extended a napkin and wiped the corner of her lips.

He might think she was crazy, but she told him, "She knows." A sudden thought came to her, and she assembled the words, realizing if she'd didn't clear the air, they wouldn't stand a chance. "I have something I'd like to say."

"I think I know what you're going to say, and I'd like to go first," he said, wiping his hands.

"Why do you always get to go first?"

"My office, my rules."

She cleaned her fingers and then stood, placing her hands on her hips. "Big deal, Mr. Cocky. You don't get to go first because you don't know what I'm going to say."

"I bet I do. Here..." He tore a slip of paper off the pad on the desk and wrote something. Then he handed her the pen and her own piece of paper. "Write down what you want to say, and we'll compare notes."

She agreed. "Ready?" she asked when she finished writing.

He returned to his original position of leaning against the desk. "Go."

"I apologize for what I've said about your business practices.

I understand what you're saying about people and the land. You'd think I'd be okay with progress, having grown up in a city like Boston, but whatever. Anyway, I do get that you build around the natural landscape, and I'm sorry for accusing you otherwise. I promise, no judgment ever again. Okay, show me your slip?"

"It can wait. Come here."

When he reached for her hand, she shook her head. "First show me what you wrote."

"In a minute. I have something else to show you." He led her around the desk and removed a cardboard tube from on top of the file cabinet.

"What's this?" she asked as he unrolled a blueprint. "*Meredith Memorial Park,*" she read. "Wait, is this the old Hancock farm?" She studied the architectural blueprint and then his pleased expression.

"Yup. I'm the new owner. Last Saturday night, I presented these plans, along with my offer, and Hancock's daughter accepted."

"But Leeann told me the Conservation Committee was trying to buy the land."

"I wasn't going to let that happen."

She stared at him as a queasiness snaked into her stomach. Had she been right about him all along? "I don't understand."

St. John rested his butt against the desk, his chuckle good-natured. "Maybe this will help: when the town purchases large parcels of land, they sell portions to MacMillan, which they were going to do to seventy-five percent of this property. I wasn't going to let happen. I'm showing you this because I want you to trust me completely, *and* I need someone to manage the project and would like that person to be you."

"You're going too fast, St. John. I'm still back at you buying the farm." She leaned over the schematic to hide her embarrassment for doubting him.

"What do you think? You can still write your blog and work with Jimbo, but this way you'll have extra money, so you can pay me back for the repairs on the house."

She gave him a WTF-look and received a robust laugh in response.

"I know you, Shannon," he said. "You'd never take the work for free. And this job is not a handout. I can't be in twelve places at once. What do you think?"

"I need time to process this."

"Fine with me. I'm not going anywhere."

"What exactly does that mean?" She folded her arms to show him she was tired of pussyfooting around.

He held open his slip of paper, revealing the words, *I Love You.*

She opened her piece and showed him what she'd written. *I'm sorry.*

She realized her mistake as soon as she saw his crestfallen expression. "No, no," she clutched his shirt. "Not that kind of 'I'm sorry.' I wrote this when you said I couldn't go first and... I don't mean I'm sorry that you love me." She bent and rewrote on the reverse side of the paper and held it up. "See, I love you too," she said and hugged him around the neck. "I love you, St. John." She sensed him pulling away. "Where are you going?"

"I have to say something first." He tried to loosen her arms.

She tightened her hold and insisted, "This isn't the time to talk. Kiss me."

"I'll kiss you in a minute, but first, you need to know something about me."

She let him go and crossed her arms. "Oh, please. I know exactly what you're going to say, and no, I'm not writing it down. You're going to say you might screw things up because that's what you do, and you don't know how to love, and you don't want to hurt me or Chad and...and... What else?"

"You left out that I snore."

"Great, so do I." If she had to shake him to get him to understand, she would, but first she'd try words. "Listen to me, St. John. We're damaged people, you and me, and we're going to screw up, but I'd rather screw up with you than without you."

"Deal," he said and enveloped her with his arms. "Oh, I forgot to mention I do have one rule."

"Of course you do." She giggled. What was one more rule among his other hundred?

He looked down at her, the renegade piece of hair hanging over his eyebrow. "Never stop loving me."

She twirled the strand. "You don't have to worry. That's not going to happen."

Their lips met, and she exhaled.

She'd done it. She'd gotten herself and Chad away from Justin, and she'd found a safe place for them. And it was in St. John's love.

Thank you, goddess.

The End

Epilogue

"Live the life you imagined."
Henry David Thoreau

October 2011

"To sum it all up, Shannon, it's over." Martin stacked the papers on the conference table into a neat pile. "Any questions?"

Shannon sat stupefied at the news. Something wasn't right. "Are you sure?"

"Except for Justin's payment to you. Once it arrives, I'll forward it on, but you have the money from the closing, correct?"

"Yes." She was being silly, but she couldn't shake the uneasiness suddenly gripping her chest. Justin had found his bliss and was living in Florida with his new wife and a baby on the way. "Justin can't change the custody arrangements, can he?" It seemed foolish to ask; he'd willingly signed over full custody and all visitation rights. She'd told him she wouldn't keep him and Chad apart, but he'd waved her off, saying she could raise 'the brat.' Plus, one of Tony's guys was keeping an eye on him to make sure he didn't take any sudden trips to Wexford. So what was eating at her?

"I wouldn't lose sleep over it. I'll send Jayla in. I have a meeting in my office. There are some papers you need to sign, and she wants to talk with you."

Marty shook Shannon's hand and left the room.

Jayla entered. "Pretty surreal, huh?" She claimed Marty's seat.

"That's putting it mildly," Shannon responded. "I don't understand why I'm not dancing on this table."

Jayla placed a pamphlet in front of her.

"This is why. Marty always wants to wait until the divorce is final before we broach this subject."

Shannon read the name of the organization. "Bridges, domestic and sexual violence support?" She reread it, this time in silence, and stared at Jayla. "You're saying I need a support group?"

"Yes, you and Chad both."

"We're fine," Shannon said, pushing the brochure back to Jayla. "I make sure to talk to Chad about his feelings, and Justin didn't really abuse me; he was just a jerk."

Jayla squeezed Shannon's hand and returned the pamphlet. "Whether you want to admit it or not, you're a survivor of domestic abuse. Justin didn't break any bones, but he abused you emotionally. You may not have physical bruises, but the scars are there just the same."

"Okay, but why now? Why didn't you give this to me in September or back in the summer, for that matter?"

"That's easy to explain: you've been occupied with the divorce, the child custody classes, meetings with the mediator, getting the house ready to move it. Plus, add in your new relationship with St. John, and your mind swept all the bad stuff aside. Now that the divorce is over, it's creeping back in, and the first indication is what you're feeling—like there's some impending doom coming your way. I've been where you are, Shannon. That's how I met St. John and Marty. I was at St. John's bar with my ex, who used me as a punching bag. He smacked me, and St. John saw it. He threw my husband out into the parking lot and took me to see Marty. I learned the hard way that unless we, as survivors, do the head work to heal, we'll doom any chance we get with a new man, or woman in my case." Jayla tapped the pink-and-blue pamphlet. "They'll help you. And they'll help Chad. And I will too. The offer to spend some girl-time together still stands."

"I'd like that." Shannon slipped the pamphlet into her purse. She had been snapping at Chad and St. John lately, and no amount of spells and circle castings seemed to help. Or had they? She'd asked for guidance, and here it was. "I'll make an appointment this week. Thank you."

"My pleasure," Jayla said. "I have some papers for you to sign, and then you're a free woman."

I still can't believe it's over.

While she rode the elevator, Shannon sent St. John a text, and received an immediate response.

Believe it. Rule number 39: Never question the universe.

The elevator doors opened, and she entered the lobby. Standing to the side, she returned her attention to her phone. *I think you're just making up rules.*

Not true. Someday I'll show you the bound copy. I keep it in the same vault where I kept my heart.

And where's your heart now?

In your hands. Handle it with care, it's pretty beaten up.

As is mine so you'll need to do the same. There was no doubt in her mind; her heart was safe.

Got it. Kid gloves. We'll celebrate tonight after we get Chad's Halloween costume. How does Chuck-E-Cheese sound? Nothing says you're free like Skee-Ball and cardboard pizza.

I'll bring my headache and stomach powders. I love you and I'll see you tonight. Go back to work.

I love you too. See you tonight, Ms. Muller (I don't know how to add the two dots over the 'u', sorry, we might need to change your last name.)

She reread the string of words. Had he just proposed? She nibbled on her lip as she contemplated asking him. She changed her mind and typed instead, *I just got my name back but if you can offer something better, be my guest.*

I have a few thoughts on the subject. I'll see you and Chad later. Oh, and I love you. Bye.

See you tonight and I love you too. Bye.

She didn't care if people passing by heard her laughing like a goof; she couldn't contain her joy. She'd succeeded in rescuing herself and Chad, and had even rescued St. John along the way.

All was becoming as it should.

Blessed be.

Dear Reader,

Writing *Breaking the Rules* was tough for me. The topic of gaslighting brought forth memories I'd long ago buried. Gaslighting isn't in the forefront when people discuss domestic violence. Although the scars aren't visible, the damage verbal abuse does to a person's self-esteem, and spirit, is real.

To my beta readers, thank you for your gentle critiques (especially you, Barb – you rock); to my sister, Dyan, thank you for sharing your own story with me; and to my son, Chris, your words of wisdom kept me pushing forward. Thank you, thank you, thank you.

And to you, dear reader, thank you for purchasing *Breaking the Rules*. I do so hope you'll leave a review on Social Media. (Shameless groveling.) ☺

I love when readers connect with me and hope you'll reach out. Until then,

Blessed be,

Tinthia

Journey Stew

Ingredients

◇ 1 Tbls extra-virgin olive oil
◇ 2 garlic cloves, minced
◇ 1 cup thinly sliced onions
◇ 1 cup each, thickly sliced carrots, celery, and mushrooms
◇ 3 medium, Yukon gold potatoes, unpeeled and roughly cut.
◇ 2 cups cooked kidney beans (If using canned beans, rise well first.)
◇ 8 ounces chunky-style, unseasoned tomatoes.
◇ 1 cup of veggie base mixed with two cups water (or 3 cups veggie broth, low sodium)
◇ 1 bay leaf
◇ 1 Tbls chopped fresh thyme and rosemary, or 1/2 tsp dry
◇ 3 Tbls flour
◇ 1/4 cup Sherry (not cooking Sherry)
◇ Salt and pepper to taste

Directions

1. Heat oil in a large, heavy saucepan over medium heat, add garlic and sauté for two minutes (don't let the garlic brown).
2. Add onions and continue sautéing until slices are translucent.
3. Add carrots, celery, and mushrooms and cook 10 minutes, stirring frequently, scraping the bottom of the pan to loosen browned bits.
4. Add potatoes, beans, tomato sauce, and veggie base/water mixture, reserving 1/4 cup of the veggie base/water mixture.
5. Stir well.

6. Use a toothpick and scratch your journey's goal into the bay leaf and add, with remaining spices, to the stew and bring to a boil.
7. Reduce heat to low and simmer 30 minutes or until vegetables are fork-tender, stirring occasionally.
8. When veggies are tender, whisk the flour into remaining broth until smooth and add to stew, along with the Sherry.
9. Simmer for an additional five minutes.
10. Adjust seasoning with salt and pepper to taste.
11. Remove the bay leaf and set aside. When you're able, bury it outside while visualizing your journey's goal. Add a prayer of thanks for the food that nourished your body and soul.
12. Serve with a rustic bread. Enjoy!

Aphrodite's Brownies

Ingredients

◊ 1 cup butter
◊ 1 cup 100% Dutch unsweetened baking cocoa
◊ 4 large eggs
◊ 1/2 tsp finely-ground sea salt
◊ 1 cup granulated sugar
◊ 1/2 cup dark brown sugar, packed
◊ 1 tsp pure vanilla extract
◊ 1 cup unbleached, all-purpose flour
◊ 1/2 tsp baking powder
◊ 1/4 tsp cayenne pepper
◊ 1 tsp ground cinnamon
◊ 1 cup 60% cacao chunks
◊ 1 cup black walnuts (optional)

Directions

1. Preheat oven to 350°F.*
2. Line a 9"x 13" baking pan with parchment paper. Allow the paper to extend from the 9" edges to form 'handles'.
3. Melt the butter in a microwave or on top of the stove in a boiling water bath (double-boiler).
4. Stir in sugars until dissolved.
5. Add cocoa to the above mixture and stir until dissolved and set aside to cool.
6. In a separate bowl mix the dry ingredients and set aside.
7. In a medium-sized mixing bowl, beat the eggs, vanilla, and salt until light and frothy.
8. Using a wide rubber spatula, gently mix the cooled chocolate mixture into the blended eggs.

9. Make a depression in the dry ingredients and fold in the egg-chocolate mixture. (Don't over-mix or your brownies will have a tough texture.)
10. Gently blend in the chocolate chunks and pour the batter into the prepared pan and bake for 25 minutes.
11. The brownies will be done when the top is shiny and cracked. The inside should be fudgy, not dry.
12. Allow to cool in the pan for five minutes then remove by lifting parchment paper using the 'handles'.
13. Allow the brownies finish cooling on wire rack before cutting.
14. Store in an air-tight container; may be frozen up to three months.

*If using a glass baking dish, decrease oven temperature by 25°

Adapted from the recipe archives of Grace DiLorenzo

Soft Sugar Cookie Bars

Ingredients

Cookie Dough

◊ 1/2 cup unsalted butter softened
◊ 1 cup granulated sugar
◊ 1 large egg
◊ 2 Tbsp. sour cream
◊ 2 tsp pure vanilla extract
◊ 2 -1/3 cups unbleached, all- purpose flour
◊ 1/2 tsp baking powder
◊ 1/2 tsp finely ground, sea salt

Frosting

◊ 1/2 cup unsalted butter softened
◊ 2 heaping cups powdered sugar
◊ 2 Tbsp. milk, half and half, or light cream
◊ 1 tsp pure vanilla extract
◊ food coloring (optional)
◊ candy sprinkles (optional)

Directions

1. Preheat oven to 375°F and line a 9X13-inch baking pan with foil and grease lightly.
2. Beat butter and sugar until light and fluffy.
3. Add the egg, sour cream, and vanilla and beat until thoroughly combined. The mixture might look slightly curdled.
4. In a separate bowl, combine dry ingredients.
5. With your mixer on low, add the dry ingredients, mixing until a soft dough forms. Avoid over-mixing.
6. Using your fingers, evenly press the dough into the pan.
7. Bake for about 15 minutes, until the top appears dry and the edges are just starting to turn light brown.

8. Make sure not to over bake, as dough will continue to cook a little after you remove the pan from the oven.
9. Leave the baked dough in the pan and set aside to cool while you prepare the frosting.

Frosting

1. Beat the butter and powdered sugar until light and fluffy.
2. Add the milk and extract and beat for several more minutes until smooth.
3. Add food coloring, if using.
4. Use an offset spatula or butter knife to spread the frosting over the cooled dough.
5. Top with sprinkles and slice into squares and remove bars from pan.
6. Store in an air-tight container; may be frozen up to one month.

Soft Sugar Cookie Bars courtesy of:

www.celebratingsweets.com

Half-Moon Cookies

Ingredients

Cookie Dough

◇ 1 cup butter, softened
◇ 2 cups granulated sugar
◇ 3/4 cup 100% Dutch unsweetened baking cocoa powder, sifted
◇ 2 large eggs
◇ 1 tsp pure vanilla extract
◇ 3-3/4 cups unbleached, all- purpose flour
◇ 2 tsp baking soda
◇ 3/4 tsp baking powder
◇ 1/4 tsp finely ground, sea salt
◇ 1-1/2 cups whole milk or 2%

Vanilla Frosting

◇ 6 Tbsp. butter softened
◇ 2-2/3 cups confectioners' sugar
◇ 1/3 cup cream, or half and half
◇ 1-1/2 tsp vanilla extract

Chocolate Frosting

◇ Half of the vanilla frosting
◇ 1/3 cup cocoa powder
◇ 2 Tbsp. cream, or half and half

Directions

1. Preheat oven to 350°F.
2. Line two baking sheets with parchment paper.
3. Beat the butter, sugar, and cocoa until light and fluffy.

4. Add the eggs and vanilla and beat until thoroughly combined.
5. In a separate bowl, combine the dry ingredients.With your mixer on low, alternately add the dry ingredients and the milk to the butter mixture, beginning and ending with the flour, until combined. Scrape down the sides of the bowl with a rubber spatula.
6. Use a large spoon to portion out 2″ mounds of dough onto the prepared baking sheets. Set mounds 2″ apart. Dough will be sticky and will flatten out as it bakes.
7. Bake 12-15 minutes or until dough is set. Don't over-bake, cookies will harden as they cool.
8. Allow the cookies to cool on the pan for 2-3 minutes and finish cooling on a wire rack while you prepare the frosting

Vanilla Frosting

1. Cream the butter in a small bowl and blend in the confectioner's sugar, vanilla, alternately with the 1/3 cup cream.
2. Beat until the consistency is creamy.
3. Reserve half to make the Chocolate Frosting

Chocolate Frosting

1. Add cocoa powder and remaining cream and blend until smooth.
2. Frost half the cookie with vanilla frosting and the other half with chocolate.
3. Store in an air-tight container; may be frozen up to one month.

Half-Moon Cookies courtesy of:

www.homeinthefingerlakes.com

Tropical Breeze Scones

Ingredients

⋄ 6 Tbsp. unsalted cold butter
⋄ 3 cups unbleached flour
⋄ 3-1/2 Tbsp. granulated sugar
⋄ 3 tsp baking powder
⋄ 3/4 tsp salt
⋄ 3/4 cup each canned pineapple and mango, drained and chopped
⋄ 1/2 cup white chocolate, chopped
⋄ 1/4 cup 2% milk
⋄ 1 tsp vanilla
⋄ 1/2 cup coconut milk
⋄ 2 large eggs
⋄ Sugar for sprinkling

Directions

1. Preheat oven to 400°F and line a baking sheet with parchment.
2. In a large bowl mix the flour, sugar, baking powder, and salt.
3. Cut-in the butter until dough is crumbly, resembling peas.
4. Add the pineapple and mango and mix just until moistened.
5. Toss in the white chocolate and mix again distributing the chocolate throughout mixture. (Avoid over-mixing)
6. In another bowl blend the milk, vanilla, coconut milk, and eggs.
7. Pour liquid ingredients, a little at a time, into the dry ingredients and mix gently.
8. Place dough onto a lightly floured mixing board and knead about 12 times.
9. Roll out dough into a circle about 3/4" thick and cut into

wedges.

10. Place dough wedges onto the baking sheet and sprinkle with granulated sugar and place into the oven.

11. Set the timer for 25 minutes. Cooking time may vary depending on the oven. When they are a golden brown they are done.

12. Take out of the oven and place on a cooling rack.

13. Enjoy warm!

14. To reheat, place in a 350°F oven for about 5-10 minutes.

15. Store in air-tight container. Can be frozen up to three months.

Tropical Breeze Scones courtesy of:

www.sugarlovespices.com

Honey Lavender Biscotti

Ingredients

◇ 2-1/4 cup unbleached, all-purpose flour
◇ 1 tsp baking powder
◇ 1/2 tsp baking soda
◇ 1/4 tsp finely ground sea salt
◇ 2/3 cup granulated sugar
◇ 3 large eggs
◇ 3 Tbsp. clover honey
◇ 1 tsp pure vanilla extract
◇ 2 Tbsp. lemon or orange zest (optional)
◇ 1 Tbsp. ground dried, culinary lavender blossoms

Directions

1. Preheat oven to 350°F.
2. Line a baking sheet with parchment paper.
3. In a medium bowl, sift flour, baking powder, baking soda, and salt together; set aside.
4. In a large bowl, whisk sugar and eggs to a light lemon color; stir in honey, vanilla extract, orange zest, and lavender blossoms.
5. Sprinkle dry ingredients over the egg mixture; fold in until a soft dough is formed. (You may have to use your hands.)
6. Lightly sprinkle flour on your work surface, on top of the dough, and on your hands, and divide the dough into two pieces.
7. Pat and shape each piece into a loaf approximately 3"-4" wide, and 10" long. Place loaves on the prepared baking sheet with 3" inches in between.
8. Bake 20-30 minutes. The loaves are done baking when they offer some resistance when touched and start to form cracks on top. Rotate halfway through baking.
9. Remove the loaves from the oven and cool 10 minutes on

a wire rack or until you can handle them.

10. While biscotti are cooling, reduce oven temperature to 275°F.

11. When biscotti loaves are cool enough to handle, use a serrated knife and cut loaves diagonally into 3/4" thick slices. Place slices, cut side down, on the baking sheet and bake another 15 minutes, turning each cookie over half-way during baking to allow even crisping. Don't over-bake, biscotti will crisp as they cool.

12. Remove from oven and cool completely on a wire rack.

13. Can be stored in an air-tight container for up to three weeks. May be frozen up to three months.

Honey-Lavender Biscotti courtesy of:

www.mylavenderblues.com

About Tinthia

Earth witch Tinthia Clemant writes with the backdrop of the Concord River flowing outside her office window. When not weaving stories about strong women, she's gardening, painting, pondering, and eating ice cream, with a splash of bourbon. She shares her paradise with her black Lab, elderly cat, flocks of Mallard ducks and songbirds, and a few brave field mice who venture into the house. (Her elderly black cat is still a heck of a mouser.)

Find Tinthia on Facebook, Twitter, YouTube, Pinterest, Goodreads, and say hello to her at www.tinthiaclemant.com and www.concordriverlady.com.

Praise for

The Summer of Annah: A Midsummer's Wish

❖ Book One in the *Seasons of Annah* Series ❖

"If you're looking for a wonderful book to pass your time, this is the one."

"I was captivated all the way through."

"This amazing book had a hold of me even after I read those sad, familiar words "THE END"!

"After I started reading I was hooked. I couldn't put it down."

"The Summer of Annah: A Midsummer's Wish is phenomenal."

Read an excerpt of *A Midsummer's Wish* at:
www.tinthiaclemant.com

Praise for

The Summer of Annah: A Labor of Love

❖ Book Two in the *Seasons of Annah* Series ❖

"Tinthia Clemant has done it again and given us a magical story about a strong woman and the power of love."

"I am rooting for Annah to realize that Eric's love is for real."

"A gripping story of love, heartache, disappointment and lies."

"Here is love in all the colors of the glorious love rainbow."

"Another wonderful page-turner."

Read an excerpt of *A Labor of Love* at:
www.tinthiaclemant.com

Praise for

You Gave Me Wings

❖ Book One in the *Isabella's Story* Series ❖

"A timeless story about a woman who sets out to find herself."

"Isabella is a brave woman who travels to Italy on her own in the hopes of finding out who she is. Empowering."

"Trust, love, forgiveness, and self-growth are all at the heart of Tinthia Clemant's newest book, *You Gave Me Wings.*"

"I was transported to Rome and could actually taste the gelato."

Read an excerpt of *You Gave Me Wings* at:
www.tinthiaclemant.com

www.ingramcontent.com/pod-product-compliance
Lightning Source LLC
Chambersburg PA
CBHW030023180626
46810CB00001B/185